C000003596

This one's for you, Aline.
Je t'aime.

Acknowledgments

A huge thank you to Aline, who, in addition to delivering frequent cups of espresso to my desk, not only read every draft almost the moment it was thrust into her hands, but was also unceasingly patient in my appalling attempts to speak and write French. To Fleur, who gives her honest opinion whether I want it or not, and to all my usual suspects—many thanks for your ongoing advice and support.

Again, special thanks to Christine at Bella Books, my editor extraordinaire!

About the Author

The daughter of a teacher, Jane was brought up with books from as early as she can remember, and to this day continues her love affair with the written word and its ability to transport the reader to places unknown.

Jane was educated in the traditional fashion, taking the path directly from school to university and gaining a Bachelor of Business degree with major studies in Marketing. Her studies took her to the marketing department of a city-based educational institution where she spent over a decade working in a creative and supportive environment.

At the time of writing this novel, Jane was in the midst of a two-year sabbatical which took her across Europe, to China and a flying visit to the United States. She has since returned to Australia and her much-missed friends and family, hopefully a little wiser, but definitely with an expanded view of the world that we all occupy together.

CHAPTER ONE

Morgan Silverstone swallowed the yawn that would advertise her inattentiveness and pushed the venetian blind aside far enough to glimpse the landscape moving beyond the window. The last time she looked, which was not too long after the train pulled out of the gray and dreary East Perth station, they had been rolling through the Swan Valley, a wine region located right on the doorstep of Western Australia's capital city. She'd watched the vines that marched in ordered rows across the plains of the valley as she munched on the not-too-bad but boring chicken and lettuce sandwiches that Kitty bought from the canteen in the diner car. Only two days ago she and her crew were filming in that very same valley, gathering footage to promote the region to the rest of the nation. A half-day had been spent at one of the more prestigious wineries, accompanying a tour that took visitors through the entire winemaking process, from the vine to the cellar. The tour ended with a gastronomic lunch at the winery's restaurant.

Memories of the fabulous cabernet sauvignon that was served with her melt-in-the-mouth fillet steak made Morgan set aside the bad-verging-on-awful coffee Kitty had also plopped on the table next to the sandwiches. But only minutes later the wine was forgotten and the bad coffee downed as she, Kitty, Mark and Nick became engrossed in a preproduction meeting.

As expected, the meeting was long. Despite the groundwork already laid before they even boarded the train that would take them the 4,352 kilometers from Perth to Sydney, there was an endless array of items to finalize for the series of segments they would film over their three-day train ride.

Now, after it seemed they had nitpicked every detail possible, Kitty declared the meeting done.

There was a collective groan of relief from around the small table as, finally, they could escape the confines of Morgan's "room." The compartment was meant to accommodate two, cozy enough when containing the standard number of persons, but positively claustrophobic with four of them squeezed in.

The exodus of the three other members of their party was led by Mark, the only smoker in their group, who was now presumably charging toward one of the few designated smoking areas in the train, a glass-encased "capsule" with its own ventilation system.

Once alone, Morgan held her arms above her head, intertwined her fingers and stretched as high as she could. On release she let out a sigh, feeling an easing of some of the stiffness in her back that sitting in more or less one spot for the last four and a bit hours had caused. Her upper body again mobile, she wriggled her toes, flexed her calf muscles and tucked away the small foldaway table that had served as their workspace. She dug into her beauty case and drew the brush she found through her long auburn hair. She cleaned her teeth at the tiny wash basin, gargled with a medicated rinse, sprayed on some perfume and reapplied a smattering of lipstick.

A mirror check revealed she was presentable, so she grabbed her handbag, locked the compartment door behind her and went to explore the train. Filming would not begin until tomorrow, but before then she was charged with the task of finding fellow travelers who would be willing to be on national television. Since a great majority of people clamored to be on camera, especially for a show with such a high profile as theirs, getting takers was not normally a problem. What did present a problem was finding those persons who could be put in front of a camera *and* talk coherently once there.

"Morgan Silverstone?"

Morgan turned to the questioning voice coming from behind her. As soon as she did a rather rotund woman clapped her hand to her mouth and gave a delighted squeal. She rushed forward.

"Oh, my God, Morgan Silverstone!" she gushed. "I thought it was you, but I can't believe it actually is. I just love *Bonnes Vacances*. I watch it every week . . . honestly, I do. Bless you, dear, you look just like on television, only maybe not as tall." The woman dug into her bag and pulled out a pocket camera, not missing a beat as she primed it to take a picture. "I can't wait until I tell the girls at the club who I met . . ."

Yep, Morgan thought as the flash from the camera made her blink. *I think I can safely cross you off my list of would-be stars.*

The woman introduced herself as Marge, who lived in Adelaide and had been in Perth to visit her sister who had taken a bit of a turn on the stairs but, bless her, was on the mend now. Marge was taking the train for the return journey because it was one of those things one really must do, wasn't it, despite the fact it meant being away a bit longer from her husband, Fred, who, bless him, was probably starving by now as he couldn't even boil an egg, even though she had left plenty of meals in the freezer and clear instructions for reheating them in the oven . . .

3

Morgan had been heading toward the front of the train, to the common areas designated for "Red" passengers, that is, those in second-class sleepers such as hers and those unfortunates committed to an upright seat for the entire journey. Marge was also heading that way, so Morgan pretended she had forgotten something in her compartment and hurriedly turned the key in the lock. She rustled around noisily for a moment, poked her head outside and found Marge beaming at her, taking a deep breath as if to begin speaking again.

"It was lovely meeting you." Morgan wrapped her hands around Marge's and flashed the television presenter smile that had sent the hearts of many of her male audience—and no doubt some of the female viewers too—beating wildly. "But I do have an appointment"—she pointed in the direction of the "Gold" carriages—"down there."

"Of course, of course." Marge bobbed her head up and down. "You must be awfully busy. Life isn't just one long *Bonnes Vacances*, is it?" She laughed loudly at her own joke and beamed when Morgan politely laughed along.

Morgan nodded an assurance she would of course visit seat twenty-seven in carriage three just as soon as she had the chance, then turned and walked with what she hoped looked like an "I'm late for an appointment" purpose toward the end of the corridor. She passed through another sleeper car similar to her own before coming to a sign that read *Gold Class Passengers only beyond this point*. Despite—with the exception of Kitty—their lodgings being in Red class, Morgan and the rest of the television crew had access to all the passenger areas of the train, so she had no hesitation in pulling on the handle and stepping into what was no doubt a different world.

Courtesy of the waistcoated and bow-tied bartender, she exited Gold class two hours later, a vodka and cranberry juice under her belt and a short list of potential ring-ins in her mind. Top of her list was a gregarious retired Scottish woman who was steadily working her way through what were popularly known as the "Great Train Journeys." Each year for the past eight years she had taken a different voyage. Last year she had traveled the Paris to Istanbul route on the famed Orient Express. The year prior she traversed Canada from Vancouver to Nova Scotia.

"Hey, Mogs."

"Hey." Morgan switched her attention from thoughts of the Scotswoman to Mark, who was approaching from the opposite direction. "How's it going?"

"No worries my end." Mark grinned laconically. "Nick's having a bit of a fit though. He's just discovered his camera's as dead as a dodo and after tearing our room apart he's come to the conclusion he must have checked his spare battery packs and charger with the rest of his luggage."

"So, what's the big deal?" Morgan shrugged. "We don't start filming until tomorrow." Cameraman Nick, despite having the steady hands required for his job, had a nervous disposition and was prone to making mountains out of molehills. A complete contrast with sound recordist Mark, who, until the urge for nicotine got the better of him, was as laid back as they come. "He can just get them when we make the stop at Kalgoorlie tonight."

Mark leaned up against the window side of the corridor, hands behind his back and one sneaker-clad foot flat to the wall. "Easier said than done. Apparently checked luggage is not accessible for the entire journey. Kitty's 'in conference' with the chief guard as we speak, trying to get him to make an exception."

"Of course they will." Kitty, as the producer, had dealt with much bigger problems than a dead battery. The weight of the show's reputation alone would be enough to sway any decision. The train management surely wouldn't keep the checked baggage under lock and key at the expense of missing out on national television coverage. Morgan waved the issue away as unimportant and changed the subject. "I thought I might check out the Red passengers. Do you want to come?"

"Looking for a Lady in Red?" Mark deadpanned.

Morgan shot him a withering look. "Very funny. Come on. We've less than two hours until they start serving dinner. We're booked in for the first sitting and I sure don't want to miss any of it."

"Gold?" Mark asked hopefully.

"Damn right." Morgan nodded happily. Although they would shoot a segment of Morgan eating in Red, their *access all areas* privilege also gave them dining rights in the Gold restaurant car. It was another perk of the job. So goodness knew why Kitty had made them suffer through their lunch of canteen sandwiches and burnt coffee. Probably for the same reason that, back in February, she had convinced the executive producer it should be Morgan who was sent underwater in a sharkproof cage for a segment on diving with the Great White shark. This was despite Morgan's terror of the creatures and despite the fact that Troy— one of the show's team of six presenters and an extreme sports enthusiast—was champing at the bit for the opportunity. Kitty did such things just because she could.

Or, more likely, she did such things because she eked some sort of grim satisfaction from making life difficult for Morgan. Morgan knew, despite Kitty's outward impression that last February's "Mai Tai Incident" in Chiang Mai was forgotten, inwardly she had never actually forgiven.

Mark and Morgan agreed all the Red action was most likely to be happening in either the diner car, where meals and snacks could be purchased, or in the lounge car with its club-type seating and bar area. Their assumption was pretty much correct. A couple of the sleeper compartment doors they passed were open, and sly glances showed the occupants to be window-gazing, reading or in quiet conversation. The corridors were surprisingly devoid of people, and thankfully the people who squeezed past them either did not recognize Morgan or chose not to acknowledge the fact.

There was an immediate change in atmosphere as soon as Mark opened the door to the lounge car. Dozens had gathered in the comparatively wide space, many clustered in tight groups along the upholstered seating that flanked either side of the carriage. Others nursed their drinks as they leaned on the high circular tables found in bars around the world. At the far end of the carriage a group of young men had discovered the video game consoles. Occasional cheers or groans came from their direction as the current player either blew something up or was himself blown to pieces.

Generally, the patrons were pretty much involved in their own activities and conversations, so Mark and Morgan's entrance did not cause a sea of heads to swivel in their direction. Morgan nodded to the bar. "My buy."

"The usual, thanks." Mark was already headed in the direction of the smoking capsule, located next to the video consoles. "I'll be right back."

Morgan ordered a vodka and cranberry for herself and a beer for Mark. The woman behind the bar opened her eyes a little wider in the body language of recognition but silently placed two coasters on the bar and attended to preparing her drinks. "There you go, Ms. Silverstone," she murmured as she placed the glasses on the coasters.

"Thank you." No doubt all the staff on this journey had been briefed about the presence of a *Bonnes Vacances* film crew, but still Morgan nodded and smiled, appreciating the woman's discretion. Five years as the anchor presenter for the travel show that constantly ripped through the ratings had long ago stripped her of her anonymity. Her fame was restricted to Australia, which meant—apart from the natural curiosity of the general public when stumbling across a working film crew—she could move relatively freely in other countries. On Australia-based assignments such as this, however, she spent a good amount of time in the presence of starstruck fans. Morgan reluctantly accepted this fact as part and parcel of her job. After all, no fans meant no ratings, which ultimately meant no show . . . and no job.

Morgan slid the glasses across the bar, moving away from the central serving area. She stayed facing the bar, sipping on her drink and enjoying a brief moment of being nobody before she had to slip back into "Morgan" mode. The moment lasted for a full minute. Then she felt the weight of someone's glance.

"Excuse me."

Here we go, Morgan thought cynically, half turning toward the voice and preparing her television presenter smile. Her efforts were wasted. The young woman standing next to her was not addressing her at all but was instead trying to get the bartender's attention. The bartender had moved to the far end of the small bar, within earshot but intent on straightening the packets of dry-roasted peanuts in a display stand of various bar snacks.

"*Pardon, madame?*" the young woman rephrased, a little louder this time.

Morgan leaned forward over the bar and waved to get the bartender's attention. "Hello?" she called.

The bartender immediately left her peanuts and rushed over. "I'm sorry Ms.—" She stopped short when Morgan shook her head and nodded to the woman next to her.

The bartender changed the focus of her attention. "How can I help you?"

"One espresso please. To take with me."

Morgan noted the young woman spoke with a strong French accent. Given that the espressos in France were among the best Morgan had ever tasted, she was tempted to tell the young woman the coffee was likely to be terrible. Instead she held her tongue, covertly eyeing the woman's profile. She liked what she saw—hair short, but not too short, strong features without being harsh, taut skin touched by the sun. The T-shirt was loose without being baggy and the pants were a stylish cargo type with multiple pockets.

Maybe? Morgan mused, idly stirring the swizzle stick in her vodka and cranberry.

Definitely, Morgan decided ten seconds later. The bartender had presented the woman with her espresso, a sugar sachet and a plastic stirrer. The woman turned to Morgan, looked her straight in the eye and smiled. It was a short, penetrating look, but it spoke volumes.

Definitely a dyke.

The coffee was held up and the woman continued to look directly at Morgan as she nodded in the direction of the bartender. "*Merci beaucoup . . .*" She smiled again as she corrected herself. "Thank you very much."

Morgan had been right. She was French, or perhaps from a French-speaking country. She delved into her memory, searching for an appropriate response in her extremely limited stockpile of French phrases. Nothing immediately came to mind, so she opted for an Australian phrase instead. "No worries."

That caused the French woman to pause then laugh softly. "No worries," she repeated, as if trying out the words for the first time. "It is an 'Aussie' saying?"

Morgan shifted to face her fully. This was not the first time she had been beguiled by an accent. It was one of her failings, and a path her globetrotting career led her down many times. She nodded, noting the woman gave her a quick once-over before returning her gaze. Morgan answered the unspoken "I'm interested" with a sultry stare. "Very Aussie."

At that moment Mark, reeking of tobacco smoke, appeared at Morgan's side. "Thanks, Mogs." He reached around her for his beer, which was still sitting on the bar. "What's very Aussie?"

"We were just talking about our 'no worries' saying." Morgan took a sip of her vodka and cranberry, discreetly checking the Frenchwoman's reaction to the interruption. As feared, she totally misinterpreted Mark's presence. The woman's eyes flicked from Morgan to Mark and immediately her demeanor changed, tightening and closing.

The little cardboard cup of espresso was held up. "I must go to my place. The coffee—it gets cold."

Morgan nodded a good-bye and dismally watched the woman fade into the crowd.

"What?" Mark asked when Morgan glowered at him. Then he said, "Oh," as he realized he had interrupted something. He slapped Morgan on the back and leaned toward her. "Just as well I came when I did then. Don't forget where we are."

"I know, I know." Morgan sighed a heavy sigh. The Australian-made closet she lived in to protect her public persona sure put the reins on her love life. "Come." She downed her vodka and cranberry in a series of swallows and placed the empty glass onto the bar. "Let's go mingle."

Forty minutes later and Morgan was desperate for a toilet break, the diuretic qualities of her drink of choice taking effect as she finished her third vodka and cranberry for the day. She excused herself from her present company—a very sweet old married couple from Adelaide—and worked her way through the crowd to Mark, who was in the process of protecting the galaxy from deadly invaders. After being stopped twice by people who had met her briefly and now assumed they had best-friend status, she finally made it to the bank of video games.

She tapped Mark on the shoulder, told him she would see him at dinner and headed out of the carriage in the direction of the nearest toilet. To her dismay, but not to her surprise, it was engaged. A sign pointed to alternate facilities in the next carriage, so Morgan continued on.

It too was occupied. Morgan figured the farther she moved from the lounge car, the more likely she would find a free toilet. She passed through to what was the first of the upright seating carriages.

"What does a girl have to do to take a pee 'round here?" she muttered on discovering that, yet again, the toilet was occupied.

10

She was at the stage of need where she'd have to cross her legs if she waited in the one spot, so she made one more desperate flee to the next carriage. The toilet was vacant. She ducked in.

A few minutes later, with her kidneys now taken care of, Morgan was able to give her immediate surrounds a bit more attention. The seats were like those of most modern long-distance trains. They looked remarkably similar to airplane seating, and with not too much more leg room. Many of the seats in this particular carriage were littered with reading matter, rugs, pillows and other nonvaluable oddments that indicated they were occupied but temporarily vacated. Morgan surmised the passengers were either crowded into the lounge or diner cars, or trawling up and down the narrow corridors, stretching their legs.

Morgan checked the number on the carriage door to see exactly where she was. Carriage four. Since she had been steadily moving toward the front of the train, that meant seat number twenty-seven in the next carriage was home for camera-wielding Marge. It was too close to dinnertime to become ensconced in another difficult-to-escape conversation, so Morgan retraced her steps. She would be passing this way tomorrow morning anyway, for an early interview with one of the train drivers, so she would call a hello to Marge on the way past.

The mere thought of Marge seemed to make her materialize. She was close at the heels of another woman of around the same age so she was only partially in view, but the voice was unmistakable. The leading woman wore a suffering expression and Morgan wondered how long she had been listening to tales of, bless him, husband Fred. Morgan's sympathy for the woman's plight was, however, not enough to provide her with an avenue of escape. Morgan noticed the two seats closest to her were vacant. She flung herself into the one next to the aisle, and although now facing the opposite direction to Marge and her companion, she picked up the magazine lying on the next seat and stuck her nose into it.

She stayed with head bent into the magazine until Marge's voice, which continued unabated, disappeared with her voluminous frame into the next carriage. With a loud sigh she tossed the magazine back where she found it. Only then did she notice the set of khaki-clad knees close to hers. Morgan lifted her gaze to the person sitting immediately opposite her, in one of the two backward-facing seats, and immediately raised her eyebrows in surprise.

It was the Frenchwoman.

Morgan gave a crooked, embarrassed smile. Of all the seats she had to dive into like a criminal, it had to be this one. Maybe she could redeem herself with some French. "*Bonjour.*"

The woman smiled back, obviously amused, if somewhat bemused, by Morgan's unexpected visit. "*Bonsoir.*"

You gotta love how the French can't help but point out your language mistakes, Morgan thought a little sourly. She nodded in acknowledgment of the correction, considered explaining her actions but decided against it, holding out her hand instead. "*Je m'appelle* Morgan."

The woman's grip was firm, warm and dry, and the eyes that met hers steady. "Marie."

"*Enchantée.*" Morgan held both Marie's hand and her gaze a little longer than necessary. It had the desired effect. There was a renewed flash of interest in Marie's eyes.

"*Parlez-vous français?*" Marie asked, her expression hopeful.

"*Pas vraiment.*" Morgan shook her head, and her lack of French language skills forced her to switch back to English. "Only enough to order a coffee and a croissant."

This time Marie's eyes lit up. "You 'ave visited my country?"

Morgan had probably been to France over a dozen times during her five years with *Bonnes Vacances*. "Once or twice. It's very beautiful . . . they make good espresso too," she said as she looked pointedly at the empty cardboard cup that lay wedged between the window and what she assumed was Marie's overnight bag.

"*Bof!*" Marie exclaimed disgustedly, "The coffee 'ere. It is 'orrible!"

Morgan laughed. "I know. I should have warned you." She searched her brain for the French version of sorry. "*Desolée.*"

Marie paused, apparently searching for words. She looked very pleased with herself as she said, "No worries."

Morgan laughed out loud. English spoken with a French accent really was delightful. "So, Marie . . . apart from our fabulous coffee, what brings you to Australia?"

Morgan learned that Marie, having finished school last June, had taken a gap year before starting university. She was using the year to travel and so far had been through India, Thailand and Indonesia. She'd flown into Perth from Bali less than a week ago. In the days since then she made a tourist-bus dash to see the otherworldly rock formations of the Pinnacles, and on the same tour saw the dolphins come into shore at Shark Bay. During a day spent at Perth's own island getaway, Rottnest, she'd fallen in love with the bohemian atmosphere in the port city of Fremantle. Her next stop was Kalgoorlie, then on to the Eastern States and, finally, New Zealand.

"So, you're leaving the train at Kalgoorlie?" Morgan asked, a little disappointed. The train was due to arrive in Kalgoorlie at around ten that night—only three hours away. That wasn't going to leave much time for—Morgan stopped that thought from developing. Nothing was ever going to happen, even if Marie was traveling the entire distance to Sydney. They were in Australia, and so Marie was out of bounds. She was also very young, maybe not even yet eighteen.

"Yes." Marie nodded. "I will stay in Kalgoorlie for four weeks. I have work there."

Morgan learned Marie must indeed be at least eighteen since she had secured work in one of the city's myriad of pubs. In exchange for her labor five days a week she would receive room and board, a little cash and a big opportunity to have a "real Australian outback experience."

"I wouldn't quite call Kalgoorlie the outback." Morgan glanced over the *Work in an Aussie Pub* promotional brochure that Marie dug from her bag. She had picked it up from the information stand at her backpacker accommodation and immediately applied, drawn in by the promise of an outback experience. "I hate to disappoint you, but while it's out in the middle of nowhere, it's actually a city. Don't get me wrong though," Morgan added quickly when Marie's face fell. "It's about as Australian a city as you can get. It's an old mining town that just happened to survive and thrive after the gold rush. They still mine gold there actually."

"You 'ave visited?" Marie asked.

Morgan used a deliberate offhand tone. "Oh, yes. New York, Paris, London, Kalgoorlie . . . I've done them all!"

Marie's unsure smile indicated she did not grasp Morgan's humor. "Did you like Kalgoorlie?" she asked finally.

Morgan took a moment to choose her words. Kalgoorlie was not a city she would visit by choice. Sure, there were plenty of permanent residents, including families, but with mining still as its primary industry, by nature the place had a substantial itinerant population. Many worked the mines to earn quickly the deposit for a house or gather funds for investment, but just as many raked in the big dollars only to piss them away at one of the pubs that could be found on almost every corner. Morgan passed the *Work in an Aussie Pub* brochure back to Marie. "It's a bit too much of a man's town for me." She almost added that she preferred the company of women but kept that thought to herself. If she were reading the signs correctly, Marie had already discounted Mark's appearance in the lounge car and figured that out for herself.

It appeared that Marie *had* done her calculations correctly. Her fingers brushed the tips of Morgan's as she accepted the brochure. "Then it will be a long month, no?" she said as she met Morgan's gaze.

Morgan shifted a little in her seat, feeling the unmistakable pull of lust in her groin. As if in sympathy, she felt her phone—which was located at the bottom of the handbag she held on her lap—begin to vibrate through the lightweight material. The caller ID announced it was Kitty. Morgan scowled at it, wishing to God she was on any other train in any other country. Then she could invite Marie to her sleeper. She had absolutely no doubt Marie would say yes. Again she chose her words carefully. "There are plenty of women in Kalgoorlie too. I'm sure you'll find some friends very quickly." Morgan emphasized the word *friends* then smiled apologetically as she snapped her phone open. "Yes?" A few seconds later she snapped it closed again. "I'm afraid I have to go."

Marie looked a little suspiciously at Morgan's phone. "*D'accord* . . . er, okay."

Morgan hesitated. Maybe Marie thought she was being given the brush-off, that since the phone had made no sound when it supposedly rang, there hadn't actually been anyone on the other end. "I'm having dinner with some colleagues of mine. You might remember Mark—you met him earlier at the bar," Morgan explained, pleased to extinguish any lingering doubts that Marie might have about his significance. "I wish I could stay and talk with you longer but . . ."

"*Non, non, non.*" Marie held up her hands. "I understand." Then she grinned playfully. "No worries."

As she had earlier, Morgan laughed, delighted. Against all her better judgment she dug into her handbag and pulled out a notebook and pen. "This is where I am." She tore off the sheet with her carriage and compartment number written on it. "I should be back there in no more than two hours. If you want you can drop by before you leave the train. We can . . . talk a bit more . . . about Kalgoorlie."

"Thank you." Marie gave the paper the merest of glances and slipped it into one of her numerous cargo pant pockets. "I would like that very much."

Morgan turned from Marie and her delicious French smile and walked down the aisle with a delicious French *à bientot* echoing in her ears.

Dinner was also delicious, but Morgan was away for longer than she anticipated and it was close to ten p.m. when she turned the key to open her compartment door. Part of her was relieved it was so late. Before she had even reached the Gold restaurant car she regretted her impulsiveness and wished she had not handed over the piece of paper. That was not entirely true. More accurately, she was wishing she were not in a position where she had to regret giving her details to a good-looking woman. Now, since there was only a half-hour or so before the scheduled Kalgoorlie stop, there seemed little chance Marie was going to visit. If Marie had already stopped by she would have been disappointed, finding no one home, except for maybe the staff member who had, in her absence, transformed the seats into a narrow bed.

Morgan sat on the edge of the mattress and tested it for firmness. It didn't feel too bad—certainly better than some of the lumpy excuses for beds she had experienced in her travels—but still she frowned. The upper bunk was also made up for the night. Since Morgan had the compartment to herself for the journey she figured it was the product of an overzealous staff member, and so she began looking for the catch or clip or other mechanism that she could activate to raise the bunk back to its daytime home near the ceiling. Morgan found the button, but she also found the sign right next to it that stated only staff were to raise and lower the bunks. Imagining the upper bunk coming crashing down on her in the middle of the night because she had not secured it properly, Morgan took heed of the sign and decided to go in search of a staff member.

She slid the door open and jumped in fright at the knuckles that appeared right in front of her face. "Holy shit!" she exclaimed, bringing her hand to the base of her neck. It was Marie, her hand poised to knock. "You scared the life out of me!"

"*Desolée* . . . sorry." Marie had her feet planted apart, her bag slung over one shoulder. She unclenched her hand, held it in empty air for a moment then ran her palm down Morgan's cheek. "I did not mean to frighten you."

"Just bad timing." Morgan closed her eyes to the caress. Marie's touch was like her handshake, firm and warm. This was a woman who was very sure of herself.

"Bad timing?" Marie took a step toward Morgan. Given that they were already standing close, this move brought their bodies within a whisper of each other. "You wish me to leave, *chérie?*"

During her pre-dinner cocktail—vodka and cranberry juice number four—Morgan had drifted into a daydream, imagining how Marie's visit would play out, *if* she actually did visit. First she fantasized how it could be if only they were not in Australia. Marie would knock and Morgan would stand aside for her to enter. She would offer her a drink and Marie would decline, (which was just as well because Morgan had nothing but a room temperature bottle of water in her bag), and they would settle into a sexually loaded conversation before finally falling into each other's arms for a brief but passionate encounter. Later, as she sipped on a crisp sauvignon blanc that perfectly comple-mented her main course of dhufish and sautéed snow peas, Morgan let the conversation of the other three crew members drift around her and daydreamed of the more realistic meeting; the one that must occur by virtue of their location. Again Marie would knock and Morgan would stand aside for her to enter. Again the drink offer and again the decline. Conversation, but this time full of subtle double entendres. The train would pull gently to a stop at Kalgoorlie, Marie would pick up her bag and they would say their good-byes—two Continental kisses on the cheek followed by a brief, light kiss on the lips. The second fantasy was very unsatisfying compared to the first, but it was all Morgan would allow herself.

This, however . . . this was entirely unexpected. Marie had seemingly interpreted Morgan's lack of response as an invitation to stay. The hand that still held Morgan's cheek swept to the back of her neck and Marie pressed her body fully against Morgan's as she met her lips with a hungry mouth.

Morgan's head told her to take a step back, to stick with fantasy number two, but her body told her otherwise, to find out what was behind door number three. She did take a step back, but only to pull Marie farther into the compartment. She groped for the sliding door, found it by touch and pulled it until she heard the latch click.

Marie left Morgan's mouth just long enough to give a knowing smile and toss her bag onto the floor. Then she returned, hands clasping Morgan's hips and the tip of her tongue tracing the edge of Morgan's lips. "You want me, *non?*"

Morgan groaned when Marie's tongue slid across hers. She grabbed Marie by the shoulders and pushed her against the now-closed door. She ignored everything about sticking to fantasy number two, ignored that they were chugging across the land of her devoted public, ignored everything except the heat of this moment. Her words were hardly intelligible as she breathed into Marie's mouth. "I want you, yes."

CHAPTER TWO

Ally cradled her takeaway cup of black coffee in both hands. The liquid itself was awful—bitter and old-tasting—but at least it seeped some warmth into her palms. Night had fallen on a clear sky, but still it was surprisingly cool, given how warm the day had been. She noted the abrupt drop in temperature with more than just a casual interest. It was a point to consider when drawing up the plans for her latest project.

Ally temporarily set aside her coffee and scribbled *cold nights* in her notebook. Usually she did not suffer from a bad memory, but with her burgeoning exhaustion it was best just to be sure. Last night she had arrived in Perth on the red-eye from Sydney and caught a few winks in an airport hotel before boarding a regional plane—a seventy-or-so-seater, but still far too small for her liking—bound for Kalgoorlie at six a.m. After the hourlong flight, she had just a moment to freshen up before being whisked away in a gigantic four-wheel-drive to a meeting with a potential client. The potential client was a Kalgoorlie-based executive for one of the nation's largest mining operations, and as such he needed a suitable house. Not just any house, however. In a move that seemed to run counter to the exploitative nature of mining, this executive wanted a house designed to be in sympathy with its surrounds—not just aesthetically, but also environmentally.

This was where she, Alison Brown, an architect who specialized in environmentally sustainable dwellings, came in. Only one day after the current month's issue of *Architectural Digest* was released—the issue that featured an almost entirely energy self-sufficient trilevel house that she had designed for a property in tropical north Queensland—she received a call from the mining executive's personal assistant. That was Friday of last week. Now, just five days later, she was sitting on the brink of what would be, to date, the largest project of her eight-year architectural career. Already, after spending the morning discussing her potential client's wants and needs and the afternoon assessing his five-acre homesite, she had some concepts forming. The creative side of her was itching to get into action, and indeed over dinner and while waiting here at the train station she had committed some sketches to paper. But lack of sleep followed by a long day had taken its toll, and eventually Ally's brain decided to shut down for the evening. It was at that point she went in search of caffeine and ended up with her cup of witches' brew.

The coffee was quickly going cold and its use as a hand-heater obsolete. Ally rose from the bench seat on the platform and went in search of a rubbish bin. She checked her watch against the large station clock and noticed with satisfaction that they were in sync. It was nine forty-nine. Technically, the train should be arriving in one minute.

No sooner had Ally deposited her cup and its contents into a bin than she heard the rumble of the train's approach. Impressed that it could be so punctual after leaving Perth nearly ten hours prior, Ally decided it was yet another reason why trains were infinitely preferable to planes.

She was very, very pleased to be taking this method of transport home and considered herself extremely lucky to have the opportunity. This train trip was pure indulgence—three nights and two days to traverse the Australian continent instead of a five-hour flight to cross the same distance. After scheduling the Kalgoorlie-based meeting, Ally had presented Josh, her boss, with what she thought was an outrageous request. Since she hated flying, and since she had been putting in such long hours lately, could she fly one way and take the train back? She had to try extremely hard not to throw her hands in the air and yell "woo-hoo" when Josh agreed, calling the journey a well-earned, brain-expanding break from the mind-numbing concrete jungle of Sydney.

As soon as Josh left her office Ally did a little victory dance around her desk. Then she called the train-booking office. She knew it was a long shot trying to get a place at such short notice, especially since she wanted a sleeper. But there was no harm in trying.

"We have one space available in our Red class sleepers, madam," the young man on the end of the line announced after Ally heard much tapping of keys on what she supposed was his computer keyboard. "It's a two-person compartment. Wait one moment, please." There were a few more key taps and the young man spoke again. "You would be sharing with another woman. Is this okay?"

"I'll take it," Ally said immediately. A compartment of her own would be preferable but she wasn't going to quibble. Goodness knew when Josh would be feeling so generous again. Ally pulled the company credit card from her wallet and in a few minutes and lots of tapping from the young man, the transaction was completed.

Ally stood back as the train approached and ground to a slow halt. She watched as those waiting on the platform surged forward, leaving little room for those who wished to disembark. While also a little impatient to discover the train, and her sleeping quarters in particular, Ally did not understand this desperate hurry to alight. After all, the train would not be leaving Kalgoorlie station for nearly three hours and everyone had an allocated place, so it wasn't a case of first come, first served.

Ally mulled over this quirk of human nature as she watched the activity taking place on the platform. Passengers who wished to take the train-operated one-hour bus tour of the city were herded from one form of transport to another and trolleys of suitcases and bags were being both loaded and unloaded from the baggage compartment.

Her attention was temporarily caught by a man and woman who passed immediately in front of her. The woman looked like she meant business, striding with a purpose and a "don't mess with me" expression. In contrast, her companion, a lean and lanky man, walked with a much less sure gait and chewed on the nail of his little finger. The pair stopped at the baggage carriage and the woman summoned one of the baggage handlers. The lanky man hung back, still chewing on his nails, while the woman stood with hands on her hips, shaking her head, obviously disliking the baggage handler's response. Next, a suited man came rushing over from the station, and even from her distance Ally could see he concurred with whatever the woman had to say. Within a few minutes the now very displeased baggage handler had retrieved a black case from the baggage compartment and presented it to the nail-biting male. He looked wildly relieved as he and the woman passed by Ally again.

With no one left on the platform except a gaggle of smokers furiously puffing and exclaiming how good it was to be back in the fresh air, Ally decided it was time to make her move. She ascended the two steep stairs into carriage number eleven and headed down the corridor, counting compartments as she went.

The door of her compartment—number five—was closed. Ally hesitated. Was the other occupant there? If she was, was she asleep? Given the hour that was a distinct possibility. Should she knock or should she try to open the door? Come to think of it, what if the door was locked? She had no key. Was she supposed to get one from the guard?

What to do?

Muffled sounds from behind the compartment door broke the silence of Ally's consideration. Listening a moment, she figured the sounds for what they were and stifled a giggle. It seemed a couple had taken the supposed romance of train travel to its extreme and the woman, at least, was thoroughly enjoying herself. Obviously this was not her compartment. Or rather, it was not her carriage, since the compartment number was definitely correct. She walked back down the corridor and carefully tackled the steep steps that took her back to the platform.

She checked the carriage number against that written on her ticket three times. It matched. She could only suppose that one half of the couple—maybe he was a miner?—was disembarking at Kalgoorlie and so they were making the most of their last moments together. *Well, that's just great, isn't it?* Ally thought. *What the hell am I supposed to do while Romeo and Juliet do their thing?*

Five minutes later, Ally was still standing on the platform, slowly beginning to seethe. Even if they were parting lovers, they'd had nearly ten hours since leaving Perth to say their good-byes. Did they really have to continue while the train had stopped and, more importantly, while Ally was waiting to get some sleep.

It suddenly occurred to her that maybe she had been issued the wrong ticket number. She looked around for a guard or some other staff member she could ask, but the platform was empty. Just as she had made up her mind to do a carriage-by-carriage search for staff she saw a tall, well-attired man descend the steps of "her" carriage. He whistled softly as he straightened his tie and confidently shot his cuffs. In fact, if you swapped his head for that of James's and trimmed down the belly a bit, Ally would swear it was her partner on the mornings after they had made love.

Maybe Romeo was exiting the castle?

Ally watched him leave. She walked the entire length of the platform and back—to give the woman she would be sharing with time to do whatever she now needed to do. Then, her irritation gone and again expectant at the prospect of her journey, Ally reascended the steep steps and headed back to compartment five. She raised her hand to knock but stopped short of her knuckles making contact. She swore under her breath as she heard more muffled love coming from the other side of the door.

"Can I help you?"

Ally turned. At the far end of the corridor was the woman Ally had seen at the baggage carriage. She was approaching fast and walked with the same purposeful manner that Ally had witnessed earlier. Remembering the effect the woman had on the station representative, Ally surmised that, even though she wore no visible signs of identification, maybe she was associated with the train.

"Actually, I was looking for a guard," Ally said. "I seem to be having a bit of trouble getting into my room."

The woman arched her eyebrows. "This compartment?"

Ally didn't like the suspicious look the woman gave her. What did she think, that she was a burglar trying to break in? "Yes. This compartment."

"You must have made some mistake."

It seemed forever since the train had pulled into the station. Ally was tired, her patience was wearing very thin, and despite having only had contact with her for less than a minute, this woman was already beginning to grate on her nerves. "Look." She tapped her ticket. "Carriage eleven, compartment five."

The woman studied the ticket for what seemed a very long time. "There must be some mistake," she repeated. "This compartment was booked for one person only."

Ally had been on the verge of being convinced the woman was not staff. If she was, then surely she would be doing something to help Ally find her quarters instead of standing around being argumentative. But then, if she *wasn't* staff, how did she know the booking status of this compartment? "If that's the case, could you please check the passenger list and tell me where I'm supposed to be?"

"Oh, I'm not with the train." The woman waved away the idea and smiled for the first time. Ally saw through the smile and sweet tone in a second. "But I'm traveling with Morgan and I can assure you, she is not sharing this compartment with anyone."

"Then can you please tell Morgan," Ally replied just as sweetly, "that she should do what she's doing . . . *alone* . . . a little more quietly."

"Excuse me?" The woman's smile fell from her face.

Ally tipped her head in the direction of the door, shrugged and turned away. "I need to find someone who can tell me where I am supposed to sleep tonight."

She didn't look back as she retraced her steps, but even before she was halfway to the carriage exit, Ally heard the woman hiss urgently, "Morgan!"

Five minutes later and Ally was beginning to wonder what sort of weird ride she'd booked herself on. Once the guard she found a few carriages farther down had checked her ticket against the passenger manifest he turned bright red and told her that he "needed to speak with his superior." He then mumbled into his walkie-talkie and within a minute the chief guard had arrived. The chief also scrutinized her ticket then hurried away to the station. He returned quickly enough, his face impassive and unreadable.

"My apologies for making you wait, Ms. Brown," he said,

nodding a dismissal to the other guard, who looked immensely relieved to make his escape. "It appears there has been a little mix-up with your booking."

"What sort of mix-up?" asked Ally, alarmed.

"Well, it seems the place you were assigned was not actually available."

"What!" Ally spluttered. "But I was told . . ." An image of having to again board that outrageously small plane made Ally's stomach turn. Surely this was not happening to her. "How . . . ? The man I spoke to said there was a vacancy in one of the sleepers."

The guard cleared his throat. "I'm dreadfully sorry, Ms. Brown. It was a mistake by our booking office. The compartment you were booked into is for single occupancy only on this trip. There are, however, a few upright seats available, of which you can have your choice. Of course you will be fully refunded and all your meals will be paid—"

"Of course." Too tired and too dazed by the news to put up an argument, Ally just nodded and said, "I'll take that one," to the first seat the guard mentioned. He wrote the carriage and seat number on the back of her ticket and also pressed a sheath of white slips into her hand.

"They're drink vouchers," he explained. "You can redeem them in our Red lounge car. Now, Ms. Brown, may I show you to your seat?"

Ally shook her head and held up the white slips. "Just point me in the direction of the bar."

"I'm sorry, Ms. Brown, but the lounge bar is not operational during this stop. It will open again at ten tomorrow morning."

Ally hoped her expression told him how much she hated him at that very moment. "I'm guessing carriage three is this way?" she said glacially as she pointed to the front of the train. He nodded and she stalked off without another word or a glance. Refund or no, the train company would soon be receiving a scathing letter.

Carriage three was in semidarkness when she entered, the lighting lowered for those who were attempting sleep. Ally picked her way down the aisle. A man who had straightened his leg by placing it in the corridor grunted in his sleep when Ally tripped over it. Next to him another man snored softly. A little farther and she turned up her nose. Someone had farted. Two rows later and she found her seat. Ally sighed. The woman in the adjacent seat was rather large and had draped over into her space. Ally carefully pushed her bag into the overhead luggage rack and settled gently into her seat. Despite her attempts, the woman next to her awoke.

"I'm sorry," Ally whispered as she arranged the thin blanket, which was supplied, over her knees.

"That's okay, dear." A well-padded hand patted Ally on the knee. "I was about through trying to sleep for the moment anyway." The woman rearranged her seat, adjusting the back so it was in more of an upright position. "I'm Marge, dear. What's your name?"

CHAPTER THREE

At one thirty-seven a.m., Morgan locked her compartment door behind her and headed in the direction of the Gold carriages. Not wanting to be delayed by anyone or anything, she walked quickly with her head down. By one thirty-nine she was standing outside Kitty's room. Kitty was the only crew member to have Gold accommodation. Not that she was especially special. She wanted a room to herself: there were no more twin sleepers available in Red, and single sleepers were only available in Gold class. Morgan could have also had a similar room, but since she had access to all the Gold facilities anyway, she had opted for the extra space.

The second hand on her watch was just ticking over to the next minute when she felt the train slowly pull out. It was at that same moment she knocked on Kitty's door.

Despite the hour, Morgan knew Kitty would be awake. After

all, it was Kitty who had called this late-night rendezvous.

"I want to see you in my quarters the *very second* the train leaves" had been Kitty's directive. She'd issued it after barging into Morgan's compartment unannounced at a *very* inconvenient moment. At that moment—just like one of those sneezes that threaten and threaten but then disappear—Morgan's approaching orgasm sucked itself back into her body and dissolved, leaving only a frustrating memory of what could have been.

That very inconvenient and also very embarrassing moment had been over an hour ago. Now, as Morgan waited for the few seconds before Kitty's door slid open, her thoughts shifted from what could have been to what was. And what she was, was in big trouble.

Kitty glowered at Morgan, giving a tilt of her head to indicate that she was to enter. With the bed pulled down there was very little maneuvering room in the single sleeper compartment and Morgan had to shuffle past Kitty to claim a bit of the floor space. She had the sinking feeling that what already promised to be a very uncomfortable meeting would prove even more so at such close quarters.

Morgan watched Kitty as she stood for a long moment facing the door, her hand still on the latch. She also saw the slow rise and fall of Kitty's shoulders, indication she was taking a deep breath. To calm her notoriously fiery temper maybe?

Morgan straightened her back and shoulders in anticipation of the onslaught. She wasn't afraid of Kitty or her temper. But she really did not like confrontation.

Kitty spun around. "Just what the fuck do you think you were doing?"

I thought I was having some of the best sex of my life. Morgan didn't voice this thought out loud but instead she met her producer's angry eyes directly. In the time since Marie had left her compartment, Morgan had decided an upfront apology was the best plan of attack. It would likely be unexpected and hence throw Kitty off-balance. "I'm sorry, Kitty. I don't know what came over me."

Her tactic was not overly effective. If anything it served to further darken Kitty's expression.

"Oh, for God's sake." Kitty threw her hands in the air in exasperation. "We both know what came over you, Morgan."

Yes. A fabulous Frenchwoman . . . twice. Morgan felt a smirk threaten to creep over her face but she held it at bay, determined to keep her expression neutral. She would let Kitty storm it out and then, when she was out of steam, she could proceed with her explanations.

And so Morgan just stood there while Kitty ranted on about how—if she'd known that being a producer effectively meant having to be a mother to three supposed adults—she might have thought twice before signing her contract with the network. And how, if it wasn't lost tickets or dead batteries or giving wake-up calls so airplanes wouldn't be missed, then it was something else. And was she really the only one who cared about keeping the reputation of their show intact? And so on.

"What is it with you, Morgan?" Kitty stood with hands on her hips and looked over the rim of her spectacles. "Don't you ever stop thinking with your clit?"

Morgan saw red. Kitty was getting far too personal.

"Only when I'm around you!" she shot back.

That was the first overt reference Morgan had made to the "Mai Tai Incident" since it actually occurred four months ago, back in February. It had been a steamy night in Chiang Mai and Morgan and the rest of the crew were sitting on the balcony of her hotel room, knocking back drinks. Morgan, having discovered mai tais a few days earlier, had declared them her new favorite drink and was on her fifth—or maybe it was her sixth—for the evening. As happens when steamy weather is mixed with little food and a lot of alcohol, the balcony talk turned rather lewd and she and Mark began comparing their tastes in women.

Mark, who had reiterated his well-known penchant for the busty blondes, stopped Morgan short from giving a description of her preferences. He put his arm around her shoulder. "Mogs likes them all, don't you, Mogs?"

Morgan had clinked her glass to his, nodding in agreement and saying, "Any woman . . . anywhere . . . anytime!" It was at this point that Kitty asked if Morgan had ever thought of her in that way. Morgan had given a theatrical pause during which she pointedly looked Kitty up and down. "Honey"—she waved her mai tai in front of her—"if you and I were the last two women on earth and it took two women to have a baby and the Goddess herself commanded us to go forth and multiply . . . I still wouldn't do it with you." She and Mark fell about laughing, Nick took a nervous sip on his beer, and Kitty placed her drink on the table, stood and left for her room. Morgan had not touched another mai tai since, and neither she nor Kitty had mentioned that night again.

So now Morgan stood silent, watching for the reaction.

Kitty averted her eyes and pinched the bridge of her nose between her thumb and index finger. She also took another long, controlled breath. When next she spoke, her voice was evenly modulated. "Okay, so it's happened. The question now is . . . what are we going to do about it?"

Morgan, while still wishing she had not made her last comment, was grateful it had at least quelled the tempest. Not that Kitty had actually been shouting. Her tirade had been delivered between clenched teeth, designed not to be heard through the thin walls of the compartment.

"There's nothing to do," Morgan said, finally able to give her side of the story, however weak. "She's gone. She left the train at Kalgoorlie. And I knew that when I invited her to my room."

Kitty rolled her eyes at the mention of the invitation. It suitably conveyed how brainless she thought that act had been. "And she's probably ringing the press as we speak."

Morgan shook her head. "Trust me. She doesn't know who I am. She's a backpacker who's been in Australia for less than a week. From what she told me she's been so busy she's probably not even looked at a television since she arrived, and with her new pub job in Kalgoorlie I doubt she'll get a moment to do anything but pull beers and sleep for the next month. And by then she'll have forgotten all about me."

Kitty wasn't convinced. "You don't exactly have a forgettable face, Morgan." She turned away from Morgan's gaze and seemingly contemplated the white bed sheets for a moment. "And how did you explain me suddenly being in your sleeper?"

Morgan sucked in her breath. Kitty was probably not going to like this one bit. "I told her you were one of the colleagues I was traveling with—"

"Yes?" Kitty said suspiciously.

"—who's got a massive thing for me and won't leave me alone."

Kitty pursed her lips. With her wire-rimmed spectacles and hair tied in a loose bun it gave the effect of a woman much older than her twenty-nine years. But then, Morgan always thought Kitty looked older than her years.

"Well, what was I supposed to say?" Morgan argued. "I couldn't exactly tell the truth, could I? And . . . you could have knocked!"

"I did knock!" Kitty blustered. "And I called to you twice. But you were obviously too busy to notice. And I can tell you right now, you're damn lucky it was me who walked in. There was another woman right outside your door who was probably on the verge of doing the same thing. If I hadn't been walking past, then goodness knows what would have happened."

Morgan placed her hands on her hips. Kitty was obviously exaggerating. Why would anyone just enter her room, or be hanging around outside it for that matter? Unless of course it was Marge stopping by for a late-night chat. *Oh, dear,* she thought. Maybe it had been Marge and she'd heard what was happening on the other side of the door. Then she'd surely have a tale to tell the girls at the club. "What did she look like?" she asked.

"Oh, about my age, about my height. About my hair color." Kitty said airily. "Not your type at all."

Touché. Morgan mentally conceded a point to her producer. But, while relieved to hear it couldn't have been Marge, she was curious to know why someone had been hanging around outside her compartment. *If* there had been anyone. She still didn't quite know if Kitty was just trying to cover for her own tactless action. "Did you speak to her?"

"Yes, I spoke to her."

"And?"

"And she was convinced it was her room. Of course I told her it couldn't be . . ."

Morgan listened to Kitty relate all that had transpired outside her compartment, including the fact that the mystery woman had shown Kitty a ticket with a carriage and compartment number corresponding to her own.

"So you're damn lucky I was there," Kitty reiterated. "Because, technically, she had every right to enter."

"So, where is she now?" Morgan asked as she folded her arms and narrowed her eyes. "If, *technically*, she was supposed to be in my room, where has she gone?"

"I don't know." Kitty waved away the question. "When she left she was looking for a guard. Obviously they found where she was supposed to be and she's happily snuggled in for the night."

Morgan stared at Kitty, still not entirely convinced. If, as she said, this woman had heard and remarked upon the activity in her compartment, then surely it should be an issue. After all, in Kitty's own words, they "had to keep the reputation of the show intact."

"When you said you were sure my room was booked for single occupancy, did you tell her why?"

"Of course not."

"Did you tell her who?"

"Who was in the room, you mean?"

"Uh-huh."

Kitty's expression showed she was recalling the conversation. "I might have called you Morgan . . ." Her voice trailed away. "Oh, shit."

"Hmm." Morgan nodded. It was doubtful there would be too many other Morgans wandering around the train. And with the filming that was to take place over the next few days, it shouldn't take the mystery woman too long to put two and two together. "We need to find this woman and find out just what she heard."

Kitty harrumphed. "She already made it quite clear what she heard."

"Maybe so," Morgan conceded. "But we don't know if she realized it was two women."

Kitty stared blankly for a moment, then the penny dropped and her face brightened considerably. "She may just assume there was a man." Morgan cringed at the thought, but she could see Kitty getting excited at this possible workaround to a potential public relations disaster. Her brow furrowed and she nodded more to herself than to Morgan. "And even if she thought she heard two women we can always convince her otherwise. Yes, yes. This may just work." Kitty nodded again, obviously thinking through all the implications. "And then, even if word did leak out we could still use it to our advantage."

"How do you figure that?" Morgan couldn't see any positives to that sort of publicity at all.

"Well," Kitty said blithely, "you'd still look like a slut, but at least you'd look like a normal slut."

Morgan was temporarily rendered speechless. In the two years since Kitty had joined the show, she had shown a tight-lipped disapproval toward Morgan's tendency to share the love around, but never before had she so blatantly voiced her opinion.

Now it was apparent that she not only disapproved of the number of partners Morgan had, but also of their gender. Morgan shouldered past Kitty. It was by sheer force of will that she managed to open the sliding door without slamming it into its cavity. "Deal with it how you want, Kitty. I'm going to bed."

CHAPTER FOUR

Ally woke with a start. She blinked quickly, trying to focus, but her world consisted only of shadowy figures, the darkness stripping her surrounds of both form and color. Unfortunately the darkness did not also strip away sounds and smells. Over the course of the night three passengers had formed a chorus of snorers, and yet others added a percussion of snorts and groans as they shifted in their sleep. And at surprisingly regular intervals the farter farted. The last fart was actually what had woken Ally from her doze. Obviously oblivious, he or she had let one go at high volume. As a thick, heavy odor once again assaulted her nostrils, Ally pressed a button on the side of her watch to illuminate the face. *Jesus.* She tilted her head back as far as the headrest would allow and stared at the black ceiling. It was not yet five a.m. How much longer did she have to endure this torture?

Ally made a quick calculation. The train was due in Sydney at ten a.m. on Saturday. Taking into account the two-hour time difference between the east and west coasts, she still had a whole fifty-one hours left to travel.

Fifty-one long, fart-filled hours.

Right now, Ally wished she had boarded that outrageously small plane from Kalgoorlie back to Perth. If she had, then in only a few hours she would have had her feet back on Sydney soil. She could have had a long post-flight soak in her bath and returned to the office, fresh and ready to begin work designing her Kalgoorlie executive residence. And tonight she would have done as James had wanted and donned "that sexy little black number" he was so fond of. She would have accompanied him to his client dinner at the Summit, an iconic Sydney restaurant set high on the forty-seventh floor of Australia Square. The 360-degree views of Sydney, the extensive local and international wine list and the innovative menu made it a venue guaranteed to impress, and it was a favored location for James's corporate entertaining. He had been slightly miffed when she announced she could not attend tonight's dinner. Especially, as he pointed out, because she didn't *need* to take "the slow boat" home. But not even Ally's favorite Summit dish—the wok-fried chili and black-pepper blue-swimmer crab—could sway her into changing her mind.

"There's no guarantee Josh will be feeling so generous again this century." Ally smoothed the traces of lines that had begun to appear on either side of James's mouth and kissed him on the nose. "It's only one dinner. And I'll be back on Saturday, so we can definitely go to the charity auction together on Sunday."

James was not one to pout, at least not outwardly. Only the taut rustle of broadsheet as he nodded and returned to his copy of *The Australian* gave any indication he was less than happy. The subject was not raised again until the actual day of her departure. "It's going to be a long week without you, Alison." He shrugged into his suit jacket and picked up his black leather briefcase. He would be the first to leave her Croyden apartment, where he slept at least a couple of nights a week. He winked. They had made love that morning and he was in a somewhat jovial mood. "Although there's some lucky crab out there that's getting a second chance this Thursday."

Ally recalled mentioning something to James about good karma befalling her for sparing the crab. And she recalled James's scoff. Despite his post-coital levity, he still didn't believe in karma and other such "hocus-pocus."

Right now, neither did Ally. *Karma, my ass*, she thought as she gently lifted herself from her seat. Marge shifted and so Ally stopped still halfway to standing. Luckily, Marge did not wake. Last night she had discovered the woman could talk the hind legs off a donkey. But, she also discovered when Marge finally stopped talking long enough for her to get a word in, she was a kindly woman with a sympathetic ear.

On hearing Ally's plight, Marge had clucked and tut-tutted and shaken her head in disgust. "That's terrible, dear." She patted her arm consolingly. "To think the booking office could be allowed to make a mistake like that. I should have a word with my friend, Morgan Silverstone, for you. Bless her, such a lovely woman. I'm sure she could do something to help you, dear."

Ally's ears had pricked up at the name. "Morgan?" she repeated.

"Oh yes, dear. You *must* have heard of Morgan Silverstone. She's traveling on the train while they do some filming for *Bonnes Vacances*. Such a wonderful show. I watch it every week."

"I think I might have heard the name." Ally didn't watch much television—she just didn't have the time—but she had caught segments of the popular travel show once or twice. Not enough to put names to the faces of any of the presenters though. She wondered if Morgan Silver-something was the same Morgan who had effectively ousted her from her compartment and into cattle-class hell. Probably. Typical trumped-up media-personality behavior. Too bloody good to share space with a plebian nobody such as herself. "I doubt she can do anything to help though."

Too tired to think anymore, Ally had closed her eyes and nodded agreement that Marge should indeed have a word with her superstar friend. Marge's voice continued to drift around her for the moments it took Ally to doze off. By the time she jolted awake only a few minutes later, Marge had fallen asleep. Ally pulled the thin blanket that lay over her knees to her chin and tried for sleep again. She had adjusted her seat as far back as it would go, but just as in an airplane, sleep proved impossible. In an airplane, her sleeplessness was largely due to a dread fear the tin can they were bolting across the sky in might at any moment fall back to earth. Despite the tin can she was currently in already being securely at ground level, sleep was no closer. Ally just couldn't sleep sitting up. Especially when surrounded with snores and grunts and farts and sneezes and all the other revolting noises that human beings make. She had dozed and woken countless times during the night.

Now, having given up on sleep altogether, she continued to rise from her seat as quietly as possible. She retrieved her overnight bag from the overhead compartment and hurried to the end of the carriage where the toilet and shower was located. At this hour, she was sure to beat the morning queue to bathe. And so far as the toilet was concerned, she wanted to get there before the farter came and expelled whatever was causing the continued production of noxious gases.

A hot shower did wonders to Ally's psyche. As did the fact she had taken her sweet time, shampooing her hair—twice—and for once leaving the conditioner in for the amount of minutes recommended by the manufacturer. She had moisturized every inch of her body, had cleansed, toned and moisturized her face, plucked a few stray eyebrows, finger-dried her hair and scrutinized her nails. Once they were buffed she dressed slowly, applied some perfume and left the bathroom clean, but with a lingering mix of floral fragrances. Outside, a man with a towel slung over his shoulder stood waiting. Fully aware of his impatience, Ally grinned a hello, flounced past him and took both herself and her overnight bag in the direction of the diner car.

As expected, it was yet too early for the breakfast service to have begun. Ally slid into one of the American diner-style booths, dug her notebook and pencil from her bag and lay them on the table. She also retrieved her mobile, tried to check her messages and realized with dismay that she was out of network range. The mobile was set aside—she would try again later—and she flipped open her notebook. Being the type that was more or less brain dead before her morning coffee, by the time she had reread the notes made the previous day, her attention had already begun to wander. She rested her chin on her hand and contemplated the view outside the window. Day was breaking over the Nullabor Plain, a vast expanse of almost-nothingness nearly four times the size of Belgium. The name was derived from the Latin *nullus* meaning none, and *arbor*, meaning tree. *Rather apt*, Ally thought as she gazed out to the famed treeless plain. It was also the home of the longest straight stretch of railway track in the world. A whole 478 kilometers—297 miles—without a bend. Ally wondered if they were traveling on the straight stretch right now. If so, she hoped the train driver had something to keep his wits about him. Like a nice hot cup of coffee. She turned her attention to the canteen-style serving area. Speaking of coffee . . . wasn't it about time this mob opened for business?

But no, the security grille was still well and truly clamped down. Ally sighed and for the umpteenth time since having her sleeper carriage privileges revoked, her thoughts turned dark. She pulled her notebook toward her and started scratching out a letter of complaint that would have even the mildest-mannered consumer advocate screaming from the rooftops.

Her letter was almost completely drafted when she heard the grille on the canteen lift. At the same moment, from the corner of her eye, she saw a middle-aged woman entering the diner car. In a move that ran completely counter to her usual hang-back nature, Ally slid quickly out of her booth and bolted to the canteen. She still had forty-nine and a bit hours to kill, but this particular morning she was damned if she was going to wait in a queue for a coffee.

Begrudgingly, she handed over one of her white drink vouchers in exchange for the coffee. She grabbed a plastic stirrer from the dispenser on the counter and was just in the middle of debating whether to take white, brown or lump sugar when she was interrupted by an "Excuse me?"

Ally decided on lump sugar and took two paper-wrapped cubes. After such a poor quality sleep she needed all the energy boosts she could get. "Yes?" she said without looking up, concentrating instead on unwrapping and depositing the lumps into her black coffee.

A hand appeared near the counter, outstretched in an offer to shake. "Kitty Bergen. I think we met last night."

Oh, great. It's you again. Ally ignored the hand, instead slowly stirring her coffee and staring into it. "Yes?" she repeated.

"I was wondering if you managed to find your compartment?"

Ally finally glanced up. Was this woman for real? "Oh, yes," she said sarcastically, returning her attention to her coffee. She took a sip and edged past Kitty, wanting only to return to her booth.

Annoyingly, Kitty followed. "Good, good," she said, either unaware of Ally's tone, or choosing to ignore it. "I'm glad that little problem got sorted out. I told my friend—"

"Morgan?" Ally offered as she sat back down.

"Yes . . . Morgan." Kitty continued, smiling a little nervously, "I told Morgan about the mix-up and she was quite . . . embarrassed by the whole affair."

Ally took a sip of her coffee. It was as disgusting as the Kalgoorlie train station brew, but it gave the caffeine hit needed to sweep aside the morning fuzziness. One more sip and Ally's brain was ticking madly. *Ah-hah.* It seemed her sexed-up not-to-be compartment companion *was* the *Bonnes Vacances* Morgan Superstar-stone . . . or whatever she was called. And it seemed she was worried she may end up in the gossip columns.

Even if Morgan had had the entire national soccer team in there, Ally couldn't care less. And she certainly wouldn't bother ringing the media about it. Hell, since her mobile phone was out of network range, she couldn't even if she wanted to. "Well, as you said, it is her compartment." Ally shrugged. "She can do whatever she likes in it"—she took another few sips of her coffee—"with whomever she likes."

When Ally glanced up to Kitty to issue her a saccharine smile, she found the woman regarding her with an oddly quizzical look. Or maybe it was just the impression given by the glow of the fluorescent strip lighting in the ceiling. Whichever it was, Kitty's demeanor changed entirely and she flashed the same too-bright smile that she had given Ally outside Morgan's compartment last night. "Actually, Morgan asked me to ask you if you would join us for lunch today."

"Oh, I don't—"

"One o'clock in the Gold restaurant." Kitty didn't give Ally time to finish her refusal. "I'll clear it so you have no trouble getting in. What's your name? I'll need it to tell the staff."

"Alison." Ally took another sip of coffee. *Why did I just tell her my name?* she wondered.

Kitty peered over the rim of her spectacles, looking for more information. "Alison . . . ?"

Now Ally felt like she was back at school, being interrogated by the headmistress. Again she spoke without conscious consent. "Alison Brown."

"Alison Brown," Kitty repeated, as if to commit the name to memory. She nodded, obviously pleased with her arrangements. "Well, I have to fly. I'll see you again soon. One o'clock. We'll be waiting."

Just as in her schooldays after receiving a scolding, Ally gave a defiant "yes, sir!" salute, but Kitty missed it, not looking back as she headed in the direction of the rear of the train.

Ally slid to the window side of the booth seat and again gazed out to the dawning landscape. So . . . now she was scheduled to have lunch with a sexed-up superstar and a frightening flashback from school. *Oh, well,* she thought. *If nothing else, at least I'll get to see how the Gold class lives.*

Wanting to see as little as possible of Kitty, Morgan purposely arrived late to breakfast. Late enough for Kitty to have already filled Mark and Nick in on the previous night's activities, it seemed. Morgan had hardly sat down when Mark elbowed her in the ribs. "Busted!" he mouthed, grinning.

It was while Morgan was buttering a piece of toast that she learned Kitty had been up and about for hours. She'd been working her way through the carriages, looking for a staff member who could tell her where Mystery Woman was, when she stumbled across her in the diner car. Morgan was reaching for a pot of thick-cut marmalade when Kitty announced she had invited the woman—Alison—to lunch. "Why?" she asked, popping the lid on the jar of conserve.

"Because she was just too offhand about the whole episode—especially with her comment that you could do what you want with *whomever* you want," Kitty replied. "I get the feeling she was letting me know she knows something she shouldn't."

"I don't see how inviting her to lunch will change anything," Morgan argued.

"Yeah, Kitty," Mark chimed in. "What are you going to do?

Get out your thumbscrews and torture it out of her?"

Morgan snickered behind her toast.

Kitty shook her head and smiled at Mark. "No. No thumb-screws today. Because, as of lunchtime today, you are officially Morgan's boyfriend."

Mark dropped his Vegemite-smothered English muffin. It made his knife clatter loudly against his plate. "No way."

"Yes way." Kitty adjusted her spectacles and gave her "don't argue with me" look. "It's the perfect solution. That way, if Alison goes mouthing off to anyone and this gets into the press, it'll just look like an office love affair. It happens all the time and no one will think twice about it."

Normally laid-back Mark set his lips in a thin line. "I'm sure Rebecca will think twice about it." He half-turned in his seat and said apologetically, "Sorry, Mogs. But I'm not wrecking my chance to get some ass just to save yours."

Morgan nodded, needing no convincing. Mark had been chasing Rebecca—the supposedly natural blonde and supposedly naturally well-endowed studio sound engineer—for at least two months now. And she was getting very close to saying yes to a date. Apart from not wanting to interfere in Mark's love life, Morgan thought Kitty's plan ill-conceived and rather adolescent. "I don't expect you to, Mark." She folded her arms, signaling that that was the end of it.

But Kitty wasn't done. "Fine." She turned to Nick, who had been staring into his juice for the duration of the conversation, apparently trying to pretend this wasn't happening. "Nick?"

"Oh, no." Nick's head jerked up and he waved his hands in front of him. "Don't look at me."

"You're not married, are you?" Kitty asked, knowing full well that he wasn't.

Nick adjusted his long legs under the table. "No."

"No girlfriend or significant other? No one special you have your eye on?"

Again Nick shifted his lanky frame. "Well . . . no."

"It's settled then." Kitty downed the last of her coffee, then folded and placed her napkin on the table. "Nick, you're it. Now come on, everyone." She motioned for Nick to stand so she could edge out of the booth. "We've got work to do."

Kitty led a very disgruntled crew out of the restaurant car. Nick followed close at her heels, protesting. Morgan took over when Nick and Mark stopped by their compartment to pick up the camera and audio equipment, and she continued with her arguments against this juvenile idea almost until the moment Kitty called "action" on her interview with the train driver.

By late morning, when the train made a refueling stop at the tiny settlement of Cook, they had all but given up on trying to sway Kitty's decision. Many of the passengers disembarked for the half-hour stop, not only to explore the place but also to watch the taping of Morgan being shown the sights by the two people who currently made up the entire population of the settlement. As soon as the train pulled out again, Kitty announced she needed to make some calls and retired to her compartment with her satellite phone and her laptop, advising she did not want to be disturbed. Morgan joined Mark and Nick in their shared accommodation. There they reviewed the footage shot that morning and bitched about their producer.

At twelve-thirty Morgan stood and stretched. "I'm going to freshen up, guys. See you at lunch."

At ten to one Morgan eased into the booth at the far end of the restaurant car and slid across the plush upholstered seating to the window. She noticed that, although the booths were technically for four-person dining, the table was set for five. Another very cozy meeting.

"I'm guessing you still haven't changed your mind about this little charade?" she said to Kitty, who slid in opposite her.

"No." Kitty picked up the menu card and scrutinized it. She peered over the rim of her spectacles at Mark when he arrived and sat down next to Morgan. "You're sitting with me today, remember. That's Nick's seat." She frowned. "Where is he, by the way?"

Mark obediently changed places but rolled his eyes at Morgan once he was out of Kitty's line of sight. "He's still in our room. He's not happy about this at all, Kitty."

"And neither am I," Morgan said for the umpteenth time since Kitty had announced her little plan over breakfast.

Kitty checked her watch, pulled out her phone and dialed. She thrummed her fingers on the blood-red linen tablecloth then spoke a very curt "where are you?" into the mouthpiece. She snapped the phone shut and announced to the rest of the table, "He'll be here in a minute."

Morgan sat in silence until she saw Nick enter the restaurant. The poor guy looked like he was going to be sick. Her heart went out to him. During their midday bitch session, Nick had told Morgan there was a reason he was behind the camera and not in front of it—namely, because he hated being the focus of attention. He also admitted he couldn't pull off a lie to save his life, and that this whole thing was going to end up in disaster. When Morgan advised him to tell Kitty this, Nick had just shaken his head and fallen into a nail-biting silence. Now, knowing it was her actions that had brought all this nonsense on, Morgan decided to tell Kitty herself. She paraphrased all Nick had told her and ended with one last plea: "Let's just forget about this. We can have a nice lunch with Alison and once she sees we're all nice, *normal* people, she'll forget any ideas she may have about spreading any rumors."

Kitty looked long and hard at Morgan. "Did you or did you not tell me last night to handle this how I wanted?"

"Yes," Morgan reluctantly acknowledged.

"Well, this is how I am handling it," she said brusquely, motioning for Nick to move a little closer to Morgan. "That's better." Kitty swiveled in the direction of the carriage's far entrance and immediately turned back to the table. "She's here," she whispered. A bright smile transformed her features and she swiveled around again, this time to give a little "we're over here" wave above the ornate clear-glass partitions that separated each booth.

Morgan watched the woman—Alison—approach. The description Kitty had given last night was accurate. She was around Kitty's middling height, and around Kitty's age, maybe a little older. She also had Kitty's slight build and the same light-brown hair. But she had none of Kitty's birdlike features and, unlike Kitty's loose bun, Alison wore her hair in a short, very urbane style. So at first glance, while they were physically similar enough that they could technically share their wardrobes, their senses of style were so different that it seemed unlikely they would own anything the other wanted to wear.

The sound of Kitty's attention-getting cough halted Morgan's scrutiny of their luncheon guest. She focused on her producer, who was fixedly eyeing both Nick and her.

"Now, for God's sake, you two," Kitty appealed. "If not for me then for the sake of the show . . . at least *try* to look like lovers."

When the waiter presented Ally with her main course, she looked intently at the crispy-skinned duck with a mandarin confit. Something was wrong. Not with the food. That looked delicious. And if her appetizer of barbequed chili king prawns with a coriander squid salad had set the standard, then her duck promised to be rather special. No, there was nothing wrong with the food. Rather, something was not sitting right with this situation. Ally waited until her dining companions had also been presented with their plates before picking up her cutlery. And then, before she took her first bite she stole another glance around the table, trying hard to pinpoint just what was niggling at the back of her brain.

Whatever it was, it just wouldn't come to the fore. Ally inwardly shrugged. Maybe she was just being overly suspicious, looking for something that wasn't there. Goodness knew the train had cut through many miles while she sat in the diner carriage that morning mulling over why she had received this unexpected invitation to lunch. Initially she wondered if she would be "made an offer" to keep quiet. But she soon discarded that theory. She'd made it very clear to Kitty that she couldn't care less what Morgan did behind closed doors, and the logical extrapolation of that was that she wouldn't waste her time telling anyone about it. So bribery was off the list. Then she wondered if Morgan was trying to appease herself for sending her to steerage. On review of her early morning conversation with Kitty, however, Ally also threw that idea out. Kitty had asked if Ally had found her correct compartment, so obviously they had no idea she was now slumming it. And since her accommodation situation had not been mentioned once since she arrived, they no doubt didn't care what corner of the train she'd been squeezed into.

Ally took a sip of her cabernet sauvignon, aware she was sinking into dark thoughts again. She made a conscious effort to sweep them away and just enjoy this for what it was, a very fine lunch in much more opulent surrounds than the cafeteria-like décor of the Red diner car. And, dark thoughts aside, she had to admit she was having a much better time than she had expected. True, she still thought Kitty was uptight and altogether false, but her presence was more than compensated by the other members of the *Bonnes Vacances* crew.

Even Morgan.

Ally had caught her first real-life glimpse of her earlier that morning, after returning to her seat next to Marge. Morgan had been walking through the carriage behind Kitty, apparently on their way to do some filming. Ally only knew this because Marge had waved wildly at Morgan, who stopped and gave a distracted hello. She had not looked at Ally at all, and in fact gave Marge only the merest of glances, saying she was on a tight schedule and that she had to fly. Afterward, Marge smiled at Ally and patted her on the hand, saying how Morgan must be so busy. But Ally could tell she was disappointed. It was at that moment her already dim view of the woman darkened even further. Marge, in contrast, was not one to dwell on negatives, and once word got around that more filming would take place at the Cook stop, she could hardly contain herself until the train drew to a standstill. Ally had followed Marge outside into suffocating heat, but she had not contributed to the audience that formed around Morgan & Co., choosing instead to meander around the settlement by herself. When she and Marge settled back into their seats Marge had been all chatter about the filming process. Apparently her efforts to get Morgan's attention when filming ceased were as unfruitful as earlier, her being "very involved" with talking to the cameraman. Ally had not commented, but her view of Morgan as the stuck-up star had been doubly reinforced.

So, when Ally arrived at the table and was in turn introduced to everyone by Kitty, she had given Morgan a cold glance combined with an even colder greeting. But despite her best efforts to keep her dislike for the woman alive, by the time they had been served their appetizers, she found her preformed opinion melting.

Ally's cynical side warned her that Morgan's welcoming demeanor and seemingly genuine interest in what Ally had to say were probably both carefully cultivated traits that could be called up at will. And it was also her cynical side—or maybe it was just the female tendency toward bitchiness that reared its head whenever confronted with a particularly beautiful woman—that told her Morgan had no doubt won her position with the television network courtesy of the casting couch. Her less cynical side admitted she was probably seeing the woman for what she really was—a genuinely likable person who had not only striking good looks, but also a keen mind and a certain charisma that drew people around her like moths to a flame. A formidable combination, and no doubt her presence was one of the reasons, as Kitty made sure to point out, *Bonnes Vacances* kept topping the ratings.

Just as likable was Mark. To Ally's mind he could have been a poster boy for the stereotypical laid-back Australian bloke. Not that he was especially handsome. His nose was a little too big and his ears stuck out a little too much from under a mop of sandy-colored sun-bleached hair. But he was obviously comfortable in his own skin, and what he lacked in looks he made up for in personality. Ally felt instantly at ease with the man and was glad he formed a buffer between her and Kitty, him squashed between them in a space meant only to accommodate two. Their close arrangement had lasted only as long as the aperitif because once the appetizers arrived it became apparent the three of them would either have to take turns eating or have a constant clash of cutlery. After consultation with the waiter, a chair materialized and Ally took her place at the head of the table, which had the advantage of now allowing her to see all of her dining companions without obstruction. But since she was now smack in the middle of the corridor—not the most convenient of locations—she had to draw her chair as close to the table as possible to allow the staff to squeeze past.

Another disadvantage of her new position was that it impinged on the legroom of Nick. Long and lanky, he had been jutting one leg into the corridor and moving it out of the way each time a waiter or fellow diner passed by. Now, after knocking knees with her on at least three occasions, he had folded his legs under the table and kept them there, unmoving. She imagined it must be quite uncomfortable as he wore a rather pained look on his face. Or maybe his pained expression was due to the intense looks Kitty kept throwing at him. For what reason the poor guy was being targeted, Ally could not surmise. Personally, she found him rather sweet and unassuming, and definitely inoffensive.

Ally shifted in her seat, and not just to avoid her head being knocked by the waiter who was about to pass behind her chair, but because she was again getting the feeling that something was not quite right. From the corner of her eye she had caught another look thrown at Nick, this time Kitty tilting her head almost imperceptibly toward Morgan as she peered over her spectacles, her brow furrowed.

What the hell was going on between those two? Ally wondered.

Her thoughts were interrupted by Mark. "How's the duck?" he asked, gazing a little enviously at her plate. "It looks really good."

"It is." Ally cut a piece of the breast, topped it with a smear of confit and held out her fork. "Do you want to try?"

"Sure." Mark took the fork from her hand. He chewed slowly before returning the fork to Ally. "Damn, that *is* good. I think I might order that tonight."

"You're as bad as a woman for changing her mind." Morgan rolled her eyes at him before glancing at Ally. "Last night he swore he would have the steak for *every* meal."

"Well, it's darn good steak." Mark shrugged, taking a bite of his fillet. He picked up his beer and took a large swallow. "But variety is the spice of life. Is it not, Mogs?"

"Definitely." Morgan winked at him as she reached across the table to clink her glass against Mark's. "I always say—"

Kitty coughed. "What do you think of the steak, Morgan?"

Morgan looked pointedly at her snapper fillet. "How would I know? I ordered the fish."

"Nick?" Kitty questioned, an edge of impatience in her voice. "How's your steak?"

Nick had been concentrating hard on the act of eating. He glanced up from his plate. "Huh?"

"I said . . ." Now there was definite irritation in Kitty's tone, even though Ally noticed she was at pains to control it. She also caught another covert tilt of her head in Morgan's direction. "Your steak looks good. Maybe someone else would like to try it, too."

"Oh." A flash of realization crossed Nick's features just at the moment Morgan accepted Mark's proffered steak-laden fork. He quickly cut a portion and offered it to Kitty. "Here you go."

For a single moment Kitty just stared at Nick, a look of disbelief on her face. Ally was almost sure she heard her mutter "Jesus Christ" under her breath. Then her demeanor changed completely and she waved coyly in Nick's direction. "Oh . . . stop joking around, Nick. Morgan's going to get jealous." She picked up her fork and loaded it with some of the herbed potato mash that accompanied her lamb cutlet. The fork was brought to her mouth, but she stopped short of eating, seemingly giving a thought some consideration before saying it out loud. "You've probably noticed by now, so there's no point trying to keep it a secret. Morgan and Nick are"—Kitty winked at Ally—"you know . . ."

Ally blinked, more than a little surprised. If Kitty meant that Nick and Morgan were lovers, then no, she didn't know. They certainly hadn't given any signs pointing in that direction. If anything, they seemed a little uncomfortable with each other. They hadn't shown any hint of intimacy during the entire time she had been present and even conversation between the pair was limited. Not that Nick said much of anything to anyone. He was a polar opposite to Morgan and definitely not someone Ally would have predicted as her choice of partner. In fact, she thought Mark to be a much more likely candidate for Morgan's affections.

Ally was in the middle of giving a noncommittal nod when she realized an apparent contradiction. Last night Nick had accompanied Kitty to the baggage carriage. How could he have been on the platform at the same time Morgan was having the time of her life in her compartment? Unless, of course, she was having the time of her life with someone other than Nick . . . *Oh, ho!* Ally's brain started fitting the pieces together. Maybe Morgan and Mark had been taking advantage of Nick's temporary absence to have a little fling? Maybe that was why Kitty had been so unnerved to find Morgan "busy" in her compartment. And maybe Nick had either found out about the affair or was having his suspicions. That would explain the distance between him and Morgan.

It still didn't explain why Ally had been invited to lunch though. Maybe she should just ask? She pondered the notion as she took a sip of her cabernet sauvignon. It was very, very good. She set the glass on the table and picked up her cutlery again. She would ask after dessert and coffee. After all, there was no point in ruining what was probably going to be her last decent meal for the remainder of her journey.

"So, what's next on your film schedule?" she asked Morgan in an attempt to change the topic completely.

"Well, after we're finished here we have a few days in the studio, editing and the like. And I'll be recording the lead-ins to the segments that will be airing in the next weeks. And then we're off to—" Morgan looked at Mark. "Where is it again?"

"Vanuatu."

"That's right . . . Vanuatu." Morgan gave a self-deprecating smile. "Sometimes I can't remember where we actually are, never mind where we're going next."

Ally sighed enviously. "You know how to make someone jealous, don't you? I would *love* to go to Vanuatu. It's supposed to be a beautiful spot."

"Very romantic," Kitty interjected quickly. She smiled at Morgan and Nick like an indulgent parent. "I'm sure I'll have trouble getting much work out of these two."

"Stop it, Kitty." Morgan glared across the table then glanced in embarrassment to Ally. "Sorry, Alison."

"Call me Ally," she reminded her. "And no need to apologize." Ally secretly thought Mark might not be getting much work done either. And although she had never had an affair and had never even considered having one, she said, "I understand."

Ally had directed her comment to Morgan, but she turned her attention to Kitty, feeling her gaze upon her. Sure enough, Kitty was regarding her with the same look that she had that morning in the Red diner car. Once again Ally felt she was back at school, being sized up by the headmistress after being caught committing some misdemeanor. Unwilling—or maybe even unable—to hold the gaze, Ally returned her attention to her plate. She had saved some of the crispy duck skin for last and now she attacked it, cutting it into small bite-sized pieces.

It was delectable, the fat rendered to perfection. Ally savored each piece slowly, happy to listen to the renewed banter between Morgan and Mark, the two of them recounting an episode in Egypt where Morgan had become hopelessly lost between leaving her hotel and reaching her destination.

"The pyramids aren't exactly small, Morgan," Mark teased. "I really have no idea how you could miss them." He turned to Ally. "Our Morgan has what you might call a 'unique' sense of direction. Haven't you, Mogs?"

Morgan nodded, giving that self-deprecating smile again. "If I didn't have gravity to keep me down, I wouldn't know which way was up."

"Sounds like rather an odd quality for a traveler," Ally commented, laughing. She was picturing Morgan rushing all over Cairo, trying to find the massive stone structures.

"Well, luckily, I usually have someone to point me in the right direction." Morgan turned to Nick and poked him in the side. "Mister here was supposed to escort me. But no, he left early to go take some happy snaps." She cast her eyes heavenward. "Cameramen. I tell you . . . they see life through a lens."

"Now, now, you two. No fighting." Kitty wagged her finger at them and then gave Ally a look that she supposed was meant to convey she was their long-suffering mediator. "They're like this with each other all the time."

Ally smiled thinly. Kitty was a pain in the ass. And what was it with the continued references to the pairing of Morgan and Nick? She wondered if a covert acknowledgment of their relationship would make the woman shut up about it. "How long have you been together?" she asked.

Nick shot a worried glance to Kitty and start biting on the nail of his little finger.

"Not long," Morgan said quickly, also shooting a glance toward Kitty.

"No, not long at all." Kitty seemed unfazed by the continued filthy stare she was receiving from Morgan. "They're still at *that* stage." She winked at Ally. "As you probably gathered from last night."

Ally had been in the process of taking the last piece of crispy duck skin to her mouth. She let the fork hover a few inches from her face, more than a little interested to see the others' reactions to what she knew to be an outright lie.

Morgan turned her attention for the first time to the view as seen through the slats of the micro-blinds. Mark sculled the last of his beer and placed the empty glass with a thud back onto the table. Most astonishing of all was Nick. Although still chewing on his fingernails, he registered no surprise at the news he was supposedly with Morgan last night.

Apparently all four were in collaboration.

"Okay." Suddenly furious, Ally placed her fork, which still held her last piece of duck skin, next to her knife on the plate. "Thank you for lunch, but I find I am no longer hungry."

"Ally?"

"Alison to you, thank you very much." Ally glared at Kitty, wishing for the world she could slap the plastic smile from her face. "Look"—she addressed the table in general—"I don't know what the hell you're all playing at and why you've involved me, but"—she held her hand above her head—"I've had it up to here! First I get thrown out of my room before I even step foot in it. Then I get shoved into stinking cattle class where I have to slum it with the great unwashed. And now, for some totally unknown reason, I'm being lied to by an entire TV crew. What is this?" She peered around the carriage and even lifted the red tablecloth and had a look under the table. "Am I on *Candid Camera* or something? Or do you all just get your kicks from tormenting random members of the public?"

There was a stunned silence around the table.

Ally noticed Kitty open her mouth to speak so she cut in before she could get a word out. "Save it for someone who cares."

She pulled her chair away from the table, only narrowly missing a collision with an unsuspecting waiter who was delivering a tray of dessert delicacies to another table. Increasingly pissed that she would now miss out on the lemon tart she had already chosen from the menu card, Ally threw her napkin onto her plate and, without looking back, stalked down the corridor.

Just as Ally had done two seconds prior, Morgan threw her napkin onto her plate and glared at Kitty. "Look where your big ideas have got us now. Nick"—she motioned for him to stand—"let me get out please."

Kitty made the same shooing motion to Mark. "I'll go after her."

"Like hell you will." Morgan slid quickly across Nick's seat to the corridor. "You've done enough damage already. I'll go."

The corridor of the restaurant car was empty except for a waiter serving drinks and another presenting some delicious-looking desserts to some very Poe-faced Brits who obviously wouldn't be impressed even if the Queen herself was serving them. Morgan strode out quickly, hoping to catch Ally before she got too far ahead.

There was no sign of her in any of the Gold carriages, and it wasn't until Morgan stepped into Red that she caught a glimpse of her. Morgan broke into a half-trot. Her own compartment was in the next carriage. Ideally, she would like to speak to Ally in the privacy of her room, not wishing an audience for what she had decided she would say. Because what she had decided to say was the truth. Whether that was to be for good or bad, Morgan did not know. She may have known the woman for only a few brief hours, but there was something about Ally that struck a chord deep within her. And the resonance of this chord told her it would be for the good.

"Ally!" she called. The irony that she was going to invite another woman into her compartment for a potentially trouble-some interaction was not lost on Morgan. "Ally. Stop!"

But Ally didn't stop, or even slow down. She continued at her rapid pace, occasionally knocking her shoulders on the walls of the corridor as she moved in opposition to the carriage's sway. Morgan, unwilling to draw any more attention to herself than necessary, ceased calling after her and watched her disappear into the next carriage. She hesitated for just a moment. Then she followed.

She followed her through the Red sleeper, lounge and diner cars, and she followed her into the first and then second of the upright seating carriages. Being close to the end of the luncheon session, there was a lot of movement in the corridors. Morgan nodded politely to all those who said hello to her and murmured, "Sorry, but I can't stop and chat at the moment," to those who appeared to want to extend the niceties beyond a greeting. She was glad she didn't bump into Marge. Morgan was aware she had brushed her off this morning and didn't want to have to do the same again now. "Oh, crap," Morgan muttered to herself. She really had to stop even thinking of Marge. Because, just as occurred yesterday when she made her mad leap into a seat opposite the fabulously French Marie, the mere thought of her made her appear. She was near the other end of the carriage and—surprise, surprise—talking to someone. The carriages were long, and luckily she was facing the other direction, but right at this moment, the distance between them was not nearly far enough.

For the second time since commencing her pursuit of Ally down the length of the train, Morgan hesitated. Then she bit the bullet, increased her speed for the few steps it took to catch up to her, reached out and grabbed her by the arm.

Not surprisingly, the reception Morgan received was even colder than when Kitty had introduced her to Ally at lunch. At the time, Morgan had wondered why Ally was so chilly toward her. Little had she known that Ally's frigid reception was at least partly due to the fact she had lost her sleeper berth and ended up in an upright seat. In fact, knowing what she did now—had Morgan been Ally—she would have told Kitty to shove her lunch invitation where the sun didn't shine. Or else she would have accepted, downed as much expensive wine she could lay her hands on and then let rip. Ally had in fact done just that—with the exception of the consumption of an excess of alcohol—but to her credit she had let fly only after realizing she had been told a barefaced lie.

Now, Morgan wondered if Ally would have even mentioned her less-than-ideal travel circumstances had Kitty not insisted on pursuing her ridiculous charade. Somehow she doubted it. Over lunch, once Ally's initial defenses came down and she relaxed, she had seemed content just to enjoy the moment and leave past events in the past.

All things considered, she didn't blame Ally one bit for the return of the icy glare. Nor was she surprised at the "Get your hands off me!" that she hissed at her.

Morgan loosened her hold on Ally's arm but quietly pleaded, "Please, Ally. Let me explain."

"Let go of me," Ally repeated.

Morgan let her hand fall. "I'm sorry."

"As well you should be." Ally looked down as she smoothed the material of her shirt where Morgan's hand had been. When she eventually met Morgan's gaze, her expression was one of angry confusion. "Can you please explain to me just what was going on in there?" She pointed back toward the rear of the train, presumably to indicate the restaurant car. "What was all that bullshit about you and Nick? Because *I know* it wasn't him with you last night."

Morgan opened her mouth to explain it was all Kitty's stupid idea, then stopped herself. No matter how little she thought of Kitty personally—bitch sessions with Nick and Mark aside—she had never bad-mouthed her in front of anyone. "We all just thought it was better—"

"Yes. I know what you all thought," Ally said bitterly. "You all thought it was better that you cover up your affair in case I decided to call the papers. Well, let me tell you, *Mogs*, I don't care what you do behind closed doors, with Mark or Nick or anyone else for that matter. I didn't care last night . . . I didn't care this morning when I told Kitty the exact same thing . . . and I don't care now. You can swing from the Gold class chandeliers if that's what turns you on, so long as you leave me out of it. But what I do care about is being lied to"—Ally pointed down the carriage—"and having to sit in here for three days when I booked a damn sleeper." For a second Ally looked like she was going to cry and instinctively Morgan reached out her hand to her. It was slapped away. "This whole trip is turning out to be a nightmare."

With that, and with one final glare at Morgan, Ally turned on her heel and stalked down the carriage.

Again Morgan followed and she stopped in front of the seat

that Ally flung herself into. Out of the corner of her eye she saw that Marge had detected her presence and was waving madly in her direction. She answered with a wave of her own then refocused her attention on Ally. "Honestly," she began quickly, fully aware that Marge was now lumbering down the corridor toward her, "I didn't know you'd ended up in here—"

"Morgan!"

"Hello, Marge." Morgan turned her attention to Marge and smiled. "I'm really sorry about having to dash off so quickly this morning, but we were all running a little late . . ." She felt the weight of Ally's scorn even without looking at her. Ally didn't have to say a word for Morgan to know that she thought she reeked of insincerity.

And she really didn't like the feeling that knowledge gave her.

"Dearie me. Don't give it a second thought." Marge's delighted smile turned even more brilliant at the acknowledgment. "Bless you, Morgan. I know how busy you are. But I'm very happy you did finally come because I've been wanting to talk to you about my friend here, Alison." Marge tut-tutted. "Dreadful treatment she's had on this train, bless her. We were talking about it most all last night, weren't we, dear?" Marge actually patted Ally on the head. She didn't seem to care that Ally neither confirmed nor denied their conversation. She just charged on. "And I told her not to worry because Morgan Silverstone from *Bonnes Vacances* was on the train and that being such an *important* and lovely woman"—Marge beamed at Morgan, not a hint of guile in her expression—"that you would be able to help."

"Actually, that's exactly why I'm here." Morgan now felt doubly sorry for Ally in the knowledge that on top of everything else she had spent a night next to chatterbox Marge. The woman had probably not had a wink of sleep. Despite the temptation not to, she met the eyes she could bet had been rolling skyward at the mention of her as "lovely" and "important." As expected, the look she received was filthy. For Marge's benefit, she twisted the truth a little. "I was told over lunch about your predicament, Alison." She saw Ally raise her eyebrows at the white lie but, like Marge when she was on a roll, she ploughed on. "All I can say is that I'm dreadfully sorry this has happened to you and I hope we can figure out something to help make the rest of your trip a little more pleasant. Maybe we can talk about this further . . . somewhere a little quieter?"

Ally's expression turned defiant. "It's okay. We can talk about it right here . . . *I* have nothing to hide from anyone."

Morgan mentally froze. Ally had her over a barrel. Maybe her lunchtime assumption of her as honest and trustworthy had been wrong and the woman tended to vindictiveness. She glanced around the carriage. It was filling quickly with returned diners and . . . *oh, shit* . . . there was Kitty. She was heading straight for them. *Damn woman.* Obviously she didn't trust Morgan to handle this herself.

Not that she had done a very good job so far. Morgan dived on the first idea that entered her head. "Well, I was thinking, since I have a double compartment all to myself, that you might like to share with me for the rest of your journey."

Marge clapped her hands together excitedly. "Oh, bless you, Morgan. What a delightful and generous offer." She placed a hand on Ally's shoulder and shook it. "See, dear. *I told you* my friend Morgan would be able to do something for you. But to actually offer to share her room. Oh, Alison, dear . . . you are one lucky duck."

Morgan noted that Ally didn't look like she was overly lucky. And who could blame her? She was only getting what she should have gotten last night anyway.

Kitty reached them just in time to hear Marge's last comment. "Who's a lucky duck?"

Morgan shuddered, wondering what Kitty would have to say when she discovered the new sleeping arrangements. She didn't have to wait long to find out. Marge, who quickly introduced her to everyone, also gushed out the news of her "most generous" offer.

"Oh, I don't think that's such a good idea." Kitty flashed Morgan a glance that clearly said, "What the fuck do you think you are doing?" It was quickly followed by her brighter-than-bright producer smile. That was aimed at Ally. "Morgan is very busy and she'll be keeping terrible hours. You won't get a moment of peace. I think it's much better if you take my sleeper and I'll bunk in with her."

"But Alison was asked first!" Marge blustered, obviously put out that this stranger was muscling in on the "berth with a star" she had managed to secure for her friend.

Kitty peered over the rim of her spectacles, her smile still plastered on her face. "Madam, I happen to be the producer of *Bonnes Vacances*."

In turn, Marge peered at Kitty over her own spectacles. "Oh . . . yes. Bless you, dear. I remember you now from the filming at Cook." She mimicked the motion of a clapperboard clapping and called out, "Action!" Then she laughed heartily.

Kitty was only momentarily taken aback, shaking her head slightly before she returned her attention to Ally. "As I said, I think it better that you take my room. It's a single so you won't be disturbed. And it's in Gold class so I'll clear it that you get use of all the Gold class facilities." She checked her watch. "We're due to start filming again in one hour. I'll organize it so the room will be ready and you can move in anytime after that. It's compartment three in the first of the Gold carriages after leaving Red. Okay?"

Ally, looking rather stunned, just nodded.

"Right. That's settled." Kitty, as usual, appeared pleased with her decision. "Morgan, you can come and help me move my things into your compartment."

Morgan, also stunned at this sudden and most unwelcome

change in plans, just nodded in acquiescence. Then she nodded a good-bye to Ally and Marge.

Marge, too, just nodded. For once she seemed to have nothing to say.

Kitty had that effect on people.

Jesus, Morgan thought sourly as she followed her producer. *How long till we get to Sydney?*

CHAPTER FIVE

One hour and ten minutes after Kitty had left the upright seating carriage with Morgan in tow, Ally knocked tentatively on the door of what was now, allegedly, her compartment. Although she had passed into Gold class without being questioned, she was still not quite certain of the legitimacy of Kitty's offer, so she waited for what seemed a reasonable amount of time for a response. When none came she slowly slid the door across and took her first peek inside the sleeper.

It certainly looked unoccupied. In fact, it looked recently prepared for a new lodger. The carpeted floor had telltale vacuum cleaner lines and the stainless steel wash basin had the squeaky-clean shine of one unused since its last polish. Ally stepped inside, dropped her overnight bag onto the floor and began examining her new space. There was a teeny wardrobe—completely empty—behind one of the sections of wood paneling that lined the entire compartment, and a little shelf and mirror above the wash basin that contained a selection of train-issued miniature toiletries. There was also a little train-issued commemorative pin attached to an elaborately folded piece of card. No toilet or shower though. Shame. According to the train-issued magazine that Ally had thumbed through that morning, private facilities were only found in the two-berth Gold class compartments.

"Oh, well." Ally spoke aloud even though she was alone. "It still beats the hell out of fart-class."

The weight of the hours since boarding the train suddenly lifted and Ally did a little victory dance on the carpet. Then, just as suddenly, she felt a different weight—that of fatigue—settle on her shoulders. She slid the compartment door closed, dropped onto the seat. It was far more plush and comfortable than the one she had spent the previous night in. She loosened her muscles so she swayed in time with the rhythmic motion of the train and, even before she could finish her thought about how glorious the seat would be once it was converted into a bed, she fell into a light, but much needed sleep.

By five p.m. she was awake again, her hour-and-a-bit nap leaving her surprisingly refreshed. Ally stretched like a cat, pulled her overnight bag within reach and dug out her toiletry bag. She took an immense amount of pleasure from the simple act of being able to brush her teeth and cleanse her face at her very own wash basin. She'd also cleansed her face and teeth in the hour before taking possession of this compartment, but the glob of toothpaste, smear of soap, splashes of some unidentifiable liquid and, grossest of all, what looked remarkably like a pubic hair left by the previous occupant had done little to enhance the sensation of having freshened up.

Next Ally again tried her phone, but it was still out of network range. Probably her best bet was to wait until tomorrow morning when they hit Adelaide, capital of the state of South Australia. Poor Adelaide had the reputation of being the dullest

Australian capital city—a claim Ally couldn't attest to since she'd never had an exciting enough reason to visit—but, dull or no, it was sure to have a mobile network. She snapped her phone shut and popped it back into her bag. Then she had another little dig through her belongings and retrieved her notebook, digital camera and sketchbook.

She took some time reviewing the numerous pictures she'd taken of every aspect of the mining executive's prospective homesite. Then she unlatched the fold-out table, opened the notebook to her pages of notes and her sketchbook to her beginnings of sketches and began reviewing them. She turned her focus to outside the window, imprinting the landscape of reds and ochres and desert tundra into her mind. Finally, she closed her eyes and let the creative side of her brain take over. As always, it came up with something fantastical but largely impractical. Nevertheless, Ally opened her eyes again and began modifying one of yesterday's sketches. As with every new architectural project she undertook, she would massage and shape her idea until the impractical became practical, the fantastical simply fantastic.

She bent her head to her work and became totally engrossed in her task.

An indeterminate length of time later, a rapping on her door interrupted Ally's train of thought. "Hmm?" she said half to herself, chewing on her pencil as she continued to frown over the sketch of the roofline. The more space in the roof cavity, the easier it was to maintain an ambient temperature in the house itself. But this roofline, while satisfying the sustainable aspect of housing design, just did not work aesthetically. It was too steep. She erased it and began a new line with less of a gradient. The change was minimal, but the effect was great. Ally held up her sketchbook and scrutinized it at arm's length. Much better.

It was then that she heard the rapping again, more insistent this time. "Yes?" she called, still somewhat distracted. She tilted her head to look at her sketch from a different angle. "The door's open."

Ally lowered her pad to find Morgan's head poking around the door. Her stomach lurched. Surely Kitty didn't want her room back and had sent Morgan to do the deed. Or—a more probable scenario crossed her mind—Morgan had already had it up to her neck with Kitty and had come to beg Ally to move out.

"Hello."

Morgan smiled. "I was just wondering how you're settling in."

"Fine, thanks." Ally registered Morgan's demeanor as a little hesitant, but definitely not so much so that it pointed to an impending eviction. She put her sketchpad down and indicated the materials strewn across the table. "I'm finally able to get down to some work."

"So I see." Morgan slid the door open a little farther but did not cross the threshold. "I won't keep you. I just wanted to make sure everything was in order."

"Everything's fine, really," Ally repeated.

"Okay then." Morgan nodded and made a move as if to leave. Then she seemed to reconsider, opening the door fully and turning so she faced Ally directly. "Actually, I was wondering . . . since lunch ended up a bit of a fiasco . . . if maybe we could start over again with dinner."

"Oh, that's really not necessary." Ally waved away the memory of lunch and everything that had preceded it. That was all in the past, and now that she was ensconced in her own compartment, she was in a much better frame of mind. And to be honest, while she could handle Morgan and Mark and Nick, she really didn't want to sit through another meal with Kitty. "Look," she said, voicing her next thought as it occurred. "Why don't you ask Marge if she wants to have dinner with you? I know it would make her year." She smiled. "But I wouldn't put her in the seat in the corridor if I were you, unless you want to block all through traffic." Her smile turned a little wicked. "Kitty would be a much better fit."

Morgan laughed. "I see what you mean. But I'd actually planned to have dinner without the others. Sometimes you can see a little too much of people, you know." She paused and it wasn't until Ally nodded in agreement that she continued. "Everyone else wanted to eat at the first sitting, so I decided to reserve a table for the second. And I'd like you to join me."

"Oh." Ally was a little taken aback. She looked down at her sketchpad and other work paraphernalia, wondering at yet another unexpected invitation. But maybe she was just being cynical again. Surely there couldn't be any more bullshit bombshells left to drop. And a bit of company while eating would be welcome. "Well, if you've already booked a table . . ."

Morgan appeared pleased. "Excellent."

"And Marge can join us?"

"Well . . ."

Ally sprang to her defense. "She's a nice woman."

"I don't doubt that," Morgan said quickly. "It's just that I was hoping . . . excuse me just a minute." She pulled a phone from her pocket, checked the caller ID and said apologetically, "Sorry. I have to take this."

"No problem." Ally guessed Morgan's phone, since it had not rung—was set to vibrate. She turned her attention back to her sketchpad, scanning her preliminary design. She did so without the benefit of her usual critical eye, part of her attention on Morgan's half of the phone conversation. Not listening in on the words, she was more attuned to the cadence of Morgan's voice, how she articulated her consonants and how her tone lowered at the end of a sentence. It was pleasant. A good voice for radio. Ally glanced toward the door, where Morgan was leaning against the frame and idly twisting a strand of glossy auburn hair around her finger. It was fashionably long and framed those striking features—slate-gray eyes, not flinty but . . . piercing; chiseled bones

68

offset by a full softness to the lips. And of course, perfect teeth, a must for her job. So, she had a good voice for radio and a good face for television. And the body . . . Ally took in the slender frame, long legs and generous bust. It was a body that, bikini-clad, could quite easily grace the cover of *Sports Illustrated.* Ally returned to her work, smiling slightly as she bent over her sketchpad. It was a wonder what a private compartment with a wash basin could do. Because in ordinary circumstances this was a woman she, like the majority of the female population, should hate on sight.

But she didn't. In fact, she thought Morgan was . . . attractive? . . . appealing? . . . appealingly attractive? Ally chewed on the end of her pencil, frowning at her inability to describe just what she thought.

Nice. Ally pounced on the benign word. She thought Morgan was . . . nice. Pleased at her description, she tried to concentrate on her work. Now, where was she? Oh, yes . . . rooflines.

Still not fully focused on the job at hand, her peripheral vision caught the moment Morgan finished her call, snapped her phone shut and slid it into a pocket. "Who's your provider?" she asked, curious as to how Morgan was able to receive and, presumably, make calls when she couldn't. "Because I've tried my phone a couple of times today and I sure can't latch onto a network out here."

"It's a satellite phone." Morgan pulled it from her pocket again and showed it to Ally. "We all get issued with one. It doesn't matter where we are on the planet, we can still make calls."

"Pretty useful when you don't know where you are on the planet." Ally grinned cheekily as she handed the phone back.

"Exactly." Morgan took the teasing in good fun. "Now they just need to invent one with built-in GPS so it can also navigate me to where I'm supposed to be." She held the phone out again. "If you need to make a call . . ."

Ally briefly considered the offer before taking the proffered phone. "Thanks." She felt Morgan's gaze upon her as she dialed. It made her feel a little self-conscious. She again picked up her pencil and rolled it between her fingers as she waited for an answer. James answered on the third ring. After exchanging hellos, Ally, sensing Morgan's curiosity, was taken by a sudden mischievous streak. "James," she said, swinging her legs over one of the armrests, "have I got some front-page news for you!" She glanced up at Morgan and noted with a certain amount of glee that her expression, although she tried to mask it, was worried.

James replied, "What is it, Alison?"

Ally looked directly at Morgan, took a deep breath, then paused, just to extend the drama. "I've been upgraded to first class!" She poked her tongue out at Morgan and slung her feet back onto the floor again.

Ally kept the call brief, not only because she was aware it wasn't her phone, but because she and James never exchanged long calls. They both tended to say what needed to be said and got off the line. She didn't mention the reason for the upgrade, or the presence of the *Bonnes Vacances* crew, deciding they were details that didn't need to be said. But she did wish James well in the business he wanted to discuss at tonight's client dinner and reminded him of the time the train was due to arrive in Sydney.

"I'll be there waiting for you. I love you, Alison."

Ally lowered her voice a little. "I love you too. 'Bye." She snapped the phone shut and handed it back to Morgan. Then she grinned slyly. "Now we're even."

"Thank God." Morgan's expression was no longer worried, but she sighed dramatically. "I'd hate to see you when you've really got it in for somebody." She nodded in the direction of the Gold lounge carriage. "Can I interest you in an aperitif?"

Ally checked her watch and noticed with some surprise that it was almost half past seven. "What time's dinner?"

"Eight thirty."

"Well, I still have to get changed and I really should run down and invite Marge before she hits the diner car—if she hasn't already."

"Why don't I run down and invite Marge while you get changed?" Morgan suggested. "Then you'll have time for a drink."

"You *will* invite her?" Ally asked a little suspiciously.

"Cross my heart and hope to die." Morgan made the motions as she said the words. "I'll see you in—"

"Twenty minutes." Ally stood, waited until Morgan had left, then closed and latched the door behind her.

Alone again, she looked to her sketchpad, lying facedown on the table. She'd been so involved in it before being interrupted. Now, feeling no more than a momentary twinge of guilt, she picked it up and shoved it into her bag. After all, had she been in Sydney, she wouldn't be working; she'd be donning her little black dress to accompany James to his client dinner.

Ally scrounged through her overnight bag. She had no little black dress in there. Having packed with only the option of Red dining open to her, she didn't really have anything considered suitable as Gold-class dinner attire. She had just worn slacks and a light jumper to lunch and was indeed still wearing them now. She emptied the contents of the bag and considered the possibilities. There was the business suit she had worn to meet the mining executive, and the jeans and light cotton shirt she had subsequently changed into to go tramping around his block. Finally, there was another pair of jeans, two more T-shirts and another cotton shirt, this one in the style that was supposed to look crinkled.

The business suit, while in a modern cut, was still a little too "businesslike," and the clothes she had worn while assessing the homesite were tainted with Kalgoorlie's red desert dust. Her other pair of jeans were a designer brand and low cut. Trendy but not restaurant garb. And, of course, she'd already dined in her current outfit.

After a brief wardrobe crisis Ally decided it didn't really matter what she wore since whatever she chose she'd still look out of place. All her meals were now to be in Gold anyway, so by the time she reached Sydney she'd have to work her way through the contents of her bag, suitable or not.

"Jeans it is." She tossed them and the crinkly shirt onto the seat and hung her business suit in the teeny wardrobe.

Another wardrobe crisis occurred once Ally had dressed. She pulled out the business suit and weighed it up against her current attire. Then she laughed derisively at herself. She hadn't given two seconds' thought to the suitability of her outfit when she dressed for lunch. Why should she be worried now? Once again the suit was hung and Ally turned her attention to the contents of her makeup bag.

By the time she'd finished with that, she was what could be called fashionably late. And that didn't worry Ally at all. In fact, she idled down her carriage, even stopping to peer into the darkness from one of the large windows that flanked the corridor. And when she entered the Gold class lounge car and was immediately greeted by a wave, she was pleased in the knowledge that Morgan had been looking out for her, even though she was already surrounded by a small group of people, one of whom was Marge.

Inexplicably, as she approached, she felt a little twinge of regret for having insisted that Marge join them for dinner. She set the feeling aside for examination at a later point, caught the eye of a wandering waiter and ordered a gin and tonic.

Hours later Ally toyed with the wrapper of the chocolate that had accompanied their post-dinner coffee. It was the best coffee she'd had since leaving Sydney, and although midnight was approaching she was seriously considering ordering another one. She looked around the table to her dining companions. "Another coffee, anyone?"

"Definitely." Morgan pushed her cup toward the middle of the table.

"Dearie me, no." Marge mimicked Morgan's actions, pushing at her cup. "If I do I won't get a wink of sleep." She clutched the strap of her handbag and edged out of their booth from her seat next to Ally. "I've had a marvelous night, bless you, dears. But this old stick had better leave you young ones to it."

Both Ally and Morgan stood, exclaiming how Marge wasn't old at all, and after lots of cheek-kissing and numerous expressions of thanks, they wished her a good night.

"I'll come to see you off tomorrow." Ally had promised to meet Marge before she disembarked at Adelaide early the next morning.

Morgan clasped Marge's hands within her own. "It's been a pleasure."

Ally smiled as she saw Marge's eyes fill with emotion and draw Morgan into a hug guaranteed to expel the air supply in her lungs. She laughed when Marge trundled toward the exit and Morgan sat down, gasping for breath.

"You've made her very happy."

Morgan clutched at her ribs, grimacing. "Any happier and I'd be dead."

Ally ignored Morgan's theatrics, motioning for the waiter and nodding when Morgan suggested they order cognac to accompany their coffee.

"I'm going to be drunk, you know." Ally looked a little dubiously to the potent alcohol when it was delivered to their table. In addition to her predinner gin and tonic, she had consumed a glass of white wine with her appetizer, a red with her main course and a port with her dessert.

"You'll be fine." Morgan picked up her cognac. "Here's to Marge."

"To Marge," Ally agreed. "I told you she was a nice woman."

"I never doubted it. In fact I never doubt anything you say,

Alison."

"Ally," Ally corrected, suddenly feeling awkward under Morgan's gaze. It seemed it was becoming a habit, her having experienced more than a few bouts of self-consciousness over the course of their dinner. One such bout had occurred when she posed with Marge for one of the numerous photos they took that night. Seated in their booth, she had leaned toward Marge, ready for the photo, when Morgan peered from behind Marge's pocket digital camera. "Perfect." The gaze that accompanied her smile had been so . . . disconcerting, Ally couldn't hold the look. On review of the digital camera display they had needed to pose again because Ally had lowered her eyes at the moment Morgan pressed the button. Similarly, when she played camerawoman and was framing a picture of Morgan and Marge, she snapped either too early or too late, again thrown off balance by Morgan's expression. Now, Ally twisted her cloth napkin in her hands. "Only James calls me Alison."

"A partner's privilege?" Morgan asked.

Ally dropped the napkin to take a sip of her cognac. "Hardly. It's his choice. He sees the shortening of names as rather crass."

"So God help anyone who would call him Jim?"

"Exactly." Ally placed her glass on the table and toyed with the handle on her cup of coffee.

She'd called him Jim once. It was during sex. James had stopped what he was doing, held himself upright over her and said, "James. My name is James." Then he began doing what he had been doing before. Ally had found this extremely funny and started giggling.

"In fact, he got so insulted the time I did it, I'm surprised he actually asked me out again."

"How long have you been together?"

Ally took a sip of her coffee and looked directly at Morgan. Instead of answering the question she asked one of her own. "Why didn't you tell Marge you were seeing Nick?"

"I . . ."

Ally held Morgan's gaze, willing her to give what she hoped was an honest answer. It was over dessert that Marge—openly curious about anything to do with her idol—had brought up the subject of partners by first inquiring of Ally's status. Upon discovering that Ally, an architect, was dating another architect, she seized onto the idea of pairing up with another of the same profession, declaring, "The last time I read *TV Week* you were seen with that lovely young man who's a reporter on the news."

"Lucas," Morgan offered.

Marge bobbed her head up and down.

"We just went to a film premiere together. Nothing more."

Marge looked disappointed that there was no romantic attachment as apparently indicated in the tabloids. "So he hadn't asked you to marry him?"

Morgan laughed disarmingly. "Not that night, he didn't."

Marge's eyes opened wide, interpreting the comment to mean that he had proposed at some stage. Ally had no idea who this Lucas was that they were talking about, but she sat a little straighter, interested to know the details of this supposed romance.

Morgan shook her head. "No. No. I was kidding. Lucas has never proposed to me."

"Bless you, dear. You shouldn't tease me like that." Marge leaned a little over the table, begging Morgan to share some secret details. "But there *is* someone special in your life?"

Morgan glanced at Ally then scooped a large spoonful of chocolate mousse and brought it to her mouth. "No. There's no one special right now." She briefly looked at Ally again before dropping her gaze and filling her mouth with mousse.

Now, Morgan again lowered her lashes.

"Morgan?" Ally prompted.

Morgan shifted a little uncomfortably. "Nick and I aren't actually together. That was just a story that Kit . . . that *we* fabricated to throw you off the trail."

Ally frowned. This whole Nick business was odder by the second. Why manufacture a romance between her and Nick if she and Mark were actually together? Ally didn't know either of them from a bar of soap so it made little difference to her which one Morgan slept with. Hmm. *Unless, of course* . . . "Is Mark married?" she asked.

Morgan appeared surprised by the question. "No."

"So why are you two hiding behind Nick?"

"Pardon?"

"You and Mark. Why do you want to keep it a secret?"

"You think it was Mark with me last night?"

Ally scoffed. "Well, it sure wasn't Nick."

Morgan seemed at a loss for words. "Mark and I are not . . ." She fell silent for a full three seconds. "Last night I was . . . um . . . I'm a—"

"It's okay." Ally discovered she was unable to watch Morgan squirm. It was all quite obvious to her now. Morgan and Mark weren't an item any more than Morgan and Nick were. It had just been a one-night thing. Good friends who momentarily became bed buddies. And while Mark may not be married, maybe he had a significant other waiting for him at home. And probably Nick didn't so he had been set up as the stooge. For some reason Ally was pleased with the thought that Morgan had never slept with Nick, and that Mark had only been a once-off. "Like I've said so many times now . . . It really doesn't matter to me. So can we just declare the topic closed?"

Morgan smiled wanly, but she made the motion of buttoning her lip.

They both lifted their cognacs and downed the contents in one swallow. And they both put their glasses on the table and curled their fingers around the handles of their coffee cups and sat in contemplative silence.

CHAPTER SIX

Morgan hovered for at least a minute in front of the compartment that Mark and Nick shared. When she did eventually knock on the door she was greeted by a bleary-eyed Nick. After apologetically explaining she wanted to talk to Mark alone, he groggily gathered his shower accoutrements and shuffled down the corridor.

"Can't it wait?" Mark yawned. He shoved his pillow over his head and snuggled deeper into the bedclothes. "I haven't even had my first cigarette yet. And you know I can't think without it."

"No. It's about last night."

"Hmm." There was another yawn followed by a muffled, "How did it go?"

"Well—" Morgan stopped short. She wasn't going to talk to a pillow. Her sudden silence worked. The pillow was thrust aside and Mark turned over to regard her sleepily from his position on the top bunk. With his attention at least partially grabbed, she took a deep breath and blurted, "Ally thinks it was you with me the other night."

Mark frowned, becoming a little more alert. "What?"

"I said—"

"I know what you said. I'm just wondering why she would think that."

"Well, she knows it wasn't Nick because she saw him on the platform at the time I was . . . busy. So, I guess she was using the process of elimination."

"But of course you set her straight." When Morgan shifted uneasily Mark's voice took a warning tone. "Didn't you?"

"Well . . ."

"Mogs!"

"I did try." Morgan shifted again, this time reaching behind her to hold onto the edge of the wash basin. "Honestly I did—"

"Well, you obviously didn't try very hard." Mark flung the covers off and swung his legs over the side of the bunk. The ceiling of the compartment was not exceptionally high, so he sat hunched over. The slumped posture was in direct opposition to his current, thoroughly rankled expression. As if to get the two in sync, he leapt from the bunk, stood up straight and squared his shoulders. "You know why I didn't agree to Kitty's pairing of us in the first place. I tell you, Morgan, if this gets out and I lose my chance with Rebecca—"

"That's not going to happen," Morgan said quickly. "Ally won't say anything. She told me she wouldn't . . . and I trust her on that."

Mark folded his arms. "If you trust her so much why didn't you come out to her like you told me you were going to?"

"I don't know." Morgan shook her head, not exactly sure of the reason herself. "It was on the tip of my tongue to tell her, and then, when the moment came, I just couldn't do it."

"Well, you sure don't have a problem with it at other times," Mark said sarcastically. "Not with that French bird, or your little Swiss Miss, or that chick in Tokyo, or—"

Morgan cut Mark short from listing the participants in her recent escapades. "That's not the same and you know it. With them it was more of a . . . mutual acknowledgment."

"Mutual acknowledgment," Mark echoed, again shaking his head. "I wish I could get some woman to 'mutually acknowledge' she wants to sleep with me."

"I know a lot of women who think you're terrific."

"Don't try to butter me up," Mark warned, although she saw his chest puff slightly at her comment. "And don't try to change the subject. Look"—he sat down on the edge of Nick's unmade bottom bunk—"I know it's hard for you, being . . . what do you call it?"

"In the closet?" Morgan offered.

"That's it. In the closet." Mark nodded. "And while I understand how you might have changed your mind about doing it at the last minute, I don't understand how you could sit back and let her believe something that directly affects *me*."

"But it doesn't, really," Morgan argued. "I truly believe she's not going to tell anyone."

"Maybe not. But maybe she'll just tell her other half and maybe he'll just casually mention it to someone. And . . . you know how these things get round. More than that," Mark continued, "I happen to think Ally is an all right chick and maybe *I* don't want to have to lie to her when I see her next." He folded his arms, his expression as serious as Morgan had ever seen it. "In fact, I *won't* lie to her when I see her next. If you don't tell her she's wrong about you and me, then I will."

"Are you threatening me, Mark Baker?"

"Damn right I am."

Morgan sagged a little. While she didn't like confrontation generally, her distaste was compounded when she was in opposition to someone she considered one of her close friends. "Okay," she said, defeated.

"Come on, Mogs." Mark stood up and gave her a friendly punch on the shoulder. "You can do it. And if you can't bring yourself to tell her you were with a woman, then just say it was someone who left the train at Kalgoorlie. You don't have to mention their sex."

"Okay," she said again, feeling a little stronger.

"Now go away and leave me alone." Mark yawned widely and scratched his stomach through the ragged T-shirt he called his pajama top. "I'll see you at breakfast."

"Okay." Morgan turned to leave the compartment, smiling for the first time since she'd entered it. She hurried back to her own compartment, announced herself through the closed door and entered to find Kitty half-dressed, facing the window and putting her hair into its usual bun.

Having shared accommodations with her producer on countless occasions, they had both seen each other in various states of undress almost as often. Normally, Morgan never paid any attention to it, her feelings toward Kitty totally sexless. But now she found herself staring at Kitty's bare back. Did Ally's muscles move in the same way when she reached up to arrange her hair? she wondered.

"You're up early," Kitty commented, half turning, a hairpin between her lips.

"Yes," Morgan stammered, her gaze sliding downward to the curve of breast that Kitty's movement had revealed. She actually had to tell herself to stop staring. "My stomach's upset." That was the truth. Her insides were suddenly gripped by a churning sensation.

"Are you sick?" Kitty turned to face her fully. "Because we've got a very full schedule today."

"I know." Despite her attempts not to, Morgan's eyes strayed to Kitty's breasts. She had to admit they were exceptional. Firm and smooth, with two cherry-red nipples that seemed to be sitting up and begging for a caress. *Every woman is different,* she told herself firmly. *Even if on the surface they are physically similar.* Goodness knew, she'd seen enough unclothed women in her life to know that to be true. Having finally convinced her brain to stop interpreting the current visual input as a preview of Ally's assets, she lifted her gaze to Kitty's face. "I'll be fine, I promise. I just have to get something out of my system."

With that, she fled the compartment, hoping Kitty would interpret her words and sudden departure as proof she was making a dash to the toilet.

The toilet was not her destination at all, which turned out to be just as well, since each facility she passed appeared to have a little queue waiting outside—even in Gold where the passenger-to-toilet ratio was much lower. Clearly, it was morning rush hour. Once outside Ally's door, Morgan wished she had made a bathroom stop as she had a sudden urge to pee. *It's just nerves,* she told herself. The very same symptom had plagued her in the early days of her on-screen career. Back then, she thought she would wet herself each time someone called "action." Now, she did as she had in the past, taking a series of calming breaths and mentally talking herself up.

She knocked.

"Just a minute." Ally's voice came from the other side of the door.

She waited.

She kept breathing.

And by the time the door slid across Morgan felt her poise return. "Hi, Ally. I wanted to speak to you, if I could."

"Oh." Ally glanced to her watch, seemingly torn. "I'm supposed to meet Marge in a few minutes to say good-bye. I was just on my way there now. Can it wait . . . or would you like to walk and talk?"

Shit. Morgan had forgotten the appointment Ally had made

with Marge last night. Morgan had already said her good-byes to Marge, explaining, truthfully, that she had a breakfast meeting scheduled this morning to run over the final details before their big day of filming. And it was a big day. At Adelaide, a special carriage would be hooked onto the train, taking an eccentric and usually media-shy English crooner to Sydney. They were to film the carriage as it was attached, have an on-camera chat with the crooner before he boarded, and another once he was settled into his private carriage with king-size bed and full-sized bathroom. Finally, Morgan would be filmed trying out the luncheon delicacies prepared by an on-board chef to the crooner's advance order. Once that was done, she had a brief respite to freshen up and change her outfit before conducting some interviews with the Red class passengers she had scouted in the lounge car on the first day of the journey. Come dinnertime, she would be filmed dining in Red, something that promised to be a big letdown after her private-carriage, chef-created lunch.

She said, "Can we meet after dinner tonight? Say at about ten p.m.?"

"Sure." Ally closed the door behind her and turned the key in the lock. She grinned. "That's right. Lucky you gets to feed at the cattle trough tonight."

Morgan barely moved out of the way when Ally stepped into the corridor and she felt the loose cotton sleeves of Ally's shirt brush against her arm. It made the hairs on her forearm stand on end. "It's not that bad, is it?"

"I couldn't comment about dinner as I've never experienced it. But if breakfast is any indication . . ." Ally trailed off, leaving Morgan to fill in the blanks. She nodded down the corridor. "Sorry, Morgan, but I really have to go."

"No worries. I'll come with you as far as my room."

The narrow corridor forced them to walk in single file. Ally led and Morgan followed at a distance that allowed them to speak comfortably but still afforded her a full-length view. By the time she had passed out of Gold she had verified what she already knew to be true: that Ally had a build very similar to Kitty's. And by the time she reached her carriage, she had also reconfirmed the other conclusion she had drawn earlier: that no two women were the same. Height, build and hair color aside, everything about Ally was different than Kitty—the way she walked, the way she talked, the way she laughed, the sincerity of her smile.

Ally turned when she reached Morgan's door. "There you go. Delivered home safely."

"Thank you, madam." Morgan made a show out of bowing, mainly to hide her eyes, which she was sure would advertise the fact she was fast becoming besotted.

"I'll see you tonight."

"I look forward to it." Morgan watched Ally turn to leave and was gripped by a sense of "now or never." She couldn't imagine sitting on her news until ten p.m. that night, or worse, having Mark niggling in her ear all day because she hadn't yet cleared the air. "Wait." For the second time in as many days she grabbed Ally by the arm, pleased that this time her hand was not slapped away. In the moments it took to steer Ally far enough away from her compartment door to be out of Kitty's earshot, her stomach started to churn again and whatever was left of her last night's dinner threatened to make an encore appearance. This coming-out business never got any easier. Although, these days, she was rather out of practice. Not counting those she worked most closely with—Mark, Nick and Kitty—it had been a good number of years since she had openly confessed her orientation to anybody. There was a culture of "don't ask, don't tell" at the network, so while others she worked alongside, including the other *Bonnes Vacances* presenters, may have had their suspicions, it was never discussed. Not when she was around, anyway. Morgan reminded herself she didn't *need* to tell Ally, that she could just go down the nameless, sexless route Mark had suggested. Then she admitted she actually *did* need to tell her. For reasons Morgan herself could not entirely fathom, she felt compelled to open up to this woman. "I have to tell you something and it really can't wait."

"Okay," Ally said slowly, obviously a little unsettled by Morgan's tone.

Morgan cleared her throat, trying to rid herself of the quaver that was audible even to her own ear. "I was not with Mark the night we stopped at Kalgoorlie."

"Okay," Ally repeated, but this time her eyes narrowed slightly. She glanced down to Morgan's hand on her arm, which Morgan promptly removed.

"I've never been with Mark . . . or Nick. They're just friends." Morgan saw Ally draw a long, slow breath, so she continued before Ally could verbalize whatever she was thinking. "I wasn't with a man, Ally. It was a woman."

There. The words were out. Well, almost out. She hadn't actually said the "L" word, but Ally was a smart woman so there was no need for that level of precision. Morgan felt lighter for having offloaded her secret. But she also felt her feet were weighted to the floor, pinning her in place as she waited for what seemed an eternity for a response.

"Okay," Ally said for the third time. She scratched a little nervously at her scalp and shifted her feet, her gaze settling onto the view outside the window. "That's really interesting to know. But, like I said, I really have to go."

"So, I'll see you at around ten tonight?" Morgan asked, trying for a casual tone. It didn't work very well. Her mouth was completely dry.

"Umm . . . sure." Ally still seemed to have trouble meeting Morgan's eyes. Now she appeared to be focusing on Morgan's chin. "I'll come knock on your door when I'm ready. 'Bye for now."

" 'Bye." Morgan watched Ally's retreating figure until it disappeared into the next carriage. She knew she had held Ally up by a few minutes, but still, her hasty exit gave the impression that she was fleeing from her, as opposed to hurrying toward her appointment with Marge.

"Did you get everything out?" Kitty asked when Morgan slid the door to her compartment open again.

"I think so." Morgan sat on the bottom bunk.

"Do you feel better?"

Morgan fingered the white cotton sheets, avoiding Kitty's eyes. *Ask me again after ten o'clock tonight.* "I don't know yet."

CHAPTER SEVEN

As at Kalgoorlie, there was also an hourlong, train-operated whistle-stop tour at Adelaide. While one could not make an informed judgment of a city in one hour—and even less so when viewed from a coach window—the previous day Ally had booked herself a place on the tour with the idea of using it as a brief reconnaissance. If she liked what she saw, she would suggest to James they pay the city a visit during the next holiday weekend.

The coach was waiting, but Ally found herself standing on the platform, unable to take the steps necessary to follow her fellow tour companions. Her current immobility was bizarre. She'd had no trouble moving her feet as she accompanied Marge onto the platform when the train pulled into the station. Neither had they caused her any problems when she and Marge walked together to retrieve her suitcase from the rows of baggage that the handlers quite efficiently extracted from the train. And so too had they obeyed the orders to put one in front of the other and cover the distance necessary to be introduced to Marge's husband, Fred. In fact her feet shifted often during the ensuing ten minutes of Marge-dominated chat, seemingly itching to get on the move again. But when Marge and Fred had disappeared through the station doors and Ally had made a slow turn, looking for the tour group, her feet stopped still the moment she was facing the tracks. And since then they had refused to respond to the directives issued by Ally's brain. Instead, they stayed put, as if suddenly glued to the cement.

Ten yards away and directly in her line of sight was the *Bonnes Vacances* crew. Nick balanced a camera on his shoulder and Mark held aloft a boom. Kitty stood a few feet back watching as Morgan shook the hand of a man that Ally presumed was the English crooner. Behind them a maroon-colored carriage that looked at odds with the relatively modern train was slowly being shunted into position.

Ally was vaguely aware of a last call for the whistle-stop tour being announced over the public address system. She really should get moving if she wanted to do her Adelaide recon. But her feet were still fastened to the platform.

And her eyes were fixed on Morgan. She had changed her outfit from the jeans and jumper she had worn that morning. Now, although the morning was cool, she was in a light, summery dress that crossed over at the cleavage and flowed out until just past the knees. She was talking animatedly to the crooner, that smile of hers lighting her face. Even from this distance, Ally could see that the smile reached her eyes. And even though the crooner's back was to her, Ally could tell by his open-bodied stance he was more than a little interested in the woman who stood before him. He was probably also weighing his chances of glimpsing more than was being offered by the current drape of material.

Men, Ally thought scornfully. *Got their minds on one thing only.*

Inexplicably, Ally felt something very close to jealousy rush through her. But what did she have to be jealous of? It wasn't as if it was James who was leering at Morgan. Actually, she'd be very surprised if James had ever leered in his life. In all their time together—nine months now—James had never done anything to make Ally feel threatened or jealous. She felt secure with him. Safe. Ally's eyes bored into the bald patch that extended almost all the way down the back of the crooner's head. *You can't blame him for being interested.* She folded her arms. *She sure is a stunning-looking woman.* Ally tilted her head to one side, refocusing on Morgan. *And she sure doesn't look like a lesbian.*

Immediately Ally felt her indignation rise at the notion that Morgan was yet again playing her for a fool. Then, just as quickly, her ire dissolved and it was with a somewhat self-effacing smile that Ally admitted she really had no idea what a lesbian looked like. She didn't even know any lesbians, or, if she did, she didn't know it. Her experience was limited to what she'd seen on television, in movies and from the sidelines two years ago at the Sydney Gay and Lesbian Mardi Gras. She could discount the likes of Sharon Stone and Elle Macpherson being cast in lesbian roles as Hollywood's catering to the male audience. But the Mardi Gras . . . if the women she had witnessed there were an indicator of real life, then lesbians came in as many varieties as their heterosexual counterparts. Including real stunners. So Morgan could be telling the truth after all.

And that surely would go a long way toward explaining why Morgan and everyone around her had been madly flapping about trying to cover up the details of her Kalgoorlie station indiscretion. It didn't fully explain it though. While Ally's "I don't care what you do behind closed doors" attitude was not shared by everybody, any dent in Morgan and her show's supposedly huge popularity would most likely be small and short-lived. After all, it wasn't the Dark Ages anymore. So why the big fuss?

Maybe there was a girlfriend in the wings? But no, Ally dismissed that idea. Just last night Morgan had told Marge that there was no one special in her life right now. Ally had a second thought. Morgan may well have a girlfriend, but she was kept as secret as her sexuality. And the secret girlfriend would be pretty pissed off to discover her partner had been cheating on her while at work.

Ally was still contemplating the likelihood of a behind-the-scenes girlfriend when she realized the filming in front of the newly attached carriage was winding up. The boom was lowered and Nick removed the camera from his shoulder to hold it by his side. Morgan shook the hand of the crooner, smiling and nodding as if in thanks. Then her face lit up again and she rushed forward, past the crooner, past Kitty, to greet what looked like yet another television crew. The camera being toted by a short, stocky woman displayed the same network logo as Nick's, as did the bag carried by the person lugging the boom. Both logos had the word *News* tacked on the end.

So, there was a news crew here.

Ally's speculation at what was possibly newsworthy at eight in the morning at the Adelaide train station came to an abrupt halt. She opened her eyes wider, a knot twisting in her belly. Right before her eyes, Morgan practically threw herself into the arms of a suited man—the reporter maybe?—who was accompanying the news crew. Whatever the newsworthy event was, it had either happened already or was yet to happen, since Morgan and the suited man started walking arm-in-arm away from the other crew members. The man—just shy of Morgan's height, probably around Morgan's age—paused for a moment, laughed and pushed a strand of hair from Morgan's eyes. It was a very familiar gesture, and one that suggested intimacy. The knot in Ally's stomach twisted. *She's damn well lied to me again.*

Morgan and the man were heading in her direction, toward the station. Ally wasn't going to hang around and find out how

Morgan would talk her way out of this one. She willed her feet to move, and finally they obeyed.

Two minutes later she was back in her compartment. She slammed the door across, fully prepared to throw herself onto her bunk. But some staff member had been in her compartment in her absence and the bunk had already been converted back to daytime seating.

Fucking efficiency freaks. Ally threw herself into the seat instead and sat with her chin on her knuckles, not knowing whether the tears that threatened were angry tears, or disappointed tears. She decided they were a little of both. She was angry at Morgan for having lied . . . again, and disappointed that she had lied . . . again. Whoever said the train was the best way to travel obviously had never traveled on one with Morgan-frigging-Silverstone.

Sitting and fuming did not make the time pass quickly and it didn't take too long before Ally was bored with it. Restless, she headed for the restaurant carriage, where they were still serving breakfast. Morgan was not present, nor was any of the *Bonnes Vacances* crew. *Just as well,* Ally thought as she took a seat in the one and only vacant booth available. As she waited for her toast and coffee to arrive, she again sat with her chin on her knuckles, dreaming up a thousand things to say to Morgan when she next saw her. None of them were particularly nice. She lingered as long as she could over her meager breakfast, ordering a second coffee and then a third, but it was still only nine a.m. when she wandered back to her carriage. There was still one more hour before the train would pull out.

Maybe she could take a stroll around the streets. Or maybe not. She wouldn't get far in an hour and since the train didn't stop at the central Adelaide station but at Keswick, they were two kilometers shy of the city proper. Even at a brisk pace she'd just reach the city before having to turn back. She'd have to visit Adelaide sight unseen with James—or, more likely, not visit at all.

James.

Ally decided to give him a call. She settled into her seat and dialed. It rang. But not too surprisingly, he didn't answer. At this hour on a Friday he was usually ensconced in one of his partner meetings. James was the "Tymeson" in Ernst, Small and Tymeson, an architectural firm that specialized in low-rise residential property. At forty, he was the youngest partner in the firm and had in fact not long been awarded partner status when Ally first met him. They met over a tray of exotic nibbles at an industry cocktail party. It may have been the high that James was on due to his promotion, but on that occasion Ally found him enthusiastic about their shared profession, charming and talkative. She agreed to a post-cocktail dinner, which he followed up three days later with another dinner invitation. At their third dinner—this time at the iconic Summit restaurant—he sealed a deal on behalf of his firm with some Singaporean property developers. That night also seemed to seal the deal on their relationship. Nothing was ever formalized—certainly not by engagement or even with a spoken agreement of their pairing. They just slipped into exclusivity. Friends began inviting them as a couple and they accepted or declined as a couple. It was assumed that Ally would attend James's client dinners just as it became the norm for them to spend their nights together, either at Ally's Croyden apartment or James's Balmain townhouse. Sometimes Ally wished the early days of their relationship had been filled with a bit more excitement, a bit more spontaneity. But as James liked to point out, excitement was usually the result of either speed or the unexpected—or the unexpected occurring at speed. And spontaneity was for those who didn't have a plan. In other words, consistency and reliability undertaken at a respectable pace was the ethos James lived by. To date it had not done him any harm. He was successful, respected, steadfast. He was a good man. He was . . . nice.

Ally held her mobile to her ear, only partially listening to the message that would lead her into James's voice mail. *Nice*. That was also the word she had used to describe someone else very recently. And that someone lived by a completely different ethos than James.

Morgan.

Ally didn't want to think about her, so she didn't. She left a short message for James then checked her own voice mailbox. There were sixteen new messages. That should keep her well occupied for a while. And after that she'd get down to some serious work on her Kalgoorlie design.

Yes. That was a good plan for the day. And come tonight she'd rap on the door of the person she wasn't thinking about and tell her just what she thought of her and her "I'm a lesbian" tale. But then, if it was untrue, why had the person she was not thinking about even bothered saying it in the first place? Surely there was nothing to gain from saying such a thing. Unless of course she did it for the attention. Maybe once the cameras stopped rolling she had to do something to keep "all eyes on me."

God, who knew. And who cared? Ally shook Morgan from her thoughts once and for all, put her ear to the phone and listened to what had been happening in her world while she was out of network range.

At ten to ten that night Ally set down her pencil and ruler, interlocked her fingers and stretched her arms out in front of her. She really should get her skates on and freshen up if she wanted to meet the person she promised not to think about—but actually had been thinking about all day—at their scheduled time. *If* was the operative word here, however. She still hadn't decided if she wanted to keep their appointment or not.

Ally stared directly in front of her, her gaze settling on a little chip some previous passenger had taken out of the wood paneling that lined her compartment. She'd studied the chip countless times since catching sight of it midmorning. In fact, she'd looked at it often enough and long enough over the course of the day that had she been asked to reproduce it on paper, she'd almost certainly draw an exact replica. Ally sighed, forcing her eyes away. Somehow, she didn't think staring at a chip in the wall was exactly what her boss had meant when he told her to use this train trip as a "brain-expanding" experience. She looked dismally down to the papers strewn across the table. She hadn't made too much progress on her Kalgoorlie design either.

Although little progress had been made on the work front, Ally did feel her mind had had a workout today. Each session of chip-staring had been accompanied by a series of mental gymnastics. Morganastics, she had named the process, her mental muscles consistently being stretched in the same Morgan-related direction. Her mind would tumble and twirl around the information it had accumulated over the past two days. Eventually it would settle gracefully on a conclusion, then, without warning, a new routine would commence and her thoughts would somersault away, to land in a completely different position.

Given the series of conflicting stories Ally's brain had been presented with since boarding the train in Kalgoorlie, she wasn't too surprised it was having problems processing them correctly. What was surprising was the amount of energy she had allowed her brain cells to expend on the process. After all, was she not the one to keep saying how she really didn't care what Morgan did behind closed doors?

Unfortunately, however, Ally did care. It was during her pre-lunch session of Morganastics that she admitted—in the time since she had been dragged kicking and screaming into the world of Morgan Silverstone—there had been a shift in her mode of thinking. She had never been impressed by celebrity. Sure, she could appreciate their work, whether it be a song, a movie or a piece of art, but she had never understood the tendency for so many people—such as Marge—to worship the ground their celebrity of choice walked on, or to want to delve into every aspect of their lives. She'd never bought a magazine or a newspaper because it headlined some celebrity morsel or scandal. She just didn't care. But now . . . Morgan the out-of-reach celebrity was well and truly within reach. Under the *Bonnes Vacances* persona was a living, breathing, three-dimensional person. Not larger than life. Just a regular person. In the short time they had spent together Ally had decided she liked Morgan. Quite a lot, actually.

Until she'd realized she'd been lied to just once too often.

Or at least she thought she'd been lied to once too often. Ally took her attention off the chip, picked up her pencil and tapped the end of it on the table top. She sighed in frustration. This was the point that had been stretching her mental capacities throughout the day. She just couldn't figure out if Morgan was telling the truth or not.

Was Morgan a lesbian?

Or wasn't she?

And did it really matter to her?

Ally tapped her pencil on the table with an increased rhythm. Normally she would say no, it didn't matter. She might not know any lesbians, but she did know she wasn't a homophobe. Or was she? The thought of Morgan being a woman who liked—loved—other women, was . . . unnerving. Maybe she was only okay if someone was a lesbian from a distance? More strangely, when Ally shifted her thoughts to the idea of Morgan *not* being a lesbian, it too sat uncomfortably. She closed her eyes and imagined Morgan standing in front of her, in the dress she had seen her wear this morning, and saying "I'm not a lesbian after all. I like men."

How would she respond to that?

Ally couldn't think of a single thing she might say. With her eyes still closed, she mentally eyed Morgan's face, her shoulders, stopping just shy of the beginning of cleavage.

Ally's eyes flew open. What she felt as she sat there imagining that Morgan was not gay was . . . disappointment.

Jesus. That really was not a good thing to be feeling. She checked her watch again. It was three minutes past ten. She was late to her appointment. But it didn't matter, because she had just decided she wasn't going to keep it.

Ally threw her pencil onto the table and grabbed her phone. Since the empty expanses were behind them and they were now traveling through the more densely populated eastern states there should be no more problems latching onto a network. There wasn't and it answered after only three rings.

"Hello, James. It's Alison." She closed her eyes again and imagined James as he relaxed in front of the television, an open book on his lap and a tumbler of Scotch by his side. His image was reliably comfortable. "I miss you."

Morgan had returned to the compartment she now shared with Kitty not too long after nine thirty—a lot earlier than expected. She had begged off joining the crew for a post-filming and post-dinner drink, preferring to be alone. The first fifteen minutes of her solitude had been used to good effect, removing her on-camera makeup, cleaning her teeth, reapplying her perfume and having a general freshen-up. She stayed in the clothes she'd worn for the filming of dining in Red, casual linen slacks and a collared, sleeveless shirt. It was a little cool so Morgan fished into one of her bags and pulled out a light cardigan. She didn't put it on, instead standing in front of the mirror again and examining her appearance. She undid one of the top buttons on her shirt, pushed out her chest a little and checked the effect.

She did the button up again.

And she put on her cardigan.

Then she sat on her freshly made bottom bunk and checked her voice mail. There were a couple of new messages since she'd last checked late that afternoon. Her agent sounded his usual excited self, announcing some "*very* exciting opportunity" and wanting her to call as soon as she got the message. She casually speculated over the reason. It wasn't about a possible pay increase with the network—they'd only finished negotiating a new contract late last year and she was locked in, at a very generous salary, thank you, for the next three years. It couldn't be because some company wanted her to endorse their product or service—that was strictly prohibited under the conditions of her contract. And it couldn't be for any acting positions. Last Christmas she had dabbled in the world of theater, via a part as the Wicked Witch in a Christmas pantomime. Her performance had been so stiff she may as well have been the witch's broomstick, so she and her agent had agreed it best she only step onto a stage when she was playing herself. So his call was probably for some new event someone wanted her to attend or host. Morgan turned up her nose. Exciting opportunity or not, she had enough things to occupy her time already. As it was, the afternoon of her one day off this fortnight—Sunday—had been booked for months. Of all things, she had agreed to be one of the "lots" at a charity auction being staged by the fundraising committee at a prestigious private school for boys in Sydney. The school was raising funds to buy computers for a very poor school in India, so it was for a good cause, but still, in addition to losing her Sunday afternoon, she would subsequently have to spend another of her precious free afternoons or evenings doing whatever the highest bidder wanted. Within reason of course. Morgan decided that whatever her agent was frothing at the mouth for her to do, she was going to decline. She also wasn't going to call him now. It could wait until tomorrow. She went on to the next message.

It was her mum. "Call me when you get home, dear."

"Yes, Mum." Morgan added her mum's name below her

agent's in her little notebook.

By the time she had finished, there was a list of five names to call. She smiled at the last on her list. Audrey.

Audrey had been, and still was, a lecturer at the university where Morgan had completed her journalism degree. She had also been the first of her four Australian lovers. Audrey, while trampling over all the boundaries in the sacrosanct teacher/student relationship, subsequently trampled all over Morgan's heart by announcing a sudden attack of teacher/student morals. The breakup was not pretty. Morgan threatened to tell the dean, an act that could only end in either the sacking or forced resignation of her lecturer. Audrey, having full knowledge of Morgan's ambitions to become a television journalist, and also knowing of the postgraduation cadetship she had managed to secure with one of the regional stations, subsequently threatened to write a revealing letter to the well-known bigot of a network manager and hence "shoot down her career" before it even got off the ground. Neither had followed through on the threats, but both kept their word not to see or speak to each other. Morgan swapped her lecture with Audrey for one at a different day and time, graduated without fuss and moved to South Australia to take up her cadetship. After a year or so, a chance meeting at Sydney's Circular Quay saw their enmity dissolve into friendship. Now they called each other regularly and saw each other when they had the chance.

Morgan never forgot the lesson Audrey's threat had taught her, and in her early days of television she kept a low, low personal profile. When temptation did get the best of her she was selective, making sure her lovers had as much, if not more, to lose than she did if word of their affair got out. When first snagging her position at *Bonnes Vacances*, Morgan went a little wild. She was akin to a starved woman and the world her buffet. She feasted at every opportunity, only shaking her head at the Australian platter.

Not that that stopped her from looking, of course. There surely was some very tasty-looking Australian eye candy out there. Speaking of which . . . Morgan checked her watch. It was five past ten.

Ally was late. But not quite fashionably so. No need to send out a search party just yet. Morgan set her phone aside and stood in front of the mirror again. She fussed with a strand of hair, aiming for a more messy, carefree look than a well-coiffed one. She removed her cardigan, undid her top shirt button again and sat back down on her bunk. She stood, paced a little in the confined space, stopped at the mirror again and once more fastened her top button.

She checked her watch. Eleven past ten. The fashionably late should be turning up by now. Morgan bit down on her impulse to open the compartment door and scan the corridor. If Ally was on her way, then she'd know Morgan had been looking out for her. And that wasn't the impression Morgan wanted to give. She wanted Ally to think her announcement this morning was no big deal, that it was simply a case of clearing the air, getting a niggling little annoyance out in the open so they could continue with their friendship.

Friendship.

Morgan plopped back onto her bunk, imagining a friendship with Ally. She dreamed of calling her for a chat, meeting her for a coffee, having lunch with her and a couple of other girlfriends. They were easy scenes to conjure. She could picture Ally reclined at her desk, one foot curled under her thigh, playing with her pencil as she smiled at whatever Morgan was relaying to her on the phone. Then her expression would become more serious and she would remove her tucked leg to sit with elbows leaning on her desk, intent on the conversation. And she could picture them at a coffee shop. They'd go to one of those bookshop cafés—the sort that always has nice comfy armchairs and low coffee tables. They'd pick a couch in a sunny spot near a window, and they'd sit facing each other, sipping on little espressos. They'd be critiquing the coffee—as they always did—and planning their next café stop, their plan being to visit every coffee venue in Sydney until they found the ultimate caffeine hit. Their lunches would be in warm, sunny spots. Modern venues with clean, cool lines, crisp napkins and oversized plates with marvelously presented food. By some unspoken agreement, they'd both always arrive early to these luncheons. Early enough for them both to share the highlights of the days since they'd last met and indulge in one or two of the private jokes they were sure to have by then. As their friends arrived, a glance would pass between them—one that spoke of regret that their company now had to be shared. And they'd linger long after their friends had gone. Not necessarily talking. But just easy with each other. Easy enough that Ally would not shy away when Morgan would reach across the table and lay her hand on hers . . .

Morgan lifted her legs onto the bunk, lay back and closed her eyes. In her mind Ally's hand had turned underneath hers and now clasped her palm lightly.

"I like that," Ally would say softly.

"That's good," Morgan would respond. "Because I like it too."

They'd sit, just like that, just holding hands and looking at each other, while the tables around them emptied and the waiters began laying the places for the evening session.

"We should go," Morgan would say finally, having felt the eyes of the staff upon them, willing them to move so they could close up for the afternoon.

Ally's hand would clasp hers a little tighter. "I don't want this to end."

"This what, Ally?" Morgan would ask. She'd gesture out the window. "This beautiful, sunny afternoon?" Then she'd look up to one of the wall-mounted speakers, through which the velvet jazz of Madeleine Peyroux was still being piped. "Or this song?"

"No." Ally would glance down to their hands. "This." Her eyes would meet Morgan's and she would lift Morgan's hand to her lips, turning it over to kiss the palm.

"It doesn't have to end," Morgan would whisper. "Come home with me."

Ally's eyes would dart over Morgan's features as if searching for something. Then her hazel eyes would appear to darken as her pupils dilated and she would whisper back, "I've been wishing you would suggest that all afternoon."

Christ. Morgan groaned, flipping onto her side and hugging herself. She was working herself into a state. And to what end, really? Ally had a partner—a male partner at that. From the little Ally had talked of him he sounded like a bit of a stuffed shirt, but still, he was there and his presence proved Ally's heterosexuality. At least, it proved it to Ally. Morgan was not so sure. She sensed something in Ally that maybe Ally hadn't even sensed herself.

Or maybe she was just suffering a severe case of wishful thinking.

Morgan checked her watch for the third time. Twenty-five past ten. Well past fashionably late and heading toward a no-show.

She stood once more and paced. The span of the compartment was covered in only three steps, two if she lengthened it to a stride, but still she walked back and forth, the movement helping her to think. So far as she could see, there were two possibilities. Either Ally was afraid to come because Morgan's disclosure that morning had made her face questions about her own sexuality. Or—and this was a very unwelcome possibility—that she had misjudged Ally completely. Instead of being an open-minded liberal she was homophobic and hence now wanted nothing more do with her.

There was a soft rap on the door and Morgan exhaled in relief. She'd been worrying over nothing.

"Morgan. It's me."

Her relief turned in on itself. It wasn't Ally. It was Kitty.

There was another rap. "Open up."

"Sorry." Morgan crossed the floor and unlatched the door. "I thought you had a key."

"I do." Kitty grinned a little lopsidedly. There was wine on her breath. "But I thought I should be careful, in case you had another woman in here."

"Yeah, right." For a single second she was glad Ally had not turned up. But then, if she had, Morgan would have taken "the Kitty factor" into account and suggested they grab some drinks and take them back to Ally's compartment. She stood aside to let Kitty pass, taking the opportunity to scan the corridor. Apart from an elderly man holding onto the handrail as he shuffled along, it was empty. She glanced back inside. Kitty had dropped onto the bottom bunk—Morgan's—and was sitting there, swaying slightly. Despite Kitty's general low tolerance for alcohol, Morgan had never seen her get so pickled in only an hour. "I think you should have an early night."

"Me, too." Kitty lifted her legs onto Morgan's bunk and lay her head on the pillow.

Morgan figured she would either have to assist Kitty up the ridiculously narrow ladder to the top berth or let her stay where she was. "You can sleep here tonight, if you want."

She checked the corridor again. The elderly man was still shuffling, but he was making progress. He was heading in the direction of Gold, and once he had taken a couple more steps—if Morgan wanted to take the same direction—she would either have to squeeze past him or shuffle along behind. She *did* want to take the same direction. So she stepped out of the compartment.

"Where are you going?" Kitty asked, already half asleep.

"To meet a woman."

"Yeah, right." Kitty turned on her side and curled into a loose fetal position. "I may be drunk, but I'm not stupid."

"Good night, Kitty." Morgan slowly slid the compartment

door across. She heard Kitty's soft snores even before it was completely closed. As she passed into Gold she rubbed her hands up and down her bare arms. She wasn't cold, but still she shivered.

Still two compartments down from Ally's, Morgan noticed a little yellow Post-it note on her door. A note for her maybe? She quickened her pace.

It read, "Thanks for your patience. You can make up my bed now." The time written in the top right-hand corner: Ten twenty p.m. Morgan frowned. She imagined that Ally might have been busy working and so did not want her seat converted at the usual time, but the note had been penned twenty minutes *after* she was due to meet her. Morgan could understand that maybe she'd just lost track of time—after all, if her enthusiasm at their dinner with Marge was any indication, Ally was very revved up about her latest architectural project. But it was now twenty to eleven. Even if she hadn't left her room until twenty past ten, where the hell was she now?

Morgan had just decided to pay a visit to the Gold lounge car, and failing that, to the Red lounge car, when she heard a rustling sound come from inside the compartment. It was not the rustle of bedclothes; it was a paper rustle. Ally was still in her room, and by the sound of it she was still working. So Ally's bunk hadn't already been made up and the note left there by mistake. The presence of the note negated any chance she had just lost all track of time. She was there because she wanted to be. Or, more accurately, because she didn't want to be with Morgan.

There were two possible courses of action that Morgan could take. She could quietly leave and hope that by morning Ally had worked through whatever was troubling her. Or she could stay and see for herself which of her theories was correct.

Option one was probably the smartest. But Morgan hadn't seen Ally since before breakfast, and knowing she was just on the other side of the door was too much of a temptation to resist, even if it meant getting yelled at . . . again.

She fingered the Post-it before she knocked. "Housekeeping," she called, mustering all of her acting skills.

The rustle stopped, followed by a moment of total silence. "Go away, Morgan."

"I'm not leaving until you tell me why you didn't keep our appointment."

Another complete silence. Then, "I didn't keep it because I've got nothing I want to say to you."

"From the sound of your tone I think you've got an awful lot you want to say to me . . . you just don't have the guts to say it." Again Morgan waited. She could feel her heart pounding in her chest. She wasn't used to being the antagonist, but here she was, provoking an argument. And Ally just didn't seem to be biting. Morgan found that extremely frustrating. *Speak to me, God damn it!* "At least tell me what I've done to upset you. Was it what I said this morning, because if it was I'm—"

The compartment door flew across and Ally appeared, her eyes flaring. "You're what, Morgan? You're sorry? You've come here to tell me you want to take it all back and in actual fact it was the King of England in your compartment that night!"

Unbalanced in the face of Ally's sarcasm, Morgan said the first thing that entered her head. "Actually, there is no King of England. There's a qu—"

"I damn well know there's a queen," Ally interrupted, scowling. "But that wouldn't stop you from trying to convince me there *is* a king." She brought her index finger to her lips as if having a sudden realization. "Oh, sorry. My mistake. You probably did mean the queen because today . . . you're gay! Now, if you don't mind . . ."

Ally grabbed the door and made as if to slam it shut. Morgan was quicker and moved her body so she was half-in, half-out of the compartment. Then she stepped inside completely, closing the door behind her.

"Excuse me." Ally put her hands on her hips. "But I would like you to get out of my room."

"No." Morgan stood directly in front of the door, blocking it in case Ally was entertaining any ideas about leaving herself. "I'm not going until you tell me what the hell you're so upset about."

"Oh, nothing." Ally batted her hand in a gesture that suggested she was shooing away the thought. The action did not jibe with her sarcastic tone. "Except maybe the fact I can't believe a single word you say. What are you going to tell me tomorrow, huh? That you were actually with a rhesus monkey?"

"What the hell . . . ?" Stung by the gross insult, Morgan's voice rose. "What do you mean you don't believe me? I was telling you the truth this morning."

"So . . . you're a lesbian, are you?"

"Yes."

"I don't believe you."

Morgan stared at her. Ally's jaw was set, jutting out slightly and her arms again folded. She was serious. Morgan was at a loss for words. She'd never been accused of *not* being a lesbian before. "Well . . . I am."

"So who was the man this morning?"

"What man?"

"The man on the platform."

"I told you about the singer I was interview—"

"Not him." Ally said impatiently. "The one you met after. The one with the network news crew."

"Oh, him! That was Lucas. Remember the one Marge was talking about at dinner?"

Ally harrumphed. "The one who *didn't* propose to you."

"Exactly." Morgan studied Ally's defensive stance. Why was she so upset about her chance meeting with Lucas? Then the penny dropped. "No, no, no. You've got it all wrong. Lucas and I are just friends."

"Oh, really? Just friends who go to film premieres together.

And whose relationship is the subject of media speculation." Ally narrowed her eyes. "And who throw themselves at each other at train stations."

"Don't exaggerate. We did not throw ourselves at each other and you know it. Look, Ally . . . I wasn't expecting to see him. He'd been there trying to get an interview with some politician who was catching the Overlander to attend some summit in Melbourne and he saw us filming so came over to say hello. We're old friends. We met at my first television gig." Morgan hesitated a moment, debating whether to tell the whole truth. Since Ally was acting more jealous than homophobic, she decided what she had to say would probably go no further than this compartment. "And if there's media speculation about us it's because we go to lots of events together. It's a convenient arrangement for both of us . . . since he's also gay."

Ally laughed out loud. "Oh, God. So he's gay too. How bloody convenient. If you're to be believed, the whole damn world is gay."

Morgan shrugged. "Well, at least ten percent of us are."

"Stop it, Morgan."

"Stop what?"

"Lying to me."

Morgan was so frustrated she stamped her foot. "I am not lying!"

Ally's response was to stick her jaw out a little farther. "Tell me the name of your girlfriend."

"Girlfriend?" Morgan uttered, thrown by the unexpected question. "I don't have a girlfriend."

Ally laughed sarcastically. "Of course you don't."

Morgan threw her hands in the air in despair. "Not having a girlfriend doesn't mean I'm not gay."

Ally met her eyes directly. She shrugged. "Whatever you say."

Morgan, overcome by the intensity of the gaze, treated it as a challenge. "Obviously there's nothing I can *say* to make you believe me."

In the tiny compartment it took but a single step for her to be body-to-body with Ally. She took hold of her by the shoulders and before she could change her mind, she bent to Ally's lips. She paused for a single moment, breathing in the scent that was Ally—a mix of floral fragrances, of shampoo and perfume and creams. And then she kissed her.

An awareness of just how important this embrace could be resonated at the back of Morgan's consciousness. And so, although her mission was partly to prove a point, she resisted the temptation to assault Ally's mouth with her own and push with her tongue until she could delve inside. Instead she met Ally's lips softly, slowly increasing pressure and becoming gradually more insistent. Ally, initially stiff as a board, melted against Morgan, her lips parting ever so slightly, inviting. When Morgan accepted the invitation, Ally faltered, her tongue fleeing to the back of her mouth. But her uncertainty was fleeting. Morgan groaned involuntarily when she felt the first tentative tip of Ally's tongue against hers. Suddenly the whole tenor of the embrace changed. Ally's tongue dove and rolled against her own, and her hands, previously held at her sides, clasped Morgan's hips. Morgan could feel Ally's breasts pressing just below hers, a dizzying softness.

Then just as suddenly, the hands that had provided a burning heat on Morgan's hips were pushing her away. "Get away from me!"

A little stunned at the abrupt rejection, Morgan took a step back, hitting the base of the door with the heel of her sandals. She watched Ally swipe at her mouth with the back of her hand then brush at her clothes like she was swatting away a terrifyingly large crawling insect. The woman was freaking out. "Ally. It's okay."

"It's not okay." Ally's voice was choked and in the brief moment she met Morgan's gaze there were tears glistening in her eyes. "I'm not like that. I'm not . . ." She turned to face the window and her shoulders heaved. "Get out, Morgan."

"Ally, please."

"I said get out!" Ally spun around. She had managed to swallow her tears, her eyes now as wild as that of a newly caged animal. "Get out now! And don't come near me again. Do you hear?"

Any words she said now were sure to be ineffective. Maybe tomorrow, after Ally had time to process what had just occurred between them . . . Morgan nodded silently and reached behind her and pulled the door open.

"Shit!"

When Morgan turned toward the corridor she discovered what had caused Ally's last curse. It was a member of the train staff, fresh linen and pillows in hand, standing directly in front of the door. Morgan wondered how long he had been there, and how much he had heard. *Fuck it*, she thought. Right now, she really didn't care. "Excuse me, please."

He took a step out of her way, his expression unreadable. Either he had heard nothing or the staff had been well trained in the art of diplomacy.

"Thank you," she said as she left. She headed straight for the Gold lounge car and ordered herself a double vodka and cranberry juice. And when that was finished, she ordered another.

CHAPTER EIGHT

Ally woke with a pounding headache. She reached over to the teeny shelf next to her bed and felt around for her wristwatch.

She groaned. It was only six a.m. A mere four hours had passed since she'd fallen onto her bed. Definitely not enough sleep for someone who'd consumed as much gin as she had the night before. In fact, given that her head spun when she sat up, she was probably still drunk. Ally lowered herself back onto her pillow and closed her eyes, hoping for sleep to return. But it didn't. She lay awake staring at the ceiling for another hour before admitting, drunk or not, she may as well rise and officially begin her day.

A hot shower helped a little, as did the two headache pills she fished out of her toiletry bag. But neither were enough to negate the alcohol still in her system and she weaved rather unsteadily back to her compartment. She really needed some food.

The acquisition of nourishment presented somewhat of a problem. Breakfast service had begun in Gold, but there was no way she was going to risk going there. That's where Morgan and Co. would take their breakfast, and, not knowing their schedule, there was a real possibility they would either be there already or arrive just as Ally was applying a layer of thick-cut marmalade to her buttered toast. The breakfast service had also begun in Red, but she had to pass Morgan's compartment to get to the diner car. She'd passed it the night before, only minutes after Morgan left her room. Since she'd seen Morgan head farther into Gold, presumably to the lounge car, she had felt safe enough, grabbed her purse and left the attendant to make up her bunk. Her purse still held a swath of drink vouchers, unused since her upgrade to Gold had also included complimentary beverages. Ally had used every single one of the remaining vouchers last night, sitting alone in a corner closest to the bar, downing gin after gin and completely ignoring anyone who attempted conversation with her. She'd staggered back to her room not long before two and fallen into the dead-like sleep that is the realm of the truly drunk.

Room-delivered breakfast packs were only available when the train was making an early-morning stop, so that was not an option today. And the chances of staying her hunger until the train arrived in Sydney at ten this morning were slim.

A protest from Ally's tummy forced a decision. She chose what she considered the least risky option—Red—and hurried through the carriages as fast as wobbly legs and a head full of cotton wool would allow. She hoped the original agreement of free meals still stood. Reverting back to Red dining was bad enough, but paying for the privilege was an outright insult.

Soon enough she discovered she had revoked her free Red dining rights with her move to Gold. She took the one seat still vacant in the diner car. It was next to a middle-aged man who smelled like he hadn't showered for the duration of the journey.

Ally poked at her watery scrambled eggs and buried her nose

into her coffee cup, preferring the aroma of the burnt fluid to that of her current companion.

There was only one consolation to her sad and sorry state— and that was that it would all be over in just over two hours. In just over two hours she could kiss this damn train and all its stinking occupants good-bye. A bad choice of words. Ally wouldn't be kissing anyone good-bye, *especially* Morgan Silverstone. After all, she'd already done that last night. Freshly mortified at her own actions, Ally buried her nose farther into her cup, wishing she could disappear into its murky brown depths. "I am not a lesbian," she repeated over and over to herself. "I am not a lesbian. I am not. I am not. *I am not.*"

And in just over two hours she could prove it. Because in just over two hours she would be off this train, out of Morgan's life and she would be with James again. Her hangover must have been particularly bad, because even that thought was not particularly comforting.

Ally picked miserably at her eggs and imagined the delectable Gold breakfast treats the *Bonnes Vacances* crew were feasting on. And she wondered if Morgan liked marmalade. The thick-cut kind. The kind that was her personal favorite.

Morgan was feeling quite crappy. Over the years she had developed a reasonably high tolerance for alcohol, but not so much so that she could punish her system as heavily as she had last night and not feel any aftereffects. Of course, her feeling out of sorts was compounded by the events immediately prior to her vodka and cranberry binge. Morgan sat with her legs dangling over the edge of the upper bunk she had miraculously managed to maneuver her alcohol-sodden body onto late last night and held her head in her hands.

A headache pounded at her temples. She needed to pee but didn't quite trust her feet to find the ladder rungs to descend from the bunk. And Ally hated her. Surely she couldn't feel any more miserable if she tried.

The urge to relieve the pressure in her bladder quickly became irresistible. Morgan clenched her pelvic floor muscles as tight as she could, ignored the ladder and launched herself from the top bunk. The resulting curse when she bent her left little toe the wrong way on landing was partially drowned out by the annoying opening chords of Beethoven's *Sixth* that Kitty had set as the tone for her mobile phone. Morgan fumbled in the half dark of the compartment for the phone, but the sound came from Kitty's pants pockets, which she was still wearing having fallen asleep fully clothed the night before.

Morgan shook her by the shoulder. "Kitty. Your phone's ringing."

She left Kitty to dig around in her own pants and hurried to the toilet hoping that, just for once, there would not be a queue. There wasn't and Morgan took that as a sign the rest of the day would pan out equally well.

Unfortunately, it seemed it just wasn't to be. Morgan slid the door of her compartment across to find Kitty—her clothes crumpled and her slept-upon bun in complete disarray—worriedly pacing the floor as she held her phone to her ear. The worried expression and pacing around was nothing new to Morgan, since Kitty always made out things to be worse than they were. But today . . . there was an added something in Kitty's demeanor that made her comply without argument when Kitty pointed to the bottom bunk and mouthed, "Sit!"

Morgan had entered toward the end of the conversation. She half listened as Kitty said, "I agree it is a very difficult situation." And then, "I understand completely, sir." And finally, "I'll speak to her right now and call you back immediately."

That last comment prompted Morgan's ears to prick up. Were they talking about her? When Kitty clipped her phone shut and turned bloodshot but highly alert eyes to meet her own bleary orbs, Morgan was convinced she had been the topic of the conversation.

"That was Joseph."

"Yes . . . ?" Morgan nodded. Joseph was the show's executive producer. "What does he want?"

"Well," Kitty said, pocketing her phone, "he was very interested to know why he had received a call from the network reception this morning relaying a message from someone who claims to have undeniable proof that you are a lesbian."

"What?" Morgan felt her insides all turn liquid and commence a stomach-wrenching whirlpool. They were in constant mobile range now. Surely Ally hadn't called? No. Despite her current anger, she was a bigger person than that. If anyone it would be the sheet-toting train attendant from last night. *Bastard.* She should have known from his poker-faced expression he was trouble.

"Yes," Kitty interrupted Morgan's thoughts. "It seems that French backpacker you were sure wouldn't have 'a single moment' to watch television found the time to catch last night's episode of the show."

"Marie?" Morgan said faintly. She'd never have thought . . .

"That's the one." Kitty nodded. She paced the length of the compartment twice before stopping immediately in front of Morgan. "I must have been completely stupid to believe your placations about her. She's a French person in a non-French-speaking country. Don't you think she would have pounced on a show called *Bonnes Vacances*? She probably thought it was some frog program and tuned in . . . and then she saw you."

Last night being a Friday Morgan thought it a definite that Marie would have been on duty at her Kalgoorlie pub. But then, they probably had televisions dotted throughout the venue. Although she'd have imagined they'd have been tuned into the latest boxing bout or football match, not a travel show. "But, even if she did, I didn't think—"

"Oh, come on, Morgan! Get with the program, will you. Just because you fuck someone doesn't mean they can automatically be trusted with your secrets." Kitty shrugged like it was a foregone conclusion. "She's a financially challenged backpacker who saw an opportunity and took it."

"You mean she wants money?"

Kitty nodded. "Ten thousand and she keeps quiet."

"Ten thousand," Morgan echoed. "Dollars?"

"No. French francs," Kitty said sarcastically. The demand would have been much less grand had it been the now defunct pre-Euro currency, their face value around six times less than that of the Euro. "Of course dollars. You're just lucky she doesn't realize you're one of the most popular faces on Australian TV, or she might have asked for more."

"And if we don't pay?"

"Apparently she's going to the press."

"Do you think she's bluffing?"

Kitty shrugged. "Who knows? It seems she's got nothing to lose."

Morgan dug into her pants pockets—like Kitty she had fallen asleep fully clothed—and pulled out her mobile phone. "I'm going to call her."

Kitty turned disbelieving eyes to Morgan. "Don't tell me you actually swapped numbers with the little tart?"

"No." Morgan dialed directory assistance and held the phone to her ear. "But I know the name of the pub she's working at—"

"It's nine in the morning! I don't think even the pubs in Kalgoorlie open that early," Kitty blustered. "Besides, what the hell good do you think talking to her is going to do?"

"It damn well can't hurt, can it? And she's got room and board where's she's working, so unless she's left for an early morning tour, she's most likely going to be there." Morgan held her hand up to stop Kitty from saying anything more and gave the name of the pub to the voice recognition machine the phone company

113

now used in their quest for efficiency and cost savings. Of course, when it repeated what it thought it had heard, it was completely incorrect, so Morgan held onto the line until she was transferred to a real person. Within a few seconds she had been switched through to the pub. "Good morning," she said to the woman who answered the phone. "May I speak to Marie, please?"

"Marie who?" the woman questioned.

Jesus, how many Maries could they possibly have running around? Morgan quickly looked at Kitty before admitting, "I don't know her last name. But she started working there a few days ago. She's French."

"Oh, yes . . . *Marie*. Just a minute. I'll go see if she's in her room. Who can I say is calling?"

"Morgan."

"Morgan . . . ?" The woman was obviously looking for a surname.

Morgan wasn't going to give her one. "Just Morgan. She'll know who I am." She put her hand over the phone again and said to Kitty, "They're going to get her."

Kitty made a grab for the phone. "Let me speak to her."

Morgan slapped her hand away and turned her body so Kitty couldn't reach the phone. She'd experienced the aftermath of her dealing with Ally, so there was no way she was going to let her loose with Marie.

A familiar voice was suddenly at her ear. "*Allo?*"

"Hello, Marie. It's Morgan."

Morgan heard Marie take a sharp intake of breath. Had the woman who passed on the message decided—since she didn't have a full name to give—not to give one at all? Or was Marie suffering a sudden case of nervousness from being in contact with the person she was trying to blackmail?

There was absolutely no need to swap pleasantries, so Morgan launched straight into it. "I received a very interesting call from my employer this morning. Marie, would you like to tell me just what the hell do you think you are doing?"

There was an extended silence, then a sob. "I 'ate it 'ere, Morgan. It is 'orrible! The men—they drink too much *biere* and they try to—" Morgan didn't find out what they tried to do as Marie's sentence was cut short by another sob. "And my room. It is worse than any 'ostel. It smells like old socks."

Morgan closed her eyes, the action a physical reinforcement for her mind, which was trying to close itself to the effect of Marie's tears. It didn't quite work, so Morgan reminded herself that this woman—upset or not at her current situation—had the power to make her life potentially very difficult. Or did she? Marie certainly didn't have the "undeniable proof" of her lesbianism that she claimed. All she had was her word—that of a young backpacker—over hers—that of a respected television personality. Morgan's eyes flew open, and she felt a sudden shift in the balance of power. "I understand that you might be very unhappy where you are," she said firmly. "But you're not under any obligation to stay. You can always just leave—"

Another sob. "But I 'ave no money to leave! I must stay 'ere until I am paid."

Morgan felt the beginnings of anger. She'd been in tight money situations when she was around Marie's age. Hell, as a student the money was always tight. She'd have been better off on the unemployment benefit than the paltry student allowance the government eked out to those trying to better themselves. But even when funds were so scarce that buying tampons was considered a luxury and she thought she could not face one more dinner of Vegemite sandwiches, she had never once asked anyone for money. Not even her parents. Instead she'd done as thousands of other students had and taken a crappy job with an even crappier hourly rate. "And so you thought I would be an easy way out for you?"

"I just thought . . . when I saw you on television—"

"That I would help you?"

"*Oui.*"

"To the tune of ten thousand dollars. Marie—that's an awful lot of help."

"But *chérie*, I didn't know your number so I called the station and asked for it. The *mademoiselle* who answered the phone would not give it to me—"

"They're not supposed to," Morgan interjected.

"—and she said she would leave a message for you to call me, but I did not believe that you would ever get it."

Morgan had to admit Marie was right in her assumption. If the network phone staff actually passed on the messages of everyone who called, she'd spend her days dealing with every crackpot and crank who wanted to speak to her. "So instead you thought you'd say something to make them sit up and pay attention?"

"I just wanted to speak to you, *chérie.*"

"Well, you are speaking to me." From the corner of her eye Morgan noticed Kitty mouthing something. Figuring it was an impatient "what's going on?" she ignored her. "So tell me what you want me to do."

"I want you to 'elp me, Morgan."

"You want me to help you?" Morgan asked incredulously. "Even after you blackmail me?"

"Blackmail?"

"What you are doing is called blackmail. I don't know what you French call it, but over here it's illegal." Morgan took advantage of the ensuing silence to play her trump card. "Look, Marie. While you might think that what you are doing is the answer to your problems, it's not. For one, I fail to see what proof you have of—"

"We slept together," Marie interrupted quickly.

"Yes," Morgan agreed. "We did. But when it comes down to it, it's your word against mine. And I'm sorry, sweetheart, but in this race I'm going to win. Without concrete evidence, you're

116

going to end up looking like a wet-behind-the-ears con artist. I, on the other hand, have got plenty of *powerful* people who will back me up against anything you say."

Morgan placed her hand over the phone as she exhaled forcefully. This was not easy.

There was an extended silence on the line followed by, "I 'ate you, Morgan Silverstone."

"Well, I don't like you very much at the moment either."

"You liked me enough to fuck me."

This time Morgan inhaled deeply, using the moment to arrange her thoughts. "I tell you what. I'll organize a ticket for you to get back to Perth. And also for a few nights accommodation at the place you were staying at before—"

"At the 'ostel?"

"Yes. At the backpacker hostel." Morgan shook her head at Marie's disappointed tone. What did she expect—the *Hilton*? "That will give you enough time to get a job and earn some money to continue your travels."

"I don't want to go back to Perth. I 'ave already seen Perth."

"Okay," Morgan said slowly, trying to keep her patience. It was like dealing with a petulant child. To think she'd found this woman sexy. "Where, then?"

"Sydney."

Morgan balked. Sydney was the location of the *Bonnes Vacances* studios. It was also the city where she lived. But she'd hardly be there over the next weeks, so there was little chance Marie would be successful in any efforts to try to see her. "Okay . . . Sydney it is. I'll make the arrangements this morning and you can be on the next train that goes through from Perth. Are you happy with that?"

"*Oui, chérie.*"

"And we can forget this ever happened?"

"I will never forget you, *chérie.*"

Morgan ignored the endearments. "You'll hear from someone about your train ticket and Sydney accommodation by the end of the day."

"You will not call me then?" Marie's voice was flat with disappointment.

"I would rather not, no. Good-bye, Marie."

"*Au revoir*, Morgan."

Morgan snapped her phone shut, Marie's accent echoing in her ears. It certainly didn't have the same effect on her as it had a few days ago. "Well." She glanced up at Kitty, who was boggle-eyed with curiosity. "That's taken care of. She's just a dumb kid who thought she'd try to grab a bigger pot of money than she could carry."

"Kid?" Kitty's expression turned to one of horror. "What do you mean, *kid*?"

"Stop being such a worrywart." Now that the emergency was averted she could relax enough to smile. "She's over eighteen. She's working at a pub, remember."

"Morgan . . ." Kitty paused, her expression one of warning. But her curiosity got the better of any lectures she might feel appropriate to give. "I want to hear *everything* that was said. Word for word."

Morgan related the entire conversation, ending with her promise to purchase a train ticket to take Marie to Sydney. "And as far as I know the next train from Perth doesn't arrive in Sydney until Wednesday. We're off to Vanuatu that day so we won't cross paths."

Kitty nodded, seemingly satisfied with the outcome. But she shook her head at Morgan's idea of also arranging short-term accommodation at a backpacker hostel. "Put her somewhere nice. Not five-star, but a decent hotel. That way she'll have trouble finding anything to complain about."

Morgan was more than a little surprised at Kitty's suggestion. It was a good one. Underpromise and overdeliver. She smiled crookedly. "You know, Kitty, sometimes you're actually handy to have around."

"Don't get too carried away though." Kitty turned to face herself in the mirror. She frowned at her reflection and removed the hairpin that was clinging onto the remains of her bun. "Since it's going onto *your* credit card."

"You mean the network's not going to spring for it?" Morgan said jokingly.

Kitty didn't see the humor. "You're damn lucky you've gotten away with this, Morgan. But just in case something does happen, we won't have to explain why the network was paying for a hotel to house your floozy."

"Nothing's going to happen."

"I hope you're right." Kitty shook her hair free, frowned at her reflection again then turned to face Morgan. She pulled her phone from her pocket. "Because I'm going to call Joseph back right now and explain to him it was all a big mistake and it's been sorted. I don't want to have to eat my words farther down the track."

"You won't." Morgan grabbed her toiletry bag and a towel. "I promise." On impulse she gave Kitty a quick hug. "Thanks."

"And don't think I'm going to make the arrangements for you," Kitty warned as Morgan slid the compartment door across. "You can do that yourself."

"I will. Right after my shower." Morgan nodded. She hurried down the corridor, adding to herself, "And right after I've found Ally and spoken to her about last night."

CHAPTER NINE

Ally was packing her bag in readiness for the train's arrival in Sydney when there was a succession of three sharp raps on her compartment door. She immediately stopped, half-folded jeans in hand, and stood motionless, willing Morgan to go away. She knew it was Morgan; she'd fully expected her to pay a visit sometime that morning. That was exactly the reason why she had locked her compartment door on her return from breakfast.

Which was just as well. The rapping ceased, replaced by a rattle as the latch was tried. That too stopped and finally Morgan's voice filtered through the door. "I know you're in there, Ally. Please just let me speak to you."

Some little part of Ally was tempted to pull the door across, but she resisted and stood steadfast, biting down on her lip so she wouldn't reply, even with a "Get lost."

There were a few more raps and another plea from Morgan

for her to open up, but Ally's technique of pretending she just wasn't there eventually worked.

Silence fell.

Not realizing she had been holding her breath, she gave a relieved exhalation. Then she drew in a sharp breath as a shuffling sound came from the base of the door and a small piece of paper appeared on the carpet.

She ignored it and turned back to her packing. But not even half of her clothes were neatly repacked into her case when she dived upon the note, unable to resist seeing what it said.

Morgan had simply written, "Call me anytime." Underneath, she'd added a mobile phone number. And that was it.

Ally stared at it. To her it smacked of the type of note men had passed to women in bars in the days before mobile phones and PDAs. "Fat chance, sweetheart," she muttered. She screwed up the piece of paper, threw it into the corner of the room and continued with her packing.

Once her belongings were organized, Ally had a quick wash at her basin and settled into her seat. Now, with only forty minutes until they pulled into Sydney station, there was nothing left to do but wait for the train to arrive. Ally sat down and immediately her gaze drifted to the crumpled up piece of paper on the floor. She forced herself to look away and focused instead on the chip in the wood paneling that she had spent so much time staring at yesterday while doing her Morganastics. Another session was the last thing she wanted right now so she opened the venetian blinds and placed her attention on the view from the window. They were already traveling through the outskirts of the city, clickety-clacking through suburbia. But which suburb Ally could not exactly tell since most of the houses that backed onto the railway line were really only notable for their rundown, almost derelict, appearance.

There was precious little chance they would pass within sight of any of Sydney's more aesthetically appealing attractions, and right now Ally found the shabbiness of the view rather depressing. So she stared down at her hands instead.

Even that was not the best of ideas. The first thing she thought of when she looked at them was how Morgan's hips had felt within their grasp. The softness, how her hands had molded so well to the womanly curve, even through the material of that very sexy sleeveless shirt she had been wearing . . .

Christ almighty! So much for avoiding the Morganastics. Ally threw her head back into the headrest and stared at the ceiling.

That particular section of the compartment was apparently safe, so Ally stared at it for the remainder of the journey. As she did, she conjured images of James and their meeting at the station. It would be a romantic meeting, she decided, just as it ought to be when couples meet on train platforms. The tails of James's knee-length overcoat would be flapping behind him as he hurried to greet her and she would drop her bag as he lifted her off the ground to twirl her 'round and 'round.

"Ha ha!" For the first time that day Ally not only smiled but laughed out loud. James may very well be wearing his knee-length overcoat, but she couldn't quite picture him in a midst of a romantic twirl. Romantic or not, it would definitely be nice to see him again though.

Nice. Ally screwed up her nose at her repeated use of that benign word. She really ought to find a more descriptive adjective. *Extremely exciting.* Yes. That was better. Ally thought it *extremely exciting* to be seeing James again.

She held on to that term until the announcement came over the PA system that they were due to arrive at Sydney's Central Station in five minutes. She could hear lots of movement in the corridor—probably the same passengers who'd been desperate to board the train were now just as desperate to alight—and so she stayed seated, with her door locked, until the train had ground to a complete halt and most of the shuffle of feet past her door had ceased. Even then she waited for a minute or two before rising from her seat and unlatching her door. On a sudden impulse she bent to the floor and picked up the screwed-up piece of paper. She shoved it into her handbag as she hurried down the empty corridor, peering out of the large windows as she walked, hoping to catch a glimpse of . . . of James.

She saw him as soon as she alighted from the carriage. He was standing back from the crowd, head slowly turning from side to side as he scanned the platform looking for her. "James!" she called, holding a hand up in the air and waving. She saw him smile and nod in recognition as he moved sedately through the crowd to greet her.

"Alison." He drew her into his arms and kissed her on the cheek. His skin felt raspy against hers. If she didn't know better she'd have assumed he'd left the house unshaven. But she did know better. James's skin—apart from the first hour immediately following his fastidious morning shave—was always like that.

Strangely, it had never bothered her as much as it did right now. Nevertheless, Ally ignored the scratchy sensation that spread around her mouth and kissed him back, not on the cheek, but on the lips. She pressed against him, feeling the strength of his body and breathing in the familiar spice of his aftershave. She held onto him, laying her cheek against his chest and feeling his heartbeat against her ear, regular and even. She hadn't got her flapping coattails or her platform twirl, but she did get his arms around her. Most importantly, she got a feeling of reassurance that this was how it should be. That order had been restored. Ally clung onto him even more tightly.

James's hands moved to her shoulders, pushing her away to hold her at arm's length, an expression of bemusement on his features. "Are you okay, Alison?"

"I'm fine." Ally laughed a little at her very uncharacteristic clinginess. She let him take her bag then latched onto the crook of his arm, steering him in the direction of the exit. "Just take me home. I want to have a bath and then I want to show you how much I've missed you."

The smile that spread across James's features displayed he was not averse to that idea at all. "Right, then. Let's go."

They walked arm-in-arm across the platform, and because Ally had no checked luggage to collect, they steered well clear of the crowded baggage-claim area. Despite her attempts not to, she could not help but cast a quick glance in the direction of the throng of people waiting to collect their suitcases. The small group on the periphery was unmistakable. Two men, one tall and lanky. Two women, one pacing around talking into her mobile phone. The other, a tall brunette with a melting mouth . . .

Ally touched her fingers to her lips, the tingly feeling that ran through them no doubt a residual effect of James's whiskers. She leaned farther into him, resting her head against his shoulder and squeezing his arm. Suddenly aware the tall brunette had turned and was looking straight at her, Ally tilted her head up to James and smiled. And she hoped, not just for James's sake but for the sake of anyone who happened to be watching, that it was a look of absolute devotion.

Two hours later—one of which had been spent sitting in Sydney's abominable traffic—Ally was home. She'd unpacked her case while the bath was filling. James had brewed a pot of Earl Grey tea while she organized her clothes, so she drank that while she soaked. Now she was in her bedroom, applying her moisturizer. She applied it in long, slow strokes, her mind attuned to the feel of her own body under her hands. Her legs: soft and smooth, with only the finest traces of hair appearing since her last date with a tub of wax. Her stomach: also soft and not quite flat, but with a gentle curve that led to another, that of her Venus mound. On the upward stroke she could feel the rigid outline of her ribs and the contrasting pliability of her breasts. Ally held one in her hand as she applied the moisturizing cream. She'd given her breasts lots of attention over the years, but always with a critical eye. She'd judged them for their size, their shape, how they looked in this bra or that, this bikini, that bathing suit. Now she closed her eyes, running her hand over the soft tissue, cupping it, stopping with her palm across her nipple and feeling it react under her own touch. She dropped the tube of moisturizer to take her other breast in hand, caressing it, feeling its weight, watching the skin pucker as she traced her fingertip around the areola. *They're beautiful,* she realized, fully appreciating their uniqueness for the first time. A flash of memory—of a similar womanly softness pressing just above hers—caused Ally's breath to catch in her throat. She stopped what she was doing and bent down to frantically rub some moisturizer into her feet.

"Don't stop."

"Wha—?" Ally jerked her head around to find James at the entrance to the bedroom. His shirt was off and he'd loosened the buckle on the belt of his trousers.

"I said"—James took a step toward the bed—"don't stop what you were doing. I liked it."

Ally watched him approach, her cheeks hot in the knowledge she had been seen. She also felt somewhat affronted. Her moment had been private and nonsexual. But from the telltale bulge in James's trousers he had seen it in a very sexual manner indeed. "Haven't you ever heard of knocking?" she asked tightly, pulling her light cotton bathrobe over her shoulders.

James rounded the bed and stopped right in front of her. From her seated position all she could now see was the bulge in his pants. "The door was open, Alison."

"Oh." Mollified at what she knew to be true, she leaned back a little so she could meet his glance instead of talking to a big protrusion. "Well, you should have come in and asked if you could put some cream on my back for me, instead of sneaking around like a randy schoolboy." She held out the tube of moisturizer.

He took it, smiling indulgently. "Lie down and turn over."

Hmm. So no flapping coattails, no platform twirls and no silken lover's language. Pretty much par for the course. Ally saluted him before turning over to lie facedown on the bed. "Yes, sir!"

It was just as well James had decided on a career in architecture, since he would never have made it as a masseur. Ally yelped at the shock of cold, him squeezing a huge dollop of the very cold cream directly onto her back. His application technique was reminiscent of his dishwashing technique—fast and furious. "Good?" he asked, placing the tube onto the bedside table and lying down next to her.

Experience had taught Ally that, if one wanted a male to repeat a certain task—such as the dishes, or a load of washing—it was wise not to criticize the current effort, no matter how crude. Right at this moment however, Ally was not certain she ever wanted him to do that again. She felt more like a scrubbed pot than anything else. And—she glanced to the bedside table—he hadn't put the cap back on the tube of cream. So her tone was rather sarcastic as she reached to the table and groped around for the cap. "Oh, yes. Very good, thanks."

James wouldn't have gotten far in a career in human behavioral sciences either, since her tone seemed to have sailed right over his head. Instead he sounded rather pleased with himself. "I'm glad to do it for you." He followed Ally's trajectory to the bedside table, pressing his chest against her bare back and rubbing his lips along the side of her neck. She could feel his erection against her buttocks. "Baby, you smell so good."

Ally shunted across the mattress a little, not yet ready for full body contact. She also moved her head away, finding James's whiskers, which seemed to have sprouted farther since their last embrace on the train platform, increasingly irritating. "That tickles," she lied.

"Do you want me to shave again?" James asked as he stuck his tongue into her ear.

"No." Ally flipped over to face him, his question triggering a realization that she was being unduly hard on him. And she couldn't pinpoint why. He was no different than normal. Maybe it was she who had changed? *No!* Ally told herself firmly. *I'm exactly the same as I was before she* . . . She grabbed James's cheeks and kissed him hard on the lips. "I like you exactly the way you are."

Even before the embrace she knew she wasn't in the mood. Now, feeling his bristles scratch across her cheek and the hardness of his body against hers, she was sure of it. She knew from previous declinations of his advances that James would accept her decision without argument. But still, she *had* kind of promised. And there was a portion of her consciously pushing her onward, telling her this was something she had to do, and do *now*. So she closed her eyes and began working her lips down his chin, to his neck. She curled her fingers through the dense covering of chest hair and trailed her nails farther down, across his stomach and past his navel, where a snail trail of dark, coarser hair began. James was breathing harder, in anticipation of what was to come next. He loved it when she slid her hand into his trousers and exclaimed over what she found.

"Alison?" he said a moment later, when her hand still rested, unmoving, on his abdomen. Getting no reply he repeated, "Alison?"

Ally just shook her head against James's chest, unable to speak. She had no words to describe the sensation that had gripped her. It wasn't just a case of not being in the mood. It was more than that. It wasn't quite fear. It wasn't quite dread. It wasn't even quite distaste. It was a . . . *wrong* kind of feeling. She was lying beside the man she declared to love and it felt . . . wrong.

She rolled off the bed and grabbed her bathrobe, which she had thrown onto the floor just before James attacked her back with moisturizer. "I'm not feeling well," she said as she dashed, with head down, into the toilet.

James knocked on the locked door a few moments later. "Alison? Are you okay?"

"Not really," she said weakly. She was sitting on the lid of the toilet seat, her head in her hands. She felt a little nauseous. Maybe she actually *was* ill and it was stopping her from thinking straight. Or maybe she was suffering a delayed hangover from all the gin she knocked back last night. "I think I might have caught something on the train."

"What can I do for you?"

"Nothing at the moment," Ally said slowly, choosing her words carefully. "But I'm sure I'll be fine tomorrow."

There was a short silence, then, "Does that mean you want me to leave?"

Ally's head was awash with contradicting thoughts. She wanted to be alone to think, but she didn't want to be alone with her thoughts.

"Alison?"

Ally flushed the toilet, not out for need, but for effect. "I think maybe it would be better if you did. You don't want to catch anything I might have."

Another silence, then, "I'll give you a call later tonight, okay?"

Ally could hear the disappointment in his tone. And no wonder either. This wasn't exactly the homecoming she had planned, or that he would have been hoping for. "I'm sorry."

"It's not your fault you are unwell."

"I'll be fine tomorrow, I promise."

"We'll take tomorrow when it comes. I'm going to put a glass of water by the door here, and then I'll get going. And I'll call you tonight."

James's concern almost made Ally want to cry. How could she be such a bitch to such a nice man? *Nice?* Jesus, there was that word again. "Okay," she replied, her voice small.

Less than a minute passed before Ally heard the clink of glass against the tiled floor. "There you go. I'll be off now."

"Okay."

"I love you, Alison."

Ally opened her mouth but no more words would come out. She pulled a wad of paper off the roll and blew her nose loudly. It wasn't entirely a ruse, since she could feel tears threatening. They appeared in a flood the moment she heard the door to her apartment open and close.

"What the hell have you done to me, Morgan Silverstone?" Ally threw open the toilet door, returned to the bedroom and threw herself on the bed. In the next moment she was off it again and dashing through the apartment, to her handbag, which she'd left on the kitchen bench. She emptied the entire contents onto the granite-look laminate and rummaged through them until she found the piece of screwed-up paper with Morgan's number on it. She smoothed the paper until it was again readable then stared at the number for a very long time.

As she stared she recalled—of all things—a snippet of advice from the very staid and totally humorless teacher who had delivered their sex education class in the second year of high school. "If you scratch an itch it will only get worse." Of course, all the students thought this hilarious, assuming she was referring to sexually transmitted diseases. But no—without a hint of a smile, the teacher explained she was talking of the desire for sex—that once you have sex you'll want to keep having it again and again. In other words, don't start having sex. Of course almost everyone, including Ally, had ignored her advice. But now her words seemed to have a ring of truth to them. Morgan was her itch. And so it was better not to begin scratching it at all. Well, she had scratched a little already. But now that her days of training were over, she could leave the itch alone. And untouched, it would just disappear.

Ally took another look at the piece of paper. It was the last link she had to Morgan. If she destroyed it, she'd effectively destroy any opportunity to get in contact with her again. She set her mouth, tore the piece of paper into tiny shreds and threw it into the dustbin.

Then she slipped into some old tracksuit pants and a wind-cheater, made herself another pot of Earl Grey tea and took it to the drafting table that dominated a good third of her little lounge room. She retrieved her Kalgoorlie executive residence sketches and set them out. When she really wanted to, she could gain a very deep level of concentration—to the point she was largely unaware of anything happening around her. In fact, she was renowned for it. Conversations could be occurring over her head, the phone could ring and ring, and even when onsite, tradesmen could bang and crash all around her and still she'd be blissfully unaware of anything but her work.

Since she had been a lot less productive over the last few days than she had planned, it seemed a useful skill to employ now. Ally bent to her task and as she became more involved she gradually forgot about the shreds of paper in the dustbin and any ideas she may have entertained about fishing them out and piecing them together again.

She wasn't so involved that she missed James's call at seven p.m. She announced she was feeling much better and they made arrangements for him to pick her up in time for the charity auction that was being held the next day—Sunday—at his old school. After hanging up from his call she heated a can of chunky vegetable soup that was supposed to taste like homemade. Maybe it did, but to Ally it could have been soggy cardboard, so she tossed it into the trash, right on top of the shreds of paper.

Then she went to bed and cried.

She slept a little but woke before midnight. She went back to her drafting table until four then fell into an exhausted sleep that took her right through until ten a.m.

Less than an hour later she was showered and dressed and

waiting for James to arrive. Ally sat at the edge of the bed, one strappy sandal on her foot, the other in her hand, her thumbnail idly snapping at the metal buckle as she stared out of the window. Her view was uninspiring, dominated by the block of post-war boom period apartments on the opposite side of the street to her own, art deco-inspired building. An observer would be certain she was intent on the young mother standing on her balcony pegging nappy after nappy onto a portable clothes airer, but they would be wrong. The young woman had caught Ally's attention for but a moment, just long enough for her to acknowledge the rare sight of cloth nappies in a world now dominated by the disposable. After that Ally entered dangerous territory and allowed her mind to wander. The focus of her vision shifted and the physical world blurred to become merely a backdrop to the sequence of images flickering at the forefront of her mind's eye.

There was Marge's face at the moment Morgan invited Ally to bunk with her—round cheeks red with a network of broken capillaries, and eyes full of excitement and life. Then there was the bob of James's Adam's apple in his throat when he jutted out his chin to shave the thick stubble that grew overnight. That image switched to the graceful curve of Morgan's neck in the moment before she had leaned in to kiss her. Then there were Morgan's hands, her fingers curled around her glass of vodka and cranberry. James again, holding himself above her, momentarily still as he said, "James. My name is James." His face disappeared to be replaced by Morgan's. Her sleeveless shirt clung to her waist as she put her hands behind her back to latch the door of a wood-paneled room. Then Marge again, shaking her head, a look of disappointment on her face. And Kitty, arms folded, peering over the rim of her spectacles, her expression one of frowning disapproval. Mark flashed by. And Nick. And the English crooner, open-stanced, wanting Morgan. And news reporter Lucas, pausing to remove a strand of hair from Morgan's face. His hand became Ally's. Her fingers caught the strand of auburn hair, gently pushing it aside as Morgan leaned toward her lips—

"Alison?"

So involved was Ally in her thoughts that she dropped her sandal at the sudden interruption. "Yes?" she squeaked, heat flooding her cheeks. She looked down to her sandal, lying upside down on the floor. "I'm sorry. I was miles away and didn't hear you come in. What did you say?"

James gave a low laugh. "I hadn't actually said anything yet." He approached the bed and stood in front of her. "I was going to ask if you were ready."

"Just about." Ally slipped her sandal on and did up the buckle. As she did she noted the high polished sheen of James's black leather shoes and the sharp edge on the legs of his freshly pressed Armani trousers. She straightened slowly, smoothing the material of her dress over her thighs. James was already in his jacket—also Armani—the stark white of his shirt broken by a tie Ally had never seen before: plain maroon with a gold crest at the base. "Your old school tie?" she asked, lifting the tie to have a closer look at the crest.

James shrugged. "It seemed appropriate."

Ally nodded, hiding a smile. She imagined Ned and Phil—his two old school buddies she would be meeting for the first time at today's charity auction—would also be sporting the same tie. It was a man thing, she guessed. She wouldn't be caught dead in any portion of her old school uniform. In fact she couldn't. Unlike James, she hadn't attended a private school, so there were no hats or ties or blazers to worry about, and she and her friends had had a ritual burning of their ugly school-issued blue wind-cheaters and shirts the night they graduated. "There." Ally straightened the knot of his tie a little. "That's better."

James held her at arm's length and his brown-eyed gaze traveled over her face. "Are you sure you're up to this?"

"Of course." Ally looked at the point just below James's eyes.

132

"I told you. I think it was just a little bug I caught on the train. But I feel fine now. Honestly."

"Good." James nodded slowly, a mixture of concern and relief crossing his features. He indicated with a slight nod in the direction of Ally's front door. "Shall we?"

Ally hooked her arm into his and nodded. "We shall."

CHAPTER TEN

Throughout the drive to the auction James was animated and talkative, obviously relishing the prospect of catching up with his school friends again. He described Phil, a talented rugby player who could have made it to the big leagues but who never realized his potential, choosing instead to follow in the footsteps of his banker father. He was married at twenty-five, had a child by twenty-six and now spent twelve to fourteen hours each day making profitable use of other people's money. Then there was Ned, also the son of a banker, but a bit of a bohemian at heart. He was not academically inclined, preferring the arts to the sciences. When his father insisted he attend university Ned complied, but to his father's immense displeasure, he opted to study toward a fine arts degree. His parents were long divorced, and his mother—in an act that probably had as much to do with upsetting her ex-husband as assisting her son—funded his purchase of a small gallery in Sydney's Blue Mountains. His own painting never progressed past that of an amateur, but he did have a flair for picking talent in others, and he turned the gallery into a reputable and lucrative concern.

James's descriptions of these two quite different characters served to pique Ally's curiosity, and by the time they reached the large iron gates of the school entrance her spirits were greatly improved.

Once they were parked she turned in her seat and smiled at James. The display of his usually controlled exuberance reminded her of the days when they first met. It brought forth a rush of affection and on impulse she reached over to kiss him on the cheek. "Thank you," she said.

"What for?" he asked.

Ally wasn't quite sure how to verbalize what she was thinking. "For pulling me out of my funk."

James looked surprised. "I didn't realize you were in one."

Ally stared at him for a moment, then shook her head and opened her car door. They were hardly halfway toward the assembly hall when they ran into Phil and his wife, Barbara. Phil certainly had the physique of a rugby player—barrel-chested, thick-necked and broad-shouldered. He also had the outward signs of an indulgent lifestyle: lots of lavish business lunches, expensive alcohol and cigars. His face was a little pudgy, his nose a little goutish, and he was suffering the spread around the middle that too many hours behind a desk brings.

In the car James had described Phil's wife as "a little stout and rather verbose." Within a minute of meeting her, Ally had refined his description to that of a "portly patronizing parrot." Barbara's physical build and tendency to chatter was reminiscent of Marge. But while Marge was a kindly woman whose incessant talk was devoid of malice, Barbara scanned her surrounds with a critical eye and used her words to strike out against anything she found disagreeable. *No wonder Phil spends so much time at work,*

Ally thought as Barbara declared the auction booklet they were handed when they reached the entrance to the venue as obviously the work of an amateur.

"Photocopied pages." She sniffed, thumbing through the publication. "And black and white photos," she continued, referring to the images that accompanied a written summary of each lot that was up for auction. "Next they'll be serving us sparkling wine and calling it champagne."

"Your son attends this school, doesn't he?" Ally asked, not even bothering to try and maintain a friendly tone.

"Oh, yes. He's in the second year of high school now. Doing very well, too, I might say."

"Maybe then you—"

"Ned! You old bastard!" Phil exclaimed suddenly, interrupting Ally from telling Barbara that—since she could obviously do so much better—maybe she should get off her ass and join the school fundraising committee.

A slightly built man with a receding hairline and a goatee grinned hugely and approached their group. Like James and Phil he also sported the maroon school tie, but his chinos and sports jacket gave him a much more casual air than that of his classically suited comrades. He dropped the hand of a woman who looked half his age to return the hearty slaps on the back that both James and Phil were bestowing upon him.

"That must be Ned's latest *friend*," Barbara murmured in a disparaging voice. "She's the fifth or sixth since his divorce. His wife ran off with an artist friend of his, you know."

No, Ally did not know that. And while James had mentioned Ned was divorced, he had not mentioned that he was currently seeing anyone. They weren't in regular contact, however, so maybe he didn't even know. She approached the woman, who was watching the men perform their welcoming rituals, pleased there was to be some other female company other than the wearisome Barbara. "Ally." She held out her hand in greeting.

"Pleased to meet you."

"Mandy." The woman smiled briefly, looked Ally up and down and turned her gaze back to the men. "So, you're here with . . . James?"

"That's right."

"And James is . . ."

"The dark-haired one."

"Oh." Mandy took a long, appraising look at James and nodded appreciatively. "Ned said he's an architect?"

"That's right," Ally repeated, glancing over to the men. Now they were guffawing over something and punching one another on the shoulder. "Once they're done beating each other up I'll introduce you."

Mandy nodded again, her gaze well and truly fixed on James. "Are you two married?"

"Goodness, no." Ally waved away the notion. "We've only known each other nine months."

"So . . . you live together?"

Ally flinched a little at the personal line of questioning. She grabbed a glass of champagne from the tray of a passing waiter and took a long draught. If she felt like giving details she would say she and James spent most nights at either one or the other's places. But she didn't feel like giving details. "Nope."

Three minutes later the men had finished hitting each other hello and everyone had been introduced. Armed with a glass of champagne each, they meandered over to the cordoned-off area that displayed the items to be auctioned. Ally held back from the group a little, pretending a little more interest in the goods than she really had. From her vantage point she could see that Mandy had already filled the gap next to James and was tittering demurely at whatever he was saying. Phil and Ned were engrossed in their own conversation and Barbara was declaring loudly that she would be bidding on Lot 14 this afternoon. Ally glanced to the item that had so taken Barbara's fancy and shuddered. It was an ugly, ugly Limoge Father Christmas box. Personally, she wouldn't give it house space.

She stopped in front of Lot 23, a brand new Vespa scooter, and speculated over how much it might fetch. Ally loved the idea of a scooter but couldn't quite picture herself darting in and out of the Sydney traffic on her way to and from work every day. She could be persuaded to indulge in the two bottles of the Krug Grande Cuvée champagne that comprised Lot 34 though. And the nighttime Sydney Harbor Bridge climb was very appealing too, despite her fear of heights. Everyone she knew who had done the climb said the views were spectacular, especially at night. And the danger of falling was next to nil, since everyone was attached to the bridge by safety ropes.

Having decided on the few items she might bid on, she joined the rest of her group, already past the end of the display area. They, along with a few other people around them, were discussing what Lot 55, the "Mystery Lot," could possibly be. Apparently last year it was the deputy headmaster. He'd been won by the father of one of the students, who'd promptly handed him over to his son. The son and his group of friends had taken the deputy paintballing.

"The poor fellow was black and blue from all the paintballs that were fired at him." Phil guffawed.

There was more hearty backslapping by the three men as they imagined being able to do the same thing to their deputy headmaster when they were at school. And that concluded the Mystery Lot speculation, them turning to a series of school days "do you remember whens?" Their reminiscing was accompanied by lots of guffaws and lots of slaps on the back.

"Phil will wake up tomorrow and wonder why he can hardly move." Barbara cackled, shaking her head. She had loosened up a little since downing her glass of champagne, even though it "wasn't quite chilled enough."

Ally laughed along, temporarily shelving the very appealing

image of Barbara being the Mystery Lot, bidding for her, winning, and then taking her for paintballing target practice. "Men," she said simply.

Mandy laughed too, raising her glass and shooting glance number two hundred and seventy eight in James's direction. "You gotta love 'em."

"Yeah. You gotta." This time Ally's laugh was just a teeny bit hollow. She craned her head to see over the men's shoulders. "I think they're about to start serving lunch. I might see if I can beat the queue."

"I'll come with you," Barbara said quickly.

Can't a woman get a minute alone? Ally thought sourly. But she nodded and smiled, leading the way as they passed through the crowd to the buffet table.

"I'd have my eye on that one if I were you," Barbara said as she picked up two plates. She held onto both of them so Ally assumed she was either very hungry, or she was going to play the role of gatherer for her husband.

"On which one?" Ally pretended she didn't know who Barbara was talking about. She picked up a single plate and eyed the selection, suddenly hungry at the sight of all the food.

"On Mandy." Barbara nodded knowingly. "She's got designs on your James."

"He's not 'my' James." Ally selected some sushi rolls and dabbed a large spoonful of wasabi onto her plate. "And if he wants her then he can have her." Sensing Barbara's open-mouthed horror at that statement, she continued, "I'm not going to get into a catfight over some man. If he decides he'd rather be with her, then I won't stand in his way."

"That's almost exactly what Ned said about his ex-wife," Barbara said in a warning tone.

"Then Ned and I must be quite alike." Ally finished off her plate with some marinated octopus and a melange of salad leaves. "I'll see you back with the group."

139

On her return trip she passed Mandy, who was purportedly heading toward the buffet. Mandy eyed her plate. "You didn't get anything for James?"

Ally shrugged. "Last time I looked both his legs were in working order." She smiled at Mandy and continued through the crowd, wondering what delicacies the little vamp would bring back for him.

By the time she was back at James's side her smile had vanished. Surely she should be feeling at least a little territorial, a little jealous? But no, she wasn't. If anything, all she felt was the concern of a sister watching a gold digger trying to get her hooks into her brother. Although maybe even that wasn't accurate. Ally had no siblings, so the notion of sisterly concern was an alien concept. Probably she wasn't feeling concerned because she had nothing to be concerned about. Goodness knew she'd told herself often enough that she trusted James implicitly. So her lack of worry now was purely her demonstrating that fact. Yes. That was it.

Pleased at the reasonable explanation for her seeming lack of care, Ally applied a decent layer of wasabi onto a salmon sushi roll and popped it into her mouth. The wasabi was potent— much more so than the one served at the Japanese takeaway near her office—and Ally felt the sudden shock of it as it spread through her nasal passages. It hit her eyes just at the moment Mandy and Barbara reappeared. Since it felt like her head was about to explode, probably she looked like it too. Mandy, who had been holding an overflowing plate in James's direction, gave her a look of alarm, retracted the offering and aimed it instead toward Ned.

Ned, who had been studying the auction booklet, was seemingly oblivious to the fact he had almost missed out on lunch. He accepted the plate. "Thanks, love."

Barbara handed a plate to Phil and then, nodding approvingly, leaned over to whisper in Ally's ear, "You go, girl. Put the bitch in her place."

That comment sounded so utterly absurd coming from Barbara that Ally had to pop another sushi roll—sans wasabi—into her mouth to avoid laughing out loud.

James, now being the only person without lunch, glanced hungrily at her plate. "That looks good."

"It is." Ally nodded in the direction of the buffet but had a sudden change of heart about telling him to go get something before it all disappeared. She held her plate in between them. "Let's share."

Morgan was halfway across the Harbor Bridge when her phone buzzed. This being the umpteenth time it had rung already today, she was tempted to ignore it. But the part of her that still held hope Ally might call glanced expectantly to the caller I.D. Her expression fell. It was only Michael, her agent. She let it ring.

It stopped and was pleasantly silent for the rest of her journey, even throughout the wrong turn she made and her subsequent unscheduled stop to check her map. But it rang again as she was turning into the gated entrance to the boys' school where she was due to be "auctioned off." It was Michael again.

"All right, already. Jesus!" Morgan pointed her Mercedes in the direction of the sign that read "Staff only" parking, pulled into the first bay she found free and cut the engine. "Yes, Michael?" she said curtly as she undid her seat belt. "I hope this is more important than last time. This *is* my one and only day off, you know."

Yesterday, after being ignored by Ally and after making Marie's transport and accommodation arrangements, she'd killed the time left before the train arrived by answering some of her phone messages. She'd rolled her eyes skyward when Michael imparted the details of the so-called "exciting opportunity" he had mentioned in his message the previous day. Apparently some biographer to the stars wanted to write her life story. She'd reminded Michael she was only thirty-five years old and hopefully hadn't already done everything that may be worth writing about. And—not being in the best of moods—she also pointed out that she was trained in journalism, so, surprise, surprise, could string a sentence together. Hence, if anyone was going to write her life story, it would be her. And she hung up.

Now, Michael gave an audible sigh before saying, "Sounds like somebody's going to get their period soon."

Morgan rolled her eyes skyward again. He could be as bitchy as any self-respecting queen. Not that he'd ever admitted to her he was a gay man. The philosophy of "don't ask, don't tell" at the network also applied to her relationship with her agent, and that aspect of their lives was never discussed. Only business and money, percentages and profile-raising opportunities. And where Morgan was in her cycle. "Yes, Michael, I am. So unless you want to be the victim of a PMS-induced crime, you'd better tell me what you want quick-smart."

"Have you ever heard of a little event called the Logies?" Michael asked primly.

Of course she'd heard of the Logies. They were the Australian television industry's equivalent to the Emmys. *Bonnes Vacances* had amassed a nice collection of the little statues over the years and had indeed added another two at this year's ceremony, held only the month prior. "Get to the point."

Michael took a deep breath before saying in a very tightly controlled voice, "What would you say if I told you I had been approached asking if you want to host next year's event? Alone."

Morgan gasped. Hosting the Logies was an honor that had been bestowed on only a select few over the years. And of that select few, even fewer were women. In fact, Morgan could think of only one time a woman had single-handedly hosted the event. All others had been in a cohosting role. Michael had to be bullshitting her. "No way!"

"I kid you not, my darling." Michael's controlled tone evaporated, replaced by his gushing, excited one. "I took the call from the head of the awards committee this morning. And you, my ever-so-popular little beauty, are their first choice."

"Oh, my God." Morgan could hardly believe her ears.

"They want to talk to you sometime this week."

Morgan nodded. "Yes, yes, of course."

"I know you're leaving again on Wednesday so I proposed tomorrow night—Monday. You *are* free?"

Morgan was scheduled for recording segment lead-ins tomorrow and Tuesday, but they should wind up around six. "Even if I wasn't, I'd make myself."

"Excellent. I'll call you back later with the venue and time." Michael sniffed, a sure indication there was a bitchy comment to come. "And this time keep your PMS monster in its cage."

Morgan hung up the phone without replying.

Oh, my God. The Logies. She shook her head in amazement as she consulted the instruction sheet that gave directions as to where she was supposed to go once having entered the school grounds. "The Logies," she said to herself in wonder as she stepped out of her car and followed the sign that pointed to the assembly hall.

Given the maze of buildings that stretched out across the impressive school grounds, she was rather surprised that she found the hall without fuss. She was late, but that didn't matter. According to the agenda, they should be serving a buffet-style lunch right now, the auction itself not due to start for another forty minutes. Morgan extended her hand to the man who welcomed her at the entrance and who announced himself as William, the organizer of the event. She smiled brilliantly in his direction. *Wow. The Logies.* And she walked beside him into the assembly hall, which was buzzing with the chatter of the quite sizable crowd.

They stopped not too far from a bank of cordoned-off white-clothed tables, upon which the auction items—with the exception of a very handsome but floor-bound Vespa scooter—were on display. It was with a slight grimace that she saw that Lot 55—the final lot—had only a gold glitter card with a black question mark on it. Since it was the only lot without an item attached, she assumed it was hers.

"I hope I'm not going to have to stand on the table and be 'viewed,'" she said only half-jokingly to William.

He gave a roar of laughter then shook his head, showing her the last page of a little booklet that gave details of each lot. "See here." He pointed to the details of Lot 55. "It's a mystery lot. No one will know what it is until the auctioneer presents you at the time." He waited for her to nod in understanding then steered her past the tables and to a small cluster of two men and a woman, all of whom held little plates of food. According to his introductions, they were the other members of the organizing committee.

After saying her hellos and accepting a glass of champagne from a wandering waiter, Morgan took a moment to size up the crowd. Lots of suits. Lots of designer dresses. And a distinct smell of money in the air. Morgan took a sip of her champagne, watching as empty glasses were placed on trays and immediately replaced with full ones. She decided—given the impressive-looking array of goods that were to go under the hammer—if the alcohol served to loosen the catches on some wallets even a little, this auction stood to make a very tidy sum indeed. She hoped they still had some money left by the time it came to the Mystery Lot. It would be rather embarrassing to be passed in.

"Would you like a little something to eat, Ms. Silverstone?"

"Please, call me Morgan." She smiled at William and nodded. She hadn't eaten any dinner the previous night, having picked all day at the trays of sandwiches and muffins that the studio provided at every meeting. And she hadn't had any breakfast, a cup of coffee her only companion as she spent the morning wandering aimlessly around her apartment, turning the events of the past few days over and over in her mind and stopping every few minutes to check her phone, which lay charging on a lamp table. Ally hadn't called.

She followed William to the buffet. It was slow progress, since he saw fit to introduce her to everyone he knew along the way, but finally she had a small plate laden with an array of very tasty little treats. While she had been making a selection from the platter of sushi, William had been tapped on the shoulder and had hurried away to tend to some pre-auction detail, so she weaved her way back through the crowd alone, aiming for the still-clustered committee members.

Not too many steps into her journey she felt compelled to turn her head, feeling the weight of someone's glance. Morgan's throat tightened. Not ten feet away from her was Ally. She held a champagne flute in one hand and a small plate in the other. Her dress was salmon-colored, adding depth to the light tan of her skin. It had spaghetti straps that accentuated the fineness of her shoulders and collarbone. Her short hair, which throughout the train journey had had an urbane, tousled look, was smoothed back and sophisticated. Morgan sucked in her breath. She looked fabulous.

Her eyes strayed to the group she stood with. Three men and two women. All the men looked to be around the same age, and all wore the maroon-colored tie she'd seen on many of the other male guests. Having earlier commented on it to William, he had explained it was the school tie. He was wearing one himself and so had held it out for examination and admiration.

It could therefore be safely assumed that the male portion of Ally's contingent was alumni. And since the alumni member she stood closest to was the same man Morgan had seen her clinging onto at the train station yesterday morning, Ally's presence at this event was explained.

Morgan didn't have to delve very far into her memory to find the name of Ally's partner. *James.* She took a quick head-to-toe glance of the man. He was tall, dark and handsome—in a genteel James Bond type of way. The Pierce Brosnan Bond, as opposed to the more rugged Sean Connery Bond.

Morgan's gaze strayed back to Ally and she hovered over the decision whether to take the half-dozen steps necessary to say hello. What would the reception be like if she did? And how should she introduce herself? Had Ally told James about meeting her on the train? Goodness, what if Ally had told him . . . everything? Morgan didn't like that thought so she ignored it, instead testing the water by sending Ally a bright smile of recognition and hello.

Initially it appeared that Ally would return the smile. The hint of one flickered at the corners of her lips, but it quickly withered and died. She set her little plate onto the tray of a passing waiter, crooked her arm into James's and turned her body slightly away. It was a subtle move, but it was as effective as if she had turned her back on Morgan completely.

Disappointment covered Morgan like a shroud. She turned and walked away, refusing to think of anything but happy thoughts. *The Logies.*

This time, however, even they could not raise her spirits.

James's voice floated into Ally's thoughts at the same time she felt his hand move to the small of her back. "Are you okay?" he asked, looking to her plate of food, which was disappearing into the crowd on a waiter's tray.

Ally wished she'd given the plate to James instead of mindlessly placing it onto the tray. He hadn't yet had the opportunity to partake of anything but a little of the marinated octopus, the appearance of another old school friend interrupting his attempts at lunch. The friend and his wife had departed their

146

group only seconds before *she* appeared. Ally took a sip of her champagne and let the bubbles fizz on her tongue before swallowing. What on earth was Morgan doing here? Was she stalking her? More importantly, why did she find the thought of being followed around by Morgan appealing?

Despite the fact that her stomach was flopping about and her knees were a little wobbly she told James, "Sure. Sure. I'm fine. I've just overdone the wasabi a bit and am no longer hungry. I'm sorry about the plate. I wasn't thinking."

His hand moved to her waist and gave it a little squeeze. "It's okay."

"Maybe there's time to get another." In a little area right at the back of her mind Ally was envisioning the possible route Morgan had taken into the crowd and calculating the probability of being able to replicate it. She twisted James's wrist a little so she could see his watch. "How much longer until the auction starts?"

"Soon." James turned to her, concern in his eyes. "You're looking a little flushed. Do you want to sit down somewhere?" He scanned the hall. "I think I saw some seats behind the tables where the lots are being displayed."

My God, he is just so nice! Ally thought guiltily. *What the hell am I thinking?* She closed the door on the little area right at the back of her mind and locked it. No itch-scratching for her today. Or any other day. "No, no. Honestly. I'm okay." Ally shook her head and stood up straight as if to prove it. She opened her little booklet and looked at it intently. "Do you know what you're going to bid on?"

Two and a half hours later and the auction was almost over. The auctioneer, borrowed from one of Sydney's more venerable auction houses, was good, and had Ally been in a different frame of mind she would have found him most entertaining. He worked the crowd well, using quick wit and sharp humor to encourage the bids ever higher. He drew attention to the bidders, frowning theatrically when someone indicated they were "out" and good-humoredly heckling them until they gave in and placed another bid. In fact, when it came time for the ugly Limoge Father Christmas Box to go under the hammer and Barbara was the only bidder, he cajoled and sweet-talked her until she actually put in a higher bid against herself. This drew howls of laughter from the crowd. Barbara, initially mortified, subsequently decided that being in the spotlight wasn't half bad. She put in a third, even higher bid against herself and beamed at the ensuing thunderous applause.

Even under normal circumstances, being on display was not something Ally relished. In fact, she avoided drawing attention to herself as much as possible. Now, knowing that Morgan was somewhere in the crowd, the last thing she wanted was the humiliation of being targeted by the auctioneer. Compounding her reticence to bid were the two men who had placed themselves immediately behind her not too long into the auction. They were too old to be students and too young to be fathers of students, but they wore that damned maroon tie, which made their presence immediately acceptable. The pair was detestable, sniggering loudly as they maligned almost every item up for bid. The scooter she had admired was described as "something only a poofter would ride" and the bottles of Krug champagne as "Frenchman's piss aerated with their foul cheese farts." What they said of the Limoge box was unrepeatable, as too was their comment about Barbara when she placed her second bid. It was at that point Ally swung around and hissed at the pair to shut up. The stares she received in return were defiant, but there was relative silence for the next two lots. Then they'd started again and continued unabated, even when James turned and fixed them with a threatening glare.

Hence Ally's checkbook was still intact.

"Almost your last chance, Alison." James pointed to the description of Lot 54—the Harbor Bridge Climb—in her auction booklet. At the same time the auctioneer began giving a colorful spiel about the same. "Would you like me to bid for you?"

Ally vacillated for a moment. She liked to think herself an independent woman, not one who hid behind her partner's coattails. "I'll do it," she said decisively, ignoring the comment from behind that half the crowd was too fat to fit into the overalls issued to each participant for use during the climb.

Three minutes later the hammer came down and she found herself the proud holder of two Bridge Climb tickets. "I'll climb your bridge, darlin'," came a voice from behind.

Nothing would have pleased Ally more than to spin around and knee the source of the voice in the groin, but she didn't. She grabbed James by the arm. He had obviously heard the comment and his face was grim as he began to turn. "Don't," she warned. "Let's just go to the cashier, pay for our things and leave."

He nodded slowly, reluctantly, not taking his eyes off the two young men, who seemed to visibly shrink under the weight of his stare. Finally he turned to Phil and told him of their intention to leave. In the next moment he and Phil were chest to chest and banging each other on the back. He and Ned were doing the same when Ally—who had given an insincere "nice to meet you" to Mandy—halted in her handshaking good-byes to Barbara. Her hand dropped away as her attention was arrested by the auctioneer's words, " . . . Morgan Silverstone."

What words had preceded them she had no idea, but Ally turned to the stage to find Morgan, unseen by Ally for the duration of the auction, walking across it.

"Cor," said one of the men standing behind Ally, "she's fucking hot."

"Tell me about it," said the other man. "I keep a supply of Kleenex nearby when she's on the telly . . . if you know what I mean."

Ally tuned out their sniggering and concentrated on the stage.

"Yes, folks." The auctioneer held an arm out in Morgan's direction, a gesture that conveyed he was presenting her to the audience. "The mystery is solved. Lot fifty-five . . . star of *Bonnes Vacances*, Morgan Silverstone!" He paused long enough that the crowd began murmuring among themselves. A couple of hoots came from the back of the room, followed by a wolf whistle from somewhere to the side. The auctioneer rested an elbow on his lectern. "Is it true, Morgan, that whoever bids highest this afternoon will get to spend an entire afternoon or evening in your company?"

"That's true," said Morgan, smiling.

"Doing whatever they want?" the auctioneer continued, giving a big wink at the crowd.

Ally felt a pressure on her arm as more hoots and wolf whistles echoed throughout the assembly hall. It was James. "Are we going?" he asked.

Ally shook his hand away, transfixed with the woman standing on the stage, waiting for her reply to the auctioneer's question. "Not quite yet."

Morgan smiled again, her voice as smooth as velvet. "Anything within reason."

"So, you're quite flexible then?" The auctioneer winked at the audience again.

Morgan didn't blink an eyelid at the double entendre. "I like to think so," she said evenly.

"Yeah, darlin'," came one of the now familiar voices from behind Ally. "I bet I can stretch you in a few ways you'd never expect."

"You gonna try an' buy her?" asked his buddy.

"Why the fuck not?" said the first one. "Wouldn't be the first time I've paid for it."

Ally clenched her fists. She should have let James loose on the pair when she had the chance. And how could Morgan stand up there and let herself be objectified like that? It was demeaning.

Weren't lesbians supposed to be against this type of thing? Women's rights and all?

"And let's not forget the reason why we're all here today, folks." The auctioneer pointed his hammer toward the banner that hung at the rear of the stage. On it was a large-eyed Indian boy sitting on a mat, chalkboard in hand. "For the kids. So let's make this, our last lot for the day, a good one." He waved his hammer in the air. "What am I bid?"

"Fifty," came the voice from behind.

"One hundred," another male voice called a few rows ahead.

"Two hundred." The voice from behind again.

"Three." Yet another male voice entered the bidding.

"Four." Another new bidder. Also male.

"Five hundred." The voice from behind. It was followed by a snigger from his friend and a comment about an expensive bang.

When the bidding reach one thousand dollars there were only two left in the race, the man who stood a few rows ahead, and the cretin behind.

"Eleven hundred."

"Twelve."

"Fourteen hundred dollars," called the cretin.

The room fell into a sudden silence. Ally could feel the crowd hold its collective breath waiting for a counterbid.

"Fifteen," the other bidder said finally and there was a collective exhalation.

"Sixteen," Cretin said immediately.

Ally cringed. The cretin was cashed-up. She watched Morgan standing there, her face impassive, as the bidding went higher and higher. At twenty-four hundred it stalled again. The bid was held by the cretin.

"Sir?" The auctioneer pointed his hammer at the other bidder. "An afternoon . . . or an evening . . . with this beautiful woman."

The man shook his head. "I'm a morning person really," he

said loudly, gaining a few chuckles from the crowd.

The auctioneer looked to Morgan. "Mornings are okay with you?"

"I'm good in the morning."

"I bet you're good at anytime of day, darlin'." The friend of the cretin sniggered.

The auctioneer turned back to the bidder. "She's good in the morning," he stated, straight-faced.

The audience laughed.

The man shook his head. "I'm out."

"Last chance, sir."

The man shook his head again and the auctioneer raised his hammer. "At twenty-four hundred dollars. Going once . . ."

"You're gonna get the bitch," the friend of the cretin whispered loudly.

The hammer stayed poised above the lectern. "Going twice . . ."

"Yeah," the cretin said smugly. "Bargain too. I would've paid twice that." He sniggered. "But she's gonna earn every cent of it."

The hammer began its descent. "Sol—"

"Five thousand dollars!"

The entire room fell into a stunned silence and Ally's skin grew hot as dozens of heads turned in her direction. Even the auctioneer seemed taken aback. "Any advance on five thousand?" he asked after a pause.

There was a sullen silence from behind and the auctioneer didn't even make an attempt at cajoling further bids. "At five thousand dollars. Going once . . ."

Less than a minute later the hammer came down to a thunderous applause that outdid that when Barbara bid against herself for the ugly Limoge.

"Sold!"

At least one person was not clapping. Ally took a half-step back and met James's eyes. They were wide with astonishment.

Ally answered his question even before he asked it. "You heard those twits behind us. I wasn't going to let them win. They were talking about her like she was a piece of meat."

"But five *thousand* dollars?" He rubbed at the stubble on his chin. "Not even the Vespa went for that much."

"It's my money," Ally said defensively, still coming to grips with what she'd just done. She hadn't even felt she was in control of her mouth when she issued her bid. It was as if some invisible force inside her had pushed the words out. "I can do what I want with it."

"Obviously," James said, his tone as sarcastic as she had ever heard it. He shook his head in disbelief. "You are one confounding woman, Alison Brown."

Ally shrugged, at a loss for a reply. It happened there was no immediate need for her to say anything, since their conversation was interrupted by a heavily made-up woman dressed in a loose Indian-influenced pant suit. A camera dangled around her neck. She introduced herself as Eva, English teacher by day and compiler of the school newsletter after hours. Before Ally knew it, she was being steered in the direction of the stage to have her photo taken.

With Morgan.

Morgan stepped down from the stage to be surrounded by a throng of people, all wishing to say hello and give their congratulations on her success at auction. As with any other of her public appearances, Morgan extended her hand to all who offered theirs and made small talk as she signed their auction booklets. But unlike most of her other public appearances, her mind was barely on what she was doing. She looked through rather than at the people she spoke to, and she could only hope that whatever words her mouth was forming made sense to those listening.

Her mind was elsewhere—somewhere in the middle of the assembly hall. On Ally and the bid that had stunned the crowd, the auctioneer and, probably most of all, her.

Morgan couldn't have been more surprised if she tried. Thank goodness the surprise had been shared by everyone in the hall, so her wide-eyed expression would not have looked too out of place. Five *thousand* dollars. Over twice the previous bid. Morgan smiled inwardly as she accepted another auction booklet. Despite Ally's earlier brush-off, her hopes could not help but be raised.

"Who do I make this out to?" she asked distractedly to the bespectacled middle-aged man with a very bad toupee.

The man cleared his throat. "Err, to Alexander . . . my son."

Morgan nodded as she began to scrawl away with her pen. It was always amazing how many men wanted autographs for their sons and women for their daughters. Not many ever admitted to wanting one for themselves. "There you go." She flashed him a smile as she handed the booklet back.

The man nodded graciously and peered myopically at the inscription. Immediately he frowned and thrust the booklet back into Morgan's line of sight. "My name . . . err . . . my son's name is Alexander. Not Ally."

"Oh, my goodness. I am *so* sorry." Morgan felt a rare blush spread up her neck and pulled her own booklet from her purse. It had been folded in half to fit into the clutch-size bag. The man didn't seem to mind a few creases, more intent on making sure that this time Morgan got the inscription correct.

"Thank you, Miss Silverstone."

"My pleasure." She watched him walk away, only to stop a few steps down, close enough that she could clearly hear him exclaiming to his companion that he had Morgan Silverstone's very own, personal copy of the auction booklet.

It was at that moment that she saw Ally approaching. She was with a very tall and slender woman with a camera slung around her neck and a notebook that poked from the top of the soft Indian-style bag hanging from a shoulder. Combined, the two items shrieked reporter.

Probably—to avoid any potentially difficult line of questioning—it was best to pretend she and Ally had no prior knowledge of each other. Morgan refined the broad, welcoming smile that had spread across her features to a more impersonal one. One more suited to greeting strangers. And she showed no outward signs of recognition when the woman—Eva—introduced her to Ally.

Thankfully Ally seemed pleased to play along with the "I don't know you" charade, nodding her hello and giving a brief handshake. Morgan thought the hand contact was too brief and she was disappointed that Ally refused to meet her eyes, but still, she had paid five *thousand* dollars to be in her company, so that kind of canceled out any residual worry that she wanted nothing to do with her.

That Eva asked if it was okay with them both that she take some photos confirmed she was the amateur school reporter she declared herself to be. A professional reporter would snap first and ask permission later.

"A little bit more now." Eva encouraged Morgan and Ally to stand closer together because she also wanted to get the banner image of the big-eyed Indian boy into the frame. She peered from behind her camera and smiled appreciatively when Morgan took a step nearer Ally and angled her body slightly toward her. "Excellent."

After half a dozen snaps, Eva let her camera dangle and pulled out her notebook. Her initial questions were aimed at Ally: What was her full name? What did she do for a living? How did she come to be at the auction? Ally was a little wide-eyed, like a doe startled by a car's headlights, but she answered the questions well, succinctly, giving no more information than necessary.

Eva went on to ask if she was a fan of *Bonnes Vacances* and, particularly, of Morgan.

Ally faltered. "I don't have much time to watch TV," she said slowly. "So I have only seen the show once or twice. And as for Morgan . . . well . . ." Ally glanced quickly over to her then looked away. "I really don't know her at all."

"So what prompted you to put in such a large bid?" Eva probed, her pencil poised over her notepad.

"Err . . ." Ally glanced at Morgan again, longer this time, as if searching for an answer. Then her gaze shifted to the banner that hung on the stage. "For the children," she said quickly.

Eva nodded approvingly as she wrote that down. "One last question, Ms. Brown . . ."

"Yes?" Ally smiled gratefully, obviously pleased the interview was soon to be over.

"Just how do you plan on spending your time with Morgan?"

Ally's smile all but vanished and the trace that was left looked strained. A blush spread up her neck. "Umm . . . I'm not really sure yet," she said finally.

"You also bid successfully on the Harbor Bridge Climb today, I believe?"

Ally looked like she didn't know whether to be pissed that Eva had exceeded her question limit or relieved at the change in topic. "Yes."

"It's supposed to be quite spectacular. Have you decided who will accompany you?"

Morgan glanced sideways at Eva. She could sense the woman would be delighted if Ally announced her as her climbing companion. It would make a nice angle for her article. But Eva was to be disappointed.

"No," Ally said flatly.

Hmm. Eva may be disappointed, but Morgan certainly wasn't. That Ally hadn't said outright she was going to take James had to be a plus—in her favor. But then again, maybe James was afraid of heights. Or maybe she had a friend, or a sibling, or a niece or nephew that she might like to take. Whatever, Morgan still thought it a plus, and she smiled brightly when Eva turned the questions in her direction.

Morgan slipped into interview mode, agreeing that it was a fabulous result and saying, quite honestly, that she'd not expected anywhere near the price she finally fetched. She answered a few more questions about her career with *Bonnes Vacances* and then, sensing Ally's impatience for this ordeal to be over, deftly brought the interview to a close.

The moment Eva had disappeared into the crowd, Ally made a move as if to leave.

"You're not going, are you?" Morgan blurted, confused. She was sure Ally would want to stay and talk to her, if only to set a date for their auction-win rendezvous.

Ally shrugged. "The reporter's gone."

"Exactly. So now we can speak openly."

Ally shook her head, looking down to her hands. "I've got nothing to say to you."

Exasperated, Morgan asked, "So why did you bid?"

Even without the benefit of being able to see Ally's expression, Morgan could sense her discomfort. "Like I told Eva . . . for the kids."

Morgan didn't believe a word of it. When Ally had finally raised her head her cheeks were a splotchy red, making a mockery of her defiant tone. "Are you okay, Ally?" she asked gently.

There was an extended pause then, "Actually, no. I'm not."

"I'm sorry if I—"

"Don't flatter yourself," Ally said sarcastically. She half turned and scanned the hall as if looking for a means of escape. She found one, standing on her tiptoes and waving in the manner meant to grab someone's attention.

Morgan followed the direction of the wave and she saw the tall figure of James working his way through the lingering crowd. Within a half a minute he would be upon them.

Desperate not to lose this chance to speak to Ally alone, she grabbed her elbow and started talking quickly. "Look, Ally. I'm sorry if I pushed myself onto you on the train. I obviously made an error of judgment and I'm sorry it has upset you. What I'd really like is for us to forget everything that has happened before and to start over"—she nearly tripped over her next words, knowing they were not altogether true—"as friends. And since you've effectively purchased three or four hours of my time . . ." She trailed off, leaving the idea hanging in the air, willing Ally to take hold of it.

Ally looked torn.

"Just think about it," Morgan urged, hating the hint of desperation in her tone. This was not like her at all. "You've got my number."

Ally shook her head. "No, I don't."

"Did you not get the paper I—"

"I did." Ally nodded. Then she said a little sheepishly, "But I kind of ripped it into shreds and poured a can of soup over it."

"Oh," Morgan replied rather dumbly, wondering at the thought processes that had led to such actions. But she didn't have time to ask or comment. James arrived to stand by Ally's side. With a feeling that was also very out of character for her—it was somewhat akin to envy—she watched Ally snake her arm around his waist and smile up to him.

"James," Ally said, nodding in Morgan's direction, "this is Morgan."

James extended his hand and shook hers warmly. "Pleased to meet you."

Ally shot a fleeting glance at Morgan. "We were just discussing how we might meet. But it seems we have a clash of schedules for the next month at least, so it's proving rather difficult." She issued Morgan a look that defied her to say otherwise.

Totally deflated that Ally was making publicly sure there would be no contact in the near future, Morgan nodded, adding apologetically, "I travel a lot."

James was in the middle of saying how that was a shame, but he was sure the schedule conflict wouldn't last forever, when Morgan regained her composure. Two could play at this game. She pulled her phone from her purse and looked Ally squarely in the eye. "As I said, my schedule's not quite set in concrete. I'll give you a call when I have it sorted. What's your phone number?"

When Ally relayed her number James pulled out his phone and asked, "Doesn't your number end in a six and not a nine?" He pressed a few buttons and was soon exclaiming in his correctness.

"I never dial my own number." Ally's voice was apologetic but the look she threw James said she was anything but . . . and that he had better watch out when they got home. She repeated the number, accentuating the final numeral, six.

Morgan quickly entered it into her phone memory and, smiling, gave her number to Ally, who reluctantly punched it into her phone.

"Correct?" Ally asked icily, presenting her phone to James.

"Correct," he confirmed, seemingly unaware or unconcerned at Ally's tone.

"Lovely meeting you both." Content in the knowledge she now had a means of contact with Ally, Morgan shook both their hands. "But I really must get going. I hope to hear from you soon . . ." She glanced at James then settled her gaze a little mischievously on Ally. "Ally."

Morgan turned away and went in search of William. When she found him he gave his heartfelt thanks, exuberantly proclaiming her a major part of the auction's success.

"No. Thank *you*," she countered, holding his hands within hers. "You have no idea how much being here has meant to me."

And she took her leave, happily smiling at everyone she passed on her way out of the hall. Once in her car she cradled her phone in her hand, tempted to try out the number she had been given, just to hear Ally's voice.

But she didn't. Instead she turned her car engine over and headed out of the school gates, determined to let Ally make the first contact.

The call Morgan had been wishing for came at eight the next evening, just minutes before Michael was due to pick her up for their dinner meeting with the Logies committee.

"Hello," Morgan breathed into her phone. She wanted to end her greeting with "Ally," not only for the personal touch, but because she liked the sound of it as it rolled off her tongue. She'd been saying the name out loud intermittently all day, each time she had a moment alone. But now she didn't indulge her desire. The caller ID might say *Ally*, but anyone could be on the end of the line. James, for example.

"Morgan?"

"Yes." Morgan sat on an arm of her couch and closed her eyes to the view of the harbor that the lounge room of her Piper Point apartment afforded. "How are you, Ally?"

"I've just called to tell you I'm deleting you from my phone memory, and I'd appreciate it if you'd do the same with my number."

"What?" Morgan's eyes flew open. The city lights twinkled and the bridge lights formed a glittering arch, well deserving of its nickname of "the coat hanger." Morgan detached herself from the familiar view and focused on the reflection in the window. She saw herself on the edge of her couch, running a hand through her hair. If she looked more closely at her eyes, they would have shown a wild desperation. This was not at all what she had expected. "Ally, please. Don't do this."

The response was flat. "I have to."

"Why?"

"Because I can't live this way."

"What way?"

"Thinking about you all the time. Wanting to call . . . wanting to see you."

"Then call me." Morgan's heart jumped to her throat. "See me."

"I can't."

"Ally . . . please!" Morgan pleaded. She thought wildly, trying to figure a way to make her change her mind. An idea jumped out at her. "What will James think if you never make a claim on what you bought at the auction?"

"What James thinks is none of your business" was the sharp reply.

"Ally!"

There was a pregnant pause during which Morgan leapt up to pace in front of her window. Finally Ally's voice resumed. It was but a whisper. "See me tonight."

Oh, God, no. Not tonight. "I can't tonight. I've got plans. But tomorr—"

"Forget it."

"Ally, please listen. Tonight is . . . important to me. Let's meet tomorrow. I should wind up around six. I can meet you anywhere you—"

"Forget it." Coldness had crept into Ally's tone and Morgan knew she had closed herself off. "I'm deleting you from memory. And I don't want you to call me ever again. Good-bye."

The line went dead. Morgan stared at her phone, and despite the explicit instruction not to call, she retrieved *Ally* from the received-calls list and set it to dial. She was switched to voice mail. Morgan left a message for her to please reconsider and call back.

Morgan left her phone switched on throughout her Logies meeting. It vibrated four times, but covert checks revealed that none of the calls were from Ally. So she ignored them. She left another voice-mail message when her meeting ended and another when she got home. She also left a message early the next morning, before she drove to the studios. But when she tried again at the first break in between her recording sessions, she was switched through to a recording that very politely suggested she should check the number she had dialed.

Morgan did—twice—and both times received the same recording. It seemed that Ally had gone further than her threat of deleting Morgan's details from her contact list. She had even gone further than blocking Morgan from calling her mobile. Evidently, she had either canceled her mobile phone contract or done something to her SIM card—the sliver of technology that sat behind the battery and contained all the subscriber information, including the phone number—that rendered it useless.

From what Morgan had gleaned of Ally during their time spent together on the train, she had a busy professional life with frequent client contact. Her phone would be an important business tool. But obviously that fact had been overshadowed by Ally's desire to have no further contact with Morgan.

Morgan turned her phone off and dropped it into her handbag, took herself to the toilets and, for the first time in goodness knew how long, she put her head in her hands and cried.

Not too long later, Morgan contemplated her reflection in the large mirror that hung above the wash basin. She would be retouched by the makeup artist before the next session of shooting began, but for now her pride told her she had to try to eliminate the evidence she had been crying. "What have you done to me, Alison Brown?" she asked under her breath as she carefully wiped away the streaks of mascara from under her eyes.

She dabbed at her eyes a few more times and discarded the mascara-stained tissue. Then she dug into her bag, found her bottle of redness-reliever formula and administered a few drops into each eye. That done, she rested her hands on the edge of the wash basin and took another long, hard look at her reflection.

Despite her efforts, any fool could see she'd shed some tears. Her mouth set into a grim line, she dug into her bag again, this time to pull out her phone.

Within the push of a few keys the *Ally* entry was deleted. She put the phone back in her bag, snapped the catch shut and thought forward in time to the next day. Come tomorrow she'd be winging her way out of Australia to Vanuatu, voted as the happiest place to live on the planet. Morgan hoped the island nation lived up to its reputation. Because she sure could use some cheering up right now.

Preferably by some delicious Vanuatu island beauty.

Or not. It didn't matter really. So long as she wasn't Australian.

Or French. For the moment she was off them too.

CHAPTER ELEVEN

Ally flinched as she closed her office door behind her. She had just finished deceiving her boss. Actually, *deception* was far too soft a word to describe what she'd done. *Destruction of company property coupled with an outright lie* was more fitting terminology. Initially she hadn't intended to cause any damage to her mobile phone. All she'd wanted to do was make sure Morgan couldn't keep calling, so, after deleting voice-mail message number four she'd put a block on her phone. But she'd very quickly realized that the block was only good if Morgan dialed from her mobile. She could call from any landline or pay phone, or any other phone for that matter. Plus, Morgan's number had to be stored in Ally's phone in order for the number to be blocked and so was sitting there for retrieval should she ever be tempted. Despite telling herself she would not be tempted, there was a niggling voice in her head telling her that she would . . . so blocking her phone was not enough. She needed a new telephone number. And the best way of getting one, without having to answer curly questions from her boss, was for her SIM card to suffer some sort of mishap. Because the card was safely tucked inside her phone and—having figured Josh would never believe it had simply grown legs and walked away—this morning she had purposely destroyed her entire mobile phone by running it under the tap in the office bathroom until some of the electronics short-circuited. It hadn't taken long.

She had blushed profusely when embarrassedly presenting her still-wet phone to Josh. She explained how she had been desperate for the toilet, made a dash with her phone still in hand, placed it on the women's sanitary bin, but accidentally knocked it when she stood to flush. And it fell in. The circumstances she described made the blush feasible and he swallowed the whole story, even her proclamation that—thank goodness—she had backed up her SIM card only the week before. In actual fact, she had arrived at the office a good half-hour earlier than normal and backed up her SIM before giving her phone a cold shower.

Ally was relieved that Josh seemed to find the incident more amusing than annoying. Deciding not to push her luck, she shut herself in her office and hardly made an appearance all day. She also refused to dwell on the reason why she had taken such a drastic and dishonest action, choosing instead to bury herself in her work.

James called her on the office line at lunchtime, both to apologize for upsetting her the night before and to see if—as they had arranged before their argument—she was still going to spend the night at his place. He also asked why he was unable to get through on her mobile. Ally broadened the audience of her lie by telling James about dropping her phone down the toilet. She also said yes, she would be spending the night with him. She hung up from the call, bent to her work again and didn't give him another thought all afternoon.

Come the end of the day she was putting the finishing touches on the first pass of her Kalgoorlie executive residence. Tomorrow she could start inputting it into the 3-D-rendering program that would enable her client to virtually "walk through" his house. She packed up her bag and flicked off the light switch in her office, feeling quite pleased with her progress. Halfway to her apartment in Croyden she remembered she was supposed to be in Balmain. She turned her car around, aimed it for James's townhouse and let herself in.

She initially kept her "waiting for James at James's place" routine, bringing in the mail and placing it on the dining table, pouring herself a glass of wine and poking her head in the fridge to see what she might use in the preparation of dinner. She found the makings for a simple stir-fry and was halfway through transferring the ingredients onto the kitchen bench when she began loading them back into the fridge. Ally took herself and her glass of wine upstairs, removed all her clothes and lay down on James's bed.

She sipped on her wine and experimented with a series of seductive postures, imagining the reaction when James discovered her. Most likely he would be very, very pleased. But he would also most likely approach the bed with caution, not only because of their argument last night, but because of late all his efforts at intimacy had been knocked flat. On the Sunday night after the auction Ally had begged a headache, blaming the champagne. James had reluctantly turned over in bed, although he had quite sarcastically mentioned it was more likely the thought of the five-*thousand*-dollar check she had written that afternoon that was causing the headache. On Monday they didn't even make it as far as the bedroom. James had been watching the evening news when a promotion for *Bonnes Vacances* came on during an ad break. The five thousand dollars was mentioned again and Ally had let fly, accusing him of being a chauvinist pig who wanted to control her life and her pocketbook, and essentially throwing him out of her apartment. He left without putting up too much of an argument, just shaking his head and once more announcing her as "one confounding woman." Ally had slammed the door behind him and dashed back to the television. She stared at it for a whole half-hour before another promotion for *Bonnes Vacances* appeared. When it did she sat rigid in her seat, holding her breath until the snippet with Morgan in it had come and gone. When it was gone Ally immediately began waiting for it to appear again. It was after another twenty minutes of staring in expectation of a fifteen-second commercial that Ally reached for her mobile phone, dialed Morgan and told her of her intention to remove her from memory.

Which is exactly what she'd done today. Via vandalism and deceit, maybe, but still, it was done and now Ally could get on with her life as it had been in the days before Morgan. She took another sip of her wine, assumed another sexy posture and focused on James's reaction to finding her naked on his bed.

Too damn bad if he wasn't into spontaneity and excitement, because that's exactly what he was in for tonight.

Two minutes later, as unbidden thoughts of Morgan kept impinging on the space she had reserved for James, she sat up and checked her wristwatch, which she'd laid on one of the bedside tables. It was three minutes to seven. Usually, James didn't arrive home until after the hour. She lay back down again.

At one minute to seven she was cold and tired of waiting. She was also feeling a little silly lying there with her legs apart. "Where the hell are you?" she muttered grumpily, her seductive mood evaporating with the last sip of her wine. By one minute past seven she was dressed again, had smoothed down the bedclothes and returned downstairs. By three past the hour James was letting himself in the front door.

"How are you tonight?" he asked rather carefully as he kissed her on the cheek.

"I'm fine." Ally held up her refreshed glass. "Want one?"

"Yes, please. Good day?"

"Fine." Ally went to the fridge to retrieve the bottle.

"That's good." James picked up his mail from the dining table and flicked through it. "What would you like for dinner?"

Ally poured wine and shrugged. "There's the makings of a stir-fry in the fridge."

"Sounds good." James extracted the contents of an envelope as he walked into the lounge area. He picked up the remote and aimed it at the television. "Do you mind if I watch the news?"

"Go ahead." For the second time that evening Ally transferred items from the fridge onto the kitchen bench. She banged them a little onto the granite surface, not exactly sure why she was so irked. After all, she was getting exactly what she had wanted—the return to life as it had been before . . . *her.*

Ally grabbed a kitchen knife and chopped viciously at the vegetables as the voice of the television news presenter droned on in the background. The television would be turned off at dinnertime and she and James would eat together at the table, discussing what had happened in each of their days. With parents who took casual dining to the extreme, Ally had grown up eating dinner from a plate on her lap while perched on the couch. After graduation she'd swapped her parents for a TV-addicted flatmate who could only conduct a decent conversation for the duration of an ad break, so this civilized method of dining was a relatively new concept that she had embraced fully.

She wondered how the conversation would go tonight.

"What did you do today?" James would ask.

"Oh, just the usual. Drew up some award-winning house plans, threw my phone down the toilet and gave up any hope of trying to stop thinking about Morgan."

James would take a piece of perfectly stir-fried chicken between his chopsticks. "Are you thinking about her now?"

"Yes," Ally would admit, poking around her bowl with her own chopsticks, looking for a still-crisp snow pea.

James would admire the perfectly cooked chicken before taking it to his mouth. "And what are you thinking?"

The snow pea would be steaming hot, causing Ally to fan her mouth with her hand. "How she was so close I could feel her breath on my face. How her breasts were so soft when she pressed against me. How her lips melted against mine when she kissed me . . ."

In the next instant Ally's knife dropped with a thud onto the chopping board and she yelped. "Fuck!"

"Let me see." James was soon by her side and holding her index finger, which was bleeding quite profusely. He directed the finger under the cold-water tap. "What happened?"

"I wasn't concentrating." Ally looked at her own watered-down blood spiraling into the plug hole. Her finger didn't hurt—too much—yet she had a terrible urge to cry. She buried her head into James's shoulder and sniffed, trying to pull back the threatening tears. She couldn't. "I cut myself." She sobbed.

"My poor love." James enveloped her in his arms and rocked her. "What with your broken phone and now your broken finger, you're not having a very good day, are you?"

That brought on a fresh rush of tears.

James bandaged her cut and ordered in some couscous, declaring the consumption of the stir-fry, now that it contained the blood of Ally's finger, equivalent to an act of cannibalism. Ally kept telling him how sorry she was for ruining *another* evening, and thanking him for being so nice.

At bedtime James turned to her, maybe sensing his chivalry had earned him more than just gratitude.

"Not tonight," Ally told him, almost regretfully. Why could she no longer drum up even the teeniest bit of amorous feeling for him? "My finger hurts." She turned onto her side at the same time he turned on his, so they lay back to back. And she lay awake for hours, listening to his breathing as it first turned rhythmic, then into snores.

"I do love you, James," she whispered softly, her back still to him. "But just not in the way you want me to."

She lay staring at the wall for quite a while longer after that, trying to think of a way to tell him that when he was actually awake.

Ally hovered around James the next morning. She hovered in the bathroom while he was taking his shower and shave, she hovered in the bedroom as he was dressing, and she hovered next to him as he stood at the kitchen bench, pouring coffee and reading the headline story in *The Australian* while he waited for his toast to pop up.

"Aren't you going in to work today?" he finally asked as he transferred his toast onto a plate. Usually their morning preparations were staggered so Ally would just be descending the stairs, showered and dressed, while he was finishing his breakfast.

"Yes, I'm going." Ally stared at the kitchen bench and trailed a finger across the polished granite surface. She'd better work up the courage to say now what she had practiced in the early hours of the morning, or she'd have to wait until tonight when she saw him again. "But I wanted to speak to you first."

James must have picked up the edge to Ally's tone because he put his plate on the bench, pushed his newspaper aside and turned to look her in the eye. "Yes?" he asked simply.

Ally would have preferred to spit out her words while James was still involved in his paper, and then turn tail and run. But that was not going to happen. "I've been thinking a lot over the past few days," she began.

"Yes?" James repeated, the darkness of worry entering his eyes. He had to know this was leading nowhere good.

"And I've come to realize that—as much as I think you are a good man and I care for you deeply—that I don't want to be in a relationship with you."

James's Adam's apple bobbed up and down in his throat as he

170

swallowed twice before speaking. "What are you saying?"

"Exactly what I just said. I'm sorry, James, but I don't want to go out with you anymore."

His Adam's apple bobbed again and he ran a hand through his dark hair. "But we're good together, Alison. I know we're having a bit of a rough patch at the moment, but—"

"James. Listen to me." Ally took his cheeks in her hands and directed his gaze, which had strayed to the fridge door, back to hers. "This isn't just a rough patch for me. I've been thinking about this all night and—"

"One night?" James interrupted, his expression incredulous. "We've been together for nine months and you tell me you want to split up based on a single sleepless night?"

"It's not like that at all. Something happened to me—"

"You're having an affair!" James's voice gained its usual timbre . . . plus a bit more. It was the first sign of a building anger. "Something . . . or some*one* happened to you while you were away and you're having an affair!"

"No!" Ally shook her head vehemently and in her attempt to defend herself her words rushed out quicker than she could think them. "I'm not cheating on you. I kissed her, but only once."

"You don't call kissing someone else cheating?" For a single moment Ally thought James was going to raise his hand to her. His face turned red and a vein in his forehead throbbed purple. But his hands, which were clenched, remained at his sides. Then his expression changed to one of utter puzzlement. "Her? What do you mean you kissed *her*?"

It was very difficult for Ally to maintain eye contact, but she did. "I kissed a woman."

James stood silent, searching Ally's face as if looking for some sign she was joking. Her continued gaze, although unsteady, seemed to convince him otherwise. "But I don't understand. You're . . . you're not like that."

Ally could not hold eye contact any longer. She looked at the floor. "That's what I thought too."

"So you're telling me you're now a lesbian?"

Ally took a long moment before replying. That very same question had plagued her thoughts ever since "the kiss," and she was still no closer to a definitive answer. Was she a lesbian, bisexual or just plain curious? She'd never before considered where she lay on the spectrum of sexuality. Ask her before she boarded that train and she'd have answered without thinking, "I'm straight." Ask her now and she wouldn't be so sure. All she knew was that something had occurred between herself and Morgan that she had never experienced with anyone—male or female— before. Their time together on the train had been brief, their physical contact even briefer, yet Ally had the distinct feeling they were moments that had the power to be life-changing. And she also knew that, wherever Morgan sat on the spectrum, there was an invisible yet extremely strong thread drawing her to the same place. "I don't know, James. The way I feel . . ." She lifted her gaze from the floor to meet James's eyes again. His gaze darted over hers, showing his desperation for her to provide the answer he wanted to hear. But she couldn't do that, any more than she could pin a label on herself. She was just Ally, a woman who felt very much that she was in danger of falling in love with another woman. "I just don't know."

James swung round to face the bench. He rested his hands on the granite, his head hanging low. "Jesus fucking Christ."

That was the first time Ally had ever heard James utter anything coarser than *bloody hell*. But then again, they had never had a conversation like this before.

James's shoulders heaved as he took a large intake of breath and exhaled it slowly. "Last week you told me you loved me," he said, his voice so tight it cracked. "And this week you tell me you don't and that you think you've turned into—I'm sorry, Alison, but things just don't all of a sudden change like that."

"I'm sorry." Ally didn't know what else to say.

"So you're telling me you never actually loved me?"

"No, James. No! I called it love because that's what it was . . . what it *is*," she corrected herself. "I do love you, but not . . ." She trailed off, at a loss for the words to adequately describe what she felt inside. "Love comes in many forms."

"And which form do I fall into?" James asked bitterly. "And this . . . this . . . *woman*. What form does she fall into?"

Ally could hear the hurt in his voice and it cut right to her core. "I don't know, James. All this is new for me. I just don't know."

James turned back around, a sudden hope glimmering in his eyes. "You said you only kissed her the once. How can you make a decision like this based on one kiss?"

"I'm not." He had just gone straight to the crux of the matter. If Ally had focused less on the embrace and more on the feelings that surrounded it, she would have come to her realization long before now. "That's the thing. I don't think I even had to kiss her the one time to know it. There was just *something* there. Something that, up until now, has been missing for me."

It was past ten a.m. when Ally finally turned her car into her parking space located at the rear of the office premises. She made a conscious effort to put a bit of spring in her step but failed. She was emotionally wrung out, having tried to explain to James something she had difficulty explaining to herself. She hadn't done a particularly good job as all he seemed able to do was to shake his head and say repeatedly, "I don't understand." But he did manage to mumble, "There's no need. I'm leaving now anyway," when Ally suggested it may be better if she showered at home today. He picked up his briefcase and was gone even before Ally reached the top of the stairs.

Over the past nine months, a sizable amount of Ally's personal possessions had found semipermanent homes at James's townhouse. She had a share of the closet space and allocated drawers in the bedroom, and she had overtaken at least half of the shelves in the bathroom. Books, CDs and even some board games and the occasional kitchen utensil lurked in various other corners of the residence. Ally had vacillated over whether to take the entire morning off work, sort through everything and load all her things into her car. Finally she decided to take the items that were in open view—such as her shampoos and perfumes—and leave the rest for later. She'd call James in the next few days to make arrangements for a suitable time to come over and take everything else, and for him to do the same at her place. Then they'd return the spare house keys and . . . that would be that. Unless—within time—she and James could become friends.

Ally dragged herself up the two steps that led to the rear entrance of her offices, thinking, regrettably, that friendship with James was unlikely. Without exception, she'd never maintained contact with any of her exes. Also without exception, she'd been the one to make the split. Maybe there was a connection there—the fragility of the male ego and all that. Or maybe it was more to do with Ally herself. Looking back, she'd never dated anyone she'd previously called a friend. Even during her school years, she either dated older boys she didn't normally mix with or ones who attended different schools and she'd met via community dances or sporting events. At uni she was often set up on blind dates or was approached in the grungy university tavern. After graduation the business of networking often turned social and she'd accept an invitation to drinks or dinner. So she dated relative strangers and—if her ability to walk out of their lives so easily after the relationship ended was any indication—she never really became friends with them even while she was in the relationship.

Maybe, since the circumstances of this particular split were a first, she could set another precedent and maintain contact with James. After all, she did genuinely like the man. She just didn't want to sleep with him anymore.

Office keys in hand, Ally gripped onto the lever-style door handle and was initially surprised to find it gave way under the pressure. Usually she was the first to arrive at work so had to unlock the door and disarm the alarm. The open door was a reminder that she was late, and a quick glance to her watch reminded her by how much. Josh was an easygoing boss and not one to quibble over a few hours here or there, but still she crept in, not really feeling up to detailing the reason why she was only just arriving for the day.

Kirsty, one of the three draftspeople who shared the open area just behind the reception, called her a loud hello. Ally nodded in greeting and quickened her step. But she hadn't reached her office before she heard Josh summoning her to his, located next to her own.

She entered to find him with cup of tea in hand, feet up on the desk, a newspaper opened across his legs. Another stark reminder of how late she was. Josh was having his ritual morning "tea and read" break.

He took a sip from his cup, reached over and placed it on a bamboo flooring sample that doubled as a coaster. "Am I paying you too much?" he asked.

"Err . . ." Ally faltered, not expecting this reaction to her tardiness. He may have been an easygoing boss but as the owner of the company, he was personally paying her salary. "I'm sorry I'm late. I should have rung. I . . . overslept."

While she was talking she watched Josh lower his feet to the floor and rearrange his newspaper so it lay on the desk facing in her direction. He shrugged as he thumbed back two pages. "Everyone deserves an illicit lie-in on occasion." He pointed to the bottom of the left-hand page of the paper, looked up and grinned. "I was talking about this."

Ally relaxed at the issue of the grin. She placed her bag on the floor, perched on the edge of the seat that fronted his desk and peered at the article. Then her eyes nearly fell out of her head. Right there in black and white was a picture of Morgan and herself. The photo was a tight head and shoulders shot, taken at the charity auction. A single paragraph article accompanied the picture.

"Five thousand dollars . . ." Josh's voice intruded on the silence as Ally read the text for the second time. "That's a bit rich, isn't it?" He paused, the twinkle in his eye in opposition to the stern set of his mouth. "Obviously, I'm paying you far too much."

Ally, stunned to see the photo there at all—wasn't it just supposed to be in the school newsletter?—stopped midsentence in her excuse about it being a donation for the children. She folded her arms. "If you paid me half of what I'm actually worth, I could have made it ten."

That caused Josh to erupt into laughter. "Nice try." He reached across the desk and presented her with a colorfully printed box. The photo on the front gave away the contents. It was a new phone. "While you were dozing this morning I was out getting you this."

"Thanks." Ally turned the box around in her hands. It looked like a pretty snazzy phone with a largish color LCD screen. From all the bullet points listed next to the picture, it was also packed with features, most of which she was never likely to use. "I'll go get it charged up straightaway." She pointed to the line of numerals printed above the barcode. "Is this my new number?"

"Only if your SIM card is as drowned as your phone." Josh grinned, obviously still finding the supposed circumstances behind the death of her phone amusing. "The sales assistant told me there's a chance—if you didn't leave your phone floating in the loo for too long—that it might still work. You did keep your SIM, didn't you?"

"Yes." Ally planned to drop her mobile into the recycling box at her nearest phone shop but as yet hadn't done so. "I'll try it as soon as the new one's charged up."

Josh nodded, closing the paper and folding it. "Tea and read" was over, his attention already moving back to the massive twenty-two-inch flat-screen monitor that sat at one end of his desk. "Any chance we can have a catch-up tomorrow afternoon, to make sure everything's in order before I leave?"

"Sure." Josh was flying to Barcelona on Friday to attend a global conference on sustainable housing. He'd be gone for nearly a week, arriving in Spain on Saturday morning, sightseeing until the two-day conference commenced on Monday, and then flying back on Wednesday, arriving in Sydney on Thursday. If it weren't for the awfully long flights both before and afterward, Ally would have loved to attend such an event and soak up a bit of Spanish sun into the bargain. But taking into account airfares, accommodation and conference fees, sending one delegate was expensive enough. Sending two, especially in a firm the size of theirs, was madness. Ally would keep an eye on things while he was gone, and he could tell her all about the new developments in their field of specialization when he returned. "Five o'clock?"

"Sure," he said.

Ally reached for her bag and stood to leave, her eyes fixed on the folded up newspaper. "Are you finished with that?"

Josh peered over the rims of his spectacles as he held it out. "I guess you may as well have some tangible evidence of your investment."

Ally snatched the paper from his hand and stalked out of his office. She closed her own office door behind her and thumbed through the paper until she found the page she wanted. She extracted it, folded it so the photo of her and Morgan was face up and placed it under her keyboard. Satisfied she could now safely glance at it whenever she felt like it; she pulled her new phone from the box and plugged it into the new charger. Then she pressed the button on the hard drive of her computer.

177

She looked under her keyboard twice in the time it took for her computer to boot up.

Within two hours her new phone was fully charged; she'd inserted her old SIM, but it was as dead as her old phone. Thank goodness she'd backed it up or she'd have to spend half the morning plugging names and numbers into her new handset. As it was, she had to contact all and sundry to advise of her new number. Plus she'd have to order new business cards.

There was one other hiccup in the transition from her old phone to the new. She'd deleted Morgan's number from her phone memory *before* she backed up her SIM. So now that she had finally admitted she actually did want to speak to her, she couldn't. Not immediately anyway. Ally closed her eyes and racked her brain, trying to recall Morgan's number. One would have thought, given she'd spent so much time staring at the piece of paper that had been slipped under her compartment door, that the number would be hard-wired into her brain. But it wasn't. Not in its entirety anyway. For the life of her she could not recall with certainty the last three digits.

Three digits effectively meant nine hundred and ninety-nine permutations. Or was that one thousand? Whichever, it was an awful lot of dialing. Even if she struck it lucky after only ten percent of the possibilities, that was still one hundred numbers. Ally sat at her desk, staring at the beginnings of her 3D rendering of the Kalgoorlie executive residence.

The television network! She could ring there. Once she'd explained who she was and that she'd bought Morgan at auction, they were sure—if not to give her Morgan's number directly—at least to pass on a message to call. Ally opened up her online phone directory, found the network number and dialed.

Fifteen minutes later, ten of which were spent on hold, she placed her receiver back on its cradle. She wasn't overly confident her message would ever reach Morgan, primarily because the woman she spoke to must have had a "tea and read" herself that morning. Either that or she was kept informed of all publicity regarding the network's stable of stars so she could effectively field incoming calls. At the mention of the words *Morgan* and *auction* the woman's tone turned suspicious, and even more so when Ally indicated she was the winning bidder and hence needed Morgan's number.

"You've yet to give me anything that anyone reading the article wouldn't already know," the woman said tiredly as Ally ran off a string of information about herself.

Ally thought furiously for something only she and Morgan would know, without it being of too personal a nature. "Tell her I've decided who I want to take on the Harbor Bridge Climb with me." No one except Morgan, the reporter and herself would know she'd also successfully bid on the bridge climb since no reference was made to it in the article.

"Harbor . . . Bridge . . . Climb," the woman said slowly, as if she were writing the details down. Her tone distinctly sounded as if she thought Ally was a nutcase. "Right, Ms. Brown. I'll pass all this on for you. Although I can't guarantee Ms. Silverstone will act on it."

"Thank you." Ally figured there was no use pushing for a firmer promise than that. And she hung up, silently cursing Eva, the school reporter, for having decided Morgan's record price at auction was worthy of a wider audience than that of her newsletter. If only the story had been published one day later . . . or Ally had had her "lightbulb moment" one day earlier. Or even better . . . if only she hadn't deleted the number from her phone in the first place.

Ally dismally admitted that random dialing was probably her best hope. Either that or by some miracle she would randomly bump into Morgan on the streets of Sydney. The odds of that were slim, given that Morgan spent so much time away. And the odds of it happening today or tomorrow were nonexistent since, if Ally's memory of Morgan's immediate schedule served her correctly, she should be halfway to Vanuatu by now.

Ally turned her attention back to her 3-D rendering. None of this speculation was getting her any closer to meeting her Friday deadline for the Kalgoorlie residence. And her business cards weren't going to order themselves.

Ally took care of the phone-related business first. She transferred all her backed-up information onto her new SIM, then sent a bulk text message to her entire phone book advising of her new number. She followed that with a quick e-mail to her entire address book. On both counts she filtered James from the list of recipients. Not the best step in light of wanting to maintain a friendship with the man maybe, but she figured that being at least a little non-contactable was best for the moment. Finally, she rang the copy shop and ordered new business cards. The copy shop handled all the firm's short-run printing needs and so had their existing business card templates on file. It was a simple matter of inserting the new number and sending the file to print. Ally would be couriered her new cards within twenty-four hours.

With all that taken care of, she took a deep, calming breath, settled her gaze and her thoughts onto her computer screen and concentrated. Except for toilet breaks and to recharge her coffee mug, she barely left her office for the rest of the day, not even stopping for lunch. Her ears were attuned to her telephone and she suffered flashes of hope each time it rang. The hope was in vain. None of the calls were from Morgan. Each time she hung up she took a little peek at the photo under her keyboard.

She left the office at six and drove straight home. Her landline was ringing as she fumbled her key in the lock, but it stopped before she reached it. The caller ID didn't recognize the number and no message was left. Ally made a pot of tea and tried telephone number permutations 000 through to 020, all to no avail.

By the time she put herself to bed just before midnight she had systematically worked her way through her apartment, gathering James's belongings. She had also systematically tried dialing up to permutation 090. And she'd found the official tourism site for Vanuatu and systematically surfed through all its contents, wondering which hotel Morgan was staying in, which beaches she was lying on, which restaurants she was eating in. Whatever she was doing, she was sure to be happy doing it since—according to the Web site—Vanuatu topped the list in the *Happy Planet Index*.

Ally fell asleep wishing she was in Vanuatu too.

Considering she was in the happiest place on the planet, Morgan wasn't feeling particularly cheerful. In fact, she was decidedly gloomy. She was alone in her hotel room and had been for hours, begging off a night on the town in favor of some peace and quiet. Kitty—currently holed up in her own room—had nodded approvingly at Morgan's decision. The fewer chicks that left their hotel nest, the less likely she was to have to go chasing after them later. Mark had been disappointed, wanting to experience the local kava—a legal narcotic drink made from the root of the pepper tree. When Morgan told him he could just go without her, or go with Nick, he had punched her on the shoulder.

"Come on, Mogs," he urged. "You're the only one here who I want to get all sleepy and numb with."

Morgan reminded him they would actually be filming her knocking back a few coconut shells of the stuff early tomorrow evening, so he could try it himself afterward. And they could be pleasantly numb together then.

"It's supposed to be a great de-stressor," Mark continued. "You've been uptight all day. You need to loosen up a bit."

"I said no." Morgan could feel her phone vibrating in her pocket. She pushed Mark toward the door of her room. "Now go away."

Mark quirked an eyebrow, sensing that a motive other than an early night was keeping Morgan in the hotel. "Did you hook up with that chick while I wasn't watching?"

"No, I did not." Almost immediately after stepping off the plane they had stepped onto a yacht moored in the harbor at Port Vila, the capital city of Vanuatu. The beauty of the natural harbor and the crystal-clear quality of the water took precedence for filming, so Morgan had numerous breaks from being in front of the camera. They shared the vessel with a half-dozen tourists, one of which was a chatty Texan. Female. Good-looking. And, as Mark pointed out when he sidled up to Morgan to see if she'd noticed the attention, definitely interested. But even the woman's slow Texan drawl couldn't arouse more than a fleeting interest. "Like I told you on the boat, I just wasn't into her." Her phone was still vibrating, but it would switch to her voice mail at any second. She opened the door and hustled Mark out of it. "Piss off. I'll see you tomorrow."

Once alone, Morgan pulled out her phone and checked the caller ID. It was an unknown number. Usually she would ignore such calls, but not now. Not since Ally had disconnected from her previous number. She answered each call with a surge of hope, praying that Ally had reconsidered and wanted to speak to her.

Her hopes plunged with the voice. It was some offshore telemarketing center wanting to know if she was happy with her car insurance. Morgan had long ago learned that a firm but polite "I'm not interested" usually did the trick. But she wasn't in the mood for polite right now. "Bugger off!" she barked and disconnected.

No more unknown callers called that evening. Morgan picked at her room service dinner and placed the nearly untouched plate outside the door. She took her phone to bed with her, and instead of turning it off as she usually did, she turned the ring volume back on and set it to maximum. That way she was sure not to miss a single call, even if it occurred in the middle of the night.

Morgan lay with her phone in hand, staring at the ceiling, hating that she was putting her life on hold in the hope of receiving a call. It was time for some proactivity. She decided—if Ally had not reconsidered and called by the time they left Vanuatu for Fiji on Friday morning—she would commandeer Kitty's laptop while they were waiting at the airport, hopefully hook up to the Internet via a wi-fi connection and Google Ally. Morgan knew her full name: Alison Brown. She knew her profession: Architect. And she knew where she worked: Sydney. Google could almost certainly find her based on that degree of information, and if not, well, she'd just have to make a directory search on all the architectural firms specializing in sustainable housing in the Sydney area. Surely there couldn't be too many. So, one way or another she was sure to get Ally's office phone number and address. Morgan was flying in from Fiji on Sunday, so on Monday morning, before she hopped back on a plane—this time to Barcelona in Spain—she'd drop into Ally's office and pay her a personal visit.

Yes, that was a damn good plan. Satisfied, Morgan turned onto her side and fell asleep with her phone still clutched in her hand.

CHAPTER TWELVE

Ally woke with a feeling of well-being on Thursday, having slept surprisingly well the night before. She bounced through her preparations for the day, ate a massive bowl of cereal, downed a coffee and an orange juice and arrived at the office feeling she could just about take on the world.

Something good was going to happen very soon. She could feel it in her bones. Maybe today she'd hit the jackpot with her permutations. Ally pulled out her phone and considered trying the next sequence of numbers. But it was a little early to be disturbing people—even strangers. Instead she booted up her computer, had a look at the picture that lay under her keyboard, made herself another coffee and got down to work.

At eight thirty she reached for her first phone call of the day. But she didn't pick it up, a glance to the display of her desk phone telling her it was James.

Ally felt rather bad for not answering but she let it ring out.

Fifteen minutes later he tried again. Ally wondered why he didn't try her mobile number and then remembered he hadn't been included in yesterday's SMS and e-mail sends. She didn't pick up.

Another fifteen minutes passed and another phone call from James. Obviously, until she spoke to him she wouldn't get a moment of peace. "Hello."

"I miss you."

"Will you please stop calling me every few minutes?"

"I haven't."

"I know you have. Your name keeps appearing on my phone."

James gave a little embarrassed cough. "I'm sorry, Alison. But I just wanted to speak to you. To see if you've reconsidered."

"No, James, I haven't."

There was a silence over the line, then, "Who is she?"

That was the first time he had asked that question. Ally was not going to answer. She changed the subject, her tone a little brusque, indicating she was not in for a discussion. "I have all your things packed and ready. When would you like to come over and pick them up?"

"Alison . . ."

"And when can I come over to pick up mine?"

"Let's have dinner tonight and we can talk about it then."

Ally hesitated. She knew if she accepted it would get James's hopes up. But she also knew if she didn't, there was a great possibility she'd be barraged by phone calls until she did.

It was time to take a tough line. "I'm transferring all my calls to reception, so there's no point calling me again today. I'll phone you tonight and we can talk a little then. 'Bye for now." She hung up before he could reply and immediately dialed Kirsty, who in addition to her drafting tasks took all the general inquiries, both over the phone and front of office. "Can you please take my calls today? If James calls, tell him I'm busy and can't be disturbed. But I'm expecting a call from a Morgan, so if she calls you can switch her straight through."

If Kirsty wondered why Ally didn't want to speak to James, she didn't ask. Ally would have to break the news of her split to staff eventually, but not right now. Right now she really wanted to get her 3-D rendering of the Kalgoorlie residence completed, hopefully before her five o'clock meeting with Josh. She wanted to wow him with her six-bedroom, four-bathroom, open-plan-living, solar-powered, ranch-style masterpiece before he left for Barcelona tomorrow.

At nine thirty she was disturbed by Kirsty, who popped her head around her door. "The boss just came in. Said he wants to see you."

"Okay." Ally looked up and frowned. Why didn't Josh just pop his own head 'round the door like he normally did? "I'll be there in one minute."

In less than that she knocked on his door.

"It's Ally."

"Come in."

"You wanted to see me?" she asked, immediately noticing he looked quite drained. Normally no one would guess he was close to fifty-five. Today he was showing every one of his years.

"Yes." Josh nodded for her to close the door and then for her to sit. He leaned forward in his chair, resting his arms on the desk and clasping his hands together. "Ally, you know my son, Paterson."

Ally nodded. Josh's teenaged son had visited the offices on dozens of occasions. She'd seen him sprout from a gangly kid to the rangy seventeen-year-old he was now. Only a month prior he'd come strutting into the office, proud as punch as he jangled the keys of his first "set of wheels," an ancient Torana sedan with holes in the upholstery, badly faded paintwork and an intermittent backfire. Ally was surprised it was even allowed on the road. Her insides froze. Surely nothing had happened to the kid in that deathtrap of a vehicle?

Josh clenched his hands more tightly together. "Paterson was arrested last night—"

"Thank God!" Ally blurted, relieved he was alive and well.

Josh threw her a very odd glance. "For possession of drugs—"

"Oh," Ally interrupted again, feeling a little foolish for her untimely outburst.

"And for driving a stolen vehicle."

"Oh," Ally repeated. She was awash with questions: were there others in the car, how was he caught, was there a chase, was anybody hurt, did Josh know his son was taking drugs, what drugs was he taking? But she didn't ask. It would be hard enough for Josh to have discovered Paterson had run off the rails, without having to suffer twenty questions about it from an employee. Come to think of it, why was Josh telling her all of this in the first place? Apart from the occasional "how was your weekend" query, they didn't usually discuss their personal lives at the office. Maybe, on this occasion, he needed a sympathetic ear. "I'm really sorry, Josh. It must have been very difficult for you and Helen."

Josh acknowledged her sympathy with a nod. "It's been a long night. But he's home with us now and his court hearing is on Wednesday, so hopefully this ordeal will soon be over."

"Really? That's fast." Ally had thought the court system was clogged with waiting periods extending into weeks and months. But maybe they fed the "simple" cases through quickly. Then she realized the timing. Josh would be on the other side of the globe next Wednesday. "Good to get it over and done with, I guess. But bad timing as far as the conference goes."

Josh shook his head. "I won't be going. I want to be there for Paterson . . . and I don't want Helen to have to deal with it all by herself."

Ally nodded. She'd also met Josh's wife, Helen, on a number of occasions. She was an artist, creating beautiful silkscreens, samples of which hung around the office. In Ally's opinion, Helen was almost as delicate as her creations. Not one to cope well in a crisis.

Josh unclasped his hands. "How's your latest project progressing?"

"Very well," she admitted, a little thrown by the abrupt change in topic. "I'll have the walk-through ready to run past you this afternoon. I promised the client initial plans by close of business tomorrow."

"Excellent." Josh nodded. "What else is on your plate at the moment?"

"Well, I'm in a holding pattern with the Boyden account while Mrs. Boyden waits until her planets are properly aligned for making a decision on the floor plan." Ally was pleased to see the eccentric behavior of one of her clients managed to raise a smile. "I've also got final plans out with the Changs, but they've promised me an answer by next Tuesday. There's a site visit for the final stages of the two-story in Quaker's Hill. That's on Friday. And also on Friday I've got an appointment with some potential new clients. I can't remember their names offhand."

"So nothing of a screaming urgency that only you can handle?"

"Not really," Ally said carefully. It was never wise to admit you were dispensable.

"And your passport is up-to-date?"

Ally glanced sharply at Josh. "Pardon?"

"You'll need a passport if you're going to take my place at the conference."

Ally's mouth fell open. She'd *known* something good was going to happen today. But Barcelona? Tomorrow? Fantastic!

Except for the thought of all that flying. And except for the fact her dialing permutations would also have to come to a halt. Maybe she could squeeze in a number here and there in between everything she would have to organize at the office. And probably a couple more tonight after she'd packed her bag and watched last Friday's episode of *Bonnes Vacances*, which, according to the television schedule, was to be repeated after the Thursday night movie finished at ten thirty p.m. But she couldn't use the phone in the plane, and she could kiss her job good-bye if Josh received a telephone bill for potentially hundreds of calls charged at international roaming costs. So all her other dialing would have to wait until she got back.

In a week.

So much for something good happening today. Barcelona. The whole idea sucked. But for Josh's sake she forced out a smile. "Really? Excellent."

CHAPTER THIRTEEN

Midmorning on Friday Morgan settled into a quiet corner of the little departure lounge at Vanuatu airport and fired up Kitty's laptop.

As suspected, her Google search for "Alison Brown Architect Sydney" was immediately successful. Morgan scanned the first ten or so results and clicked on one particular entry that caught her eye. "Wow," she exclaimed softly when the page from the *Architectural Digest* Web site had loaded. If Ally had designed the house represented in the single photo then she was good, *very* good, at what she did. The short paragraph of text that accompanied the picture—it seemed one must subscribe to the magazine to get the full story—was enough to glean that Ally had indeed designed the featured home. It also gave the name of the company she worked for. Design for Tomorrow. Morgan immediately opened a new browser window and navigated to the White Pages phone directory. Within seconds she had a number and an address.

She glanced at her watch. Fifteen minutes before boarding would begin. Plenty of time to make a quick call. But should she?

Morgan pondered the options. Ally could hang up on a phone call. But it would be a bit more difficult for her to avoid Morgan in person—especially in an office environment.

She decided to give her a surprise visit on Monday.

Within less than a minute Ally's office details had been transferred into Morgan's notebook. Then she closed down the laptop and hurried to the tiny newsstand to scour the shelves for the *Architectural Digest* magazine. She tucked a copy of the most recent edition—that which featured Ally's design—under her arm for closer examination on her flight to Fiji.

Mark, who was seated next to her during the flight, quirked an eyebrow when he discovered Morgan's latest taste in reading matter. "You looking to upgrade from that harbor-side shack you call home?" he asked.

"Something like that," Morgan said evasively, closing the pages a little so his view of the content was restricted.

Mark responded by shifting in his seat and peering more closely at the magazine. "Hey, is that *our* Alison Brown?" he asked, pointing to a caption next to the main picture on the first page of the six-page article.

Morgan feigned surprise and made a show of pretending to read it for the first time. "Why, I think it is."

"Great house," he said simply, without a trace of sarcasm. "She's good."

Morgan nodded, trying very hard to keep the enthusiasm from her voice and a smile from creeping across her features. She wasn't very successful. "Seems so."

Three days later her smile had yet to fade. She entered the small reception area of Design for Tomorrow and was greeted almost immediately by a young woman, probably in her twenties, with a shock of bright red hair and a nose ring.

"Good morning," the woman chirped, a cup of coffee in hand. She frowned a little, as if she recognized Morgan but couldn't quite place her. "How can I help you?"

"Good morning." Morgan couldn't help but focus on the nose ring. She had to force her gaze to shift to the woman's eyes. "I was hoping I could speak with Alison Brown, please."

"I'm sorry, but she's not here at the moment."

"Oh." Morgan glanced at her watch. It had only just gone nine a.m. Maybe she hadn't yet arrived at the offices. Or—and this was an eventuality she hadn't figured into her plans—maybe she was off-site. After all, architects had to go visit their projects. "What time will she be here?"

"No time soon, I'm afraid. She won't be back until Friday."

"Friday?" Morgan echoed. This wasn't an eventuality she had figured on either. Where was she? Had she flown back to Kalgoorlie to present her client some house plans? Morgan's heart sank. This was not going at all how she'd imagined.

The woman nodded, now looking a little worried. She opened the large diary that sat on the reception desk and peered at Monday's date. "There's no record of any Monday appointments for Ally—"

"Oh, no. I didn't have an appointment," Morgan assured her. "I just popped in on the off-chance I could see her." She thought hard for some reason why she would do so. "I was recommended to her by a friend," she said a little lamely.

"Would you like me to make an appointment for you now?" The woman, relaxing again, sipped from her mug as she turned pages. "She's rather busy on Friday but next Monday afternoon is looking good."

Morgan would just be arriving back in Sydney next Monday. If she hurried off the plane and didn't get held up in customs she might just make it to the offices before closing time. The moment the woman raised her head again Morgan honed in on the nose ring. "Is five thirty too late?"

Apparently not.

Five minutes later Morgan left Ally's offices with a Monday afternoon appointment . . . and one of Ally's business cards.

"This is her new mobile number?" Morgan had asked when it was presented. She figured the card was brand new, since the woman had to rip open a padded courier bag to get to the box of cards.

The woman assured her it was. She didn't ask how Morgan would know Ally had a new number and that the couriered cards were not just reprints.

Back in her car, Morgan turned the card over in her hand. Her original plan of a surprise visit was dead on the ground. And, since her name was now staring up from the company diary, her Monday appointment held no element of surprise. So she may as well dial and hope for the best.

She did. And she held her breath as it rang once, twice, three times.

"Hello?" The voice that came through the line was sleepy, as if its owner had been woken. But it was definitely Ally's voice.

Morgan's breath caught in her throat at the sound. Had it really only been less than a week since she last heard it? It seemed like an eternity. But why so sleepy? she wondered. Was Ally on vacation? Or was she home from work, sick? "Hello, Ally. It's me, Morgan."

Ally sat bolt upright in bed, the fog of sleep lifting almost immediately. She hadn't been in too deep a sleep, the change in time zone and her preoccupation with her private thoughts working together to prevent quality rest. But still she had to ask, to ensure she wasn't dreaming, "Morgan?"

"Yes." There was a pause on the other end of the line, then, "Did I wake you?"

"It's okay," Ally said quickly. She rubbed at her eyes and

groped for her watch on the bedside table. It wasn't even midnight yet. Another reason she was so quick to wake. She'd been in bed for less than an hour. "I'd only just gone to bed." She sighed happily. "I'm really glad you called."

"I'm really glad you're glad." Another slight pause followed. "Are you unwell?"

Ally smiled at the concern in Morgan's voice. "No." Right at this moment Ally was feeling better than she had for days. "A bit jet-lagged, but apart from that I'm fine."

"Jet-lagged?"

Ally realized Morgan had no idea where she was. When they'd last spoken Ally had had no idea she'd be in Barcelona either. "I'm in Spain."

"Spain?" Morgan echoed softly. "Where in Spain?"

"Barcelona. I'm here for a conference."

This time there was a gasp. "I don't believe this. Ally, how long will you be there?"

"Until Wednesday morning." Ally's stomach lurched, imagining arriving back in Sydney just as Morgan was leaving. "Where are you?"

"I'm in Sydney. I have to be at the airport in a couple of hours."

Ally couldn't help the curse that escaped her lips. "Fuck."

"Ally, I'm leaving for Barcelona. I'll be there Tuesday morning."

"You're coming here?" Ally asked, feeling a little faint.

"Yes."

There was yet another pause, extended such that Ally wondered if it had been left intended for her to fill. She decided it was. After all, she had been the one to break contact. Morgan was probably unsure if she wanted to reconnect. "I really would like to see you," she said softly.

Morgan's reply was immediate. "That's good. Because I really would like to see you, too."

CHAPTER FOURTEEN

Morgan walked a few steps, stopped on her mark and started talking into the camera. "Another piece of Gaudi architecture on the same street as La Pedrera is the Casa Batllo, otherwise known as the 'house of bones.'" She turned slightly and gazed behind her to the façade of the building, which had balconies and supports that did look remarkably like skulls and bones. Then she turned back to the camera. "It was originally built for a wealthy aristocrat who lived on the lower floors and rented out the upper levels. Now it's open to the public." She turned again and walked toward the entrance as if she was going to visit. In actual fact she already had visited earlier that day. They were just filming out of sequence.

At step six Kitty called, "Cut."

"Is that it this time?" Morgan asked hopefully, eager to get this, the last shot for today, over and done with. This was the fifth time she'd had to do her introduction to the Casa Batllo, Kitty finding something wrong with each of the other takes—first Morgan's expression was "odd," second a pedestrian stopped behind her right shoulder and stared idiotically into the camera. On the third and fourth takes she fluffed her lines.

Kitty declared she was happy.

"Thank Christ for that," Mark muttered as he lowered the boom. He was in a rare bad mood and had been all day. So the repeated takes at the tail end of their day of filming had done nothing to improve his humor. "I need a beer." He turned to Morgan. "How about you?"

Morgan checked her watch. It was already nearly seven thirty p.m. Had they kept to their planned schedule they'd have wrapped up nearly an hour ago. She and Ally had arranged to meet at eight, so now there was only half an hour to get back to her hotel, freshen up and head out again to their designated meeting place—at the junction where the Plaza de Catalyuna met the beginning of the famous pedestrian strip of the Rambla. Luckily Morgan's hotel was only a few minutes' walk away from where they were now as well as the agreed meeting spot, but still she would be cutting it fine. She shook her head. "I can't right now. I'm meeting Ally, remember?"

"Yeah, I remember." Mark scowled and strode away, recording equipment in hand, in the direction of the hotel.

Morgan hurried after him. "Come on." She repeated what she'd told him on the plane on the leg from Milan to Barcelona. That was when she'd told him Ally was going to be in the city at the same time as they were and that she was taking the opportunity to catch up with her. "This is the one chance I have to meet with her before she leaves. You and I can have drinks tomorrow."

"I still don't see why I can't come along too. Just for a little while."

Morgan sighed, knowing this was at least partly the reason he was in a mood. The other was that Rebecca—the busty blond sound engineer he'd been panting after—had taken up with a balding studio manager while they were island-hopping in Fiji and Vanuatu. But she thought they'd worked through the Ally portion of his huff already. "You really are very unattractive when you sulk."

"And ever since you've fallen in love you've become a real pain in the ass."

Morgan stopped walking.

Mark didn't. She watched his back as the distance between them increased. "I'm not in love," she called to his retreating figure.

"Try and tell that to anyone looking from this side," he called back without turning.

Morgan broke into a half-trot and ended back beside him. "I've changed my mind. You can come to say hello."

Immediately Mark broke into a smile.

"One drink. That's it."

Mark's smile turned into a grin.

"You're worse than a child for getting your own way."

Mark just shrugged.

"I'm not in love."

Mark shrugged again. "Whatever you say, Mogs."

"I'm not," Morgan repeated, more to convince herself than Mark. Just because she *really* liked Ally and happened to think about her most of her waking hours didn't mean she was in love. Nor did the fact she'd been wandering around in a gloom from the moment Ally disconnected from her life and walking on cloud nine from the moment they reconnected again. And that strange flip-flopping sensation that happened in her stomach whenever she heard her voice or laid eyes on her wasn't love either. Was it?

Morgan didn't have time to contemplate life, love and the universe right now anyway. They entered the hotel and waited for the elevator.

"I'll meet you in the lobby in fifteen minutes sharp," she said to Mark before he got out on the second floor. "If you're not there I'll leave without you."

Mark was on time and they hurried out of the hotel together. Morgan caught sight of Ally when they were still a good twenty meters away from her. As arranged, she was standing near the entrance to the Metro, just out of the way of the mass of humanity entering and exiting the hole in the ground. She wore a black and lace dress, a sleeveless halter top style with a very flattering below-the-knee hankie hem. She carried a sequined evening bag. She had her hair slicked back. Morgan sucked in her breath. She looked . . . fantastic.

"Admit it." Mark knocked his shoulder against hers as they walked. "You love her."

"Shut up." Morgan hurried her step, determined to be the first to reach Ally. Mark also lengthened his stride.

The bastard overtook her in the last five meters. Despite her high heels, Morgan broke into a run. Ally, who had by now seen them, laughed a hello to them both, amused by their speedy arrival. If she was disappointed that Morgan was not alone, she did not show it, smiling broadly and accepting kisses on the cheek from the both of them.

"Damn. You're a sight for sore eyes." Mark took hold of her hands and held her at arm's length. "How are you, Ally?"

"Much better for having seen you again." Ally glanced at Morgan, briefly meeting her gaze before looking back to Mark. "Are you coming to have a drink with us?"

"That's the plan." Mark grinned.

"Excellent." Ally glanced quickly at Morgan again. Her expression was unreadable. But if Morgan was asked to choose whether it was irritation or relief, she would lean toward relief.

Was Ally a little afraid of her? she wondered. If she was, then it appeared her knight in shining armor had arrived. Mark manoeuvred between them, crooking both his arms and inviting them to take one each.

"Come, ladies." He steered them in the direction of the Rambla. "Let's go see how the Spanish beer measures up to the Australian."

An hour later they were sipping on their second drinks while seated in an open-air café on the Rambla. It was near the section where all manner of birds were on sale, from day-old chicks to canaries and quail, exotic parrots, love birds and even a toucan. Combined, their various chatter and screeches and songs were loud to the point of piercing. Personally, Morgan found the din rather irritating. Or maybe she was just annoyed that Mark had well and truly muscled in on her evening. Morgan stabbed at the ice in her vodka and cranberry with her straw while she listened to Mark tell yet another tale of their travels. Or, more accurately, another tale that made her appear a fool. This time he was recounting the "spider episode" in Malaysia. They'd been traipsing through the rainforest in the Taman Negara National Park on a guided tour. Morgan was being filmed talking with the guide about the value of the eco-tourist to the park when a spider dropped from the trees into her hair. She'd nearly knocked Nick flat as she ran down the trail, thrashing at her hair and screaming, "Get it off me! Get it off me!"

"It was a huge spider," she said sulkily in her own defense, shuddering just at the memory of it. She'd had spider-related nightmares for a week afterward.

Mark scoffed and rolled his eyes in Ally's direction. "It was a teeny little thing."

"Actually, I would have done the same thing," Ally admitted. "I hate spiders. Almost as much as I hate flying."

Morgan, infinitely pleased that Ally had rallied to her defense, jumped onto the change in topic before Mark could. He was busy lighting up another cigarette. "How was your flight over here?"

"Ask the poor people I got stuck next to on each of the three legs. I think they suffered almost as much as me."

"You should take a sleeping tablet," Mark suggested in between puffs.

"I do. But it doesn't kick in until well after takeoff. And by then the person sitting next to me has almost lost their hand from having it squeezed so hard."

If Mark hadn't been there, Morgan would have said something about not minding if she was the one having her hand squeezed by Ally. But he was there, so she didn't.

"Anyway," Ally continued, "even the tablets don't work very well. I sleep badly for a few hours then that's it." She pointed to her eyes, which had faint lines of fatigue around them. "As you can see."

This time Morgan didn't stop to think about Mark's presence. "I think you look fantastic."

In the next second Morgan was wishing she had openly complimented Ally long before now. Mark stubbed out his cigarette and sculled the remains of his beer. He stood and hoisted up his faded jeans. "Me too. But I've a date with Nick and Kitty over a plate of paella." His cigarette packet was popped into a shirt pocket and he leaned down to kiss Ally on the cheek. "Great to catch up with you again." Morgan got a punch on the arm. "Mogs, I'll see your ugly mug tomorrow morning."

Morgan nodded, stealing a glance at Ally, who was looking a little startled at Mark's abrupt departure. "Good night."

"Good night," Ally also said, her gaze following him as he weaved between the tables out to the street. He was out of sight before she returned her attention to Morgan. She smiled, albeit a little nervously. "Hello."

"Hello." Morgan hoped her smile and her tone conveyed how pleased she was that they were finally alone. She also hoped it conveyed there was no need for Ally to be afraid of being alone with her. "Are you hungry?"

Ally nodded convincingly, rolling her empty wineglass

between her palms. "I'm half starved. Why on earth the Spanish eat so late I'll never know."

Morgan laughed. "Tell me about it. Last trip here, when we were in Madrid, we were invited to dinner by some bigwigs trying to curry favor and have us promote their hotel chain. The restaurant booking was for *eleven* p.m., and so by the time our first course arrived it was close to midnight. I tell you, I was almost ready to start chewing on my arm." She nodded to the menu board leaning against a pillar. "We can eat here, if you like."

Ally screwed up her nose at the menu. "I wouldn't mind some tapas actually. If the concierge at the hotel is to be believed, there's supposed to be a good place not too far from here. Apparently the locals eat there too, so it's not too touristy."

Morgan downed the last of her drink and stood. "Lead the way."

"So did they manage to curry your favor?" Ally asked as they walked down the Rambla in the direction of the harbor.

"The bigwigs?" Morgan stopped at one of the bird stalls. "No. We don't work that way. We're more of a video guidebook than a paid advertisement." She pointed to a cage sitting directly on the pavement. "Are they baby emus?"

Ally nodded. "I saw these when I walked the Rambla on Sunday. Poor buggers. Look"—she pointed to a sign above the cage—"they're promoting them as good eating. Goodness knows where they got hold of emus over here."

"Maybe brought over from the U.K. or somewhere. They farm them there now."

"Really?" Ally exclaimed. "I didn't know that." She peered sadly into the cage then turned and pulled Morgan away. "I hate seeing birds in cages. Even the ones smart enough not to fly." She guided Morgan off the Rambla and into a side street, all the while talking about the pet budgerigar she'd been given on her fifteenth birthday and had for the next eight years. "Axel had free run of the house and then my first apartment when I went to uni. His cage door was always open, except at night when I covered it over, and he hopped in and out as he pleased. He used to love having baths and would often sit in a corner of the shower stall when I was taking a shower."

"Lucky bird," Morgan said, thinking more of the Ally shower-sharing aspect than its liberated lifestyle. "Do you have any pets now?"

"When Axel died I decided it was too hard. Emotionally, that is. I think I cried more for him than when my grandma passed away."

"The bond with a pet is a very special one." Morgan understood completely what Ally was saying. She'd gone to pieces for days when the family cat died. Tom had been eighteen and around for longer than she had herself.

"Do you have any pets now?" Ally asked, pointing them down another side street.

"Goodness, no. With my schedule even the houseplants are in constant threat of extinction. It's a bit of a shame though," Morgan said almost wistfully. "It would be nice to come home to a friendly greeting instead of an echo."

"Don't you ever get tired of the traveling?" Ally asked, shuddering. "I know I'm about the only person on the planet who'd say this—but I don't envy your job at all. In and out of planes. It's nightmare material."

Morgan laughed. "I *do* think you're about the only person who hasn't fallen into a jealous swoon over my job. I do love it, even though it's not all glamor and chic hotel rooms like most people think. But sometimes I get jacked with the whole thing—especially all the hours spent in airports and planes—and wish I had a 'normal' nine-to-five job. Probably I'll have a serious rethink of my position when my contract's up in three years. If the show's still going then, of course. If there's one thing certain in television, it's that nothing's ever certain."

Ally glanced up to check the street name on the side of a building at a three-way junction. She hesitated a moment then pointed to the right, to a street even narrower than the last. Morgan hoped Ally knew where she was going. Although, come to think of it, she didn't really care. She couldn't think of a single person she'd rather get lost with.

"I watched your show last Thursday," Ally said a little shyly. "I don't think there's too much chance of a cancellation anytime soon. You're very good at what you do."

"You wouldn't say that if you'd seen me today," Morgan admitted, unaccountably pleased that Ally had seen the show. Given that Ally hardly ever watched television she doubted she had just caught it by accident. "I really sucked. Kept stuffing up my lines, forgetting place names. And I kept calling Gaudi gaudy."

"His work was a bit on the wild side of architectural design." Ally laughed. "Maybe your mouth just kept popping out what your brain was really thinking."

"Maybe." Morgan would have liked nothing better than for her mouth to pop out what her brain was thinking right now. But it would likely send Ally scurrying away in fright. It was almost enough to make Morgan scurry away herself. Because her brain was telling her what her heart—and Mark—already knew. It was telling her there was no point trying to deny it: she was in love with this woman. "But I think it was more because I was distracted by something other than work today."

Morgan knew that Ally knew exactly what she was talking about. She watched for the reaction and waited for her to ask the obvious question: *what distracted you?*

After Ally had asked it she'd smile knowingly in her direction and say simply, "You."

It would be a gentle easement into intimacy that would hopefully not freak Ally out.

But she was disappointed. It seemed Ally was not ready to

203

take the conversation to a more personal level. She just shrugged and said, "We all get days like that." Then she pointed a little farther down the street, to a building with a brightly painted façade and the words *Casa de los Tapas* daubed across a varnished wooden shingle hanging from a cast iron bracket. "That's the place. The House of Tapas." She turned to Morgan. "Totally unoriginal name but the food's supposed to be good."

"Who cares about originality? I'm just impressed you managed to find this place at all." Morgan looked around her. "I've got no idea where we are."

Ally put her hands on her hips and set her feet apart. "Then you'd better not say anything to upset me tonight, or I'll leave you here to forever wander the back streets of Barcelona."

God, the woman was just so damned cute when she was trying to be tough. Especially in that dress and those heels. "I'll consider myself warned." Morgan held back a smile as she headed for the entrance.

"Maybe the place isn't that great after all," Ally whispered a bit dubiously once they were inside. "It's not exactly full."

Morgan shrugged, scanning the premises and pinpointing where she wanted to sit. There was a cozy little table tucked into the far corner. It was pleasantly out of range of the bar and the toilets. And all the other diners—all seven of them—were clustered toward the front. "It's Spain, remember. Only we tourists eat so early. All the locals are still digesting lunch."

Once settled at the tucked-away table, they studied the menu card. Thankfully there was an English translation under the Catalan. Morgan spoke a smattering of Spanish, but her Catalan was nonexistent.

"What grabs your fancy?" she asked.

"I don't know. Everything sounds good. Except for the beef tripe." Ally put the menu card down. "Let's be bad and get one of everything else."

Morgan laughed. There were dozens of choices. "We'll be

here all night if we do that."

"I've got all night."

So do I, but I hope not all of it will be spent eating. Morgan's gaze strayed to Ally's lips. Her greatest wish right now was to taste them again. She put her menu card on the table. "I'll let you decide what we have. Just make sure you include some chicken croquettes. They're my favorite."

Ally settled on a selection of ten different dishes and a jug of sangria.

"Oh, my God," Ally said when the waiter quickly returned with their drink. "I didn't realize the jug would be so big." She tipped it toward Morgan's glass. "I hope it's good 'cause there's plenty of it."

"There's no rule that says we have to finish it." Morgan touched her glass to Ally's. "Here's to . . . tapas in Barcelona."

"And to us being together eating tapas in Barcelona."

Morgan's stomach started doing its flippy-floppy thing. She smiled into Ally's eyes. "A happy coincidence."

Ally nodded and took her glass to her lips. But she put it back on the table before taking a sip. "I left James," she said quickly, as if wanting to get the words out as fast as she could.

Morgan put her own glass back on the table, her heart leaping at this admission. She wasn't too surprised at the news—Ally had already hinted around the edges of the subject when they talked on the phone on Monday. But since it was only minutes ago she had skated over her attempt to up the gears, she hadn't been expecting this sudden turn in this conversation. "I kind of guessed that was the case when you told me not *everyone* had been given your new mobile number. Since you'd already said you were trying to get back in contact with me, it didn't take too long to figure who you were talking about."

"I didn't leave him for you. I mean"—the glass of sangria was lifted but again it never made it to Ally's mouth—"you were part of the reason but not the whole reason. It was something I had to do for myself."

Morgan watched as Ally's glass finally made it to her lips. In the moment it took for her to take a large swallow she managed to fit in an "I understand." But the rest of what she wanted to say would have to remain unsaid. Ally was obviously not yet finished speaking.

"I just wanted you to know in case it was something that would stop you from . . ." She looked as if she were searching for the correct words.

"The reasons you left James are yours alone," Morgan said gently. "They're not for me to judge." Ally glanced at her sharply, which made her realize she was interrupting again. "Sorry." She made the motion of zipping her lip and throwing away the key.

Ally smiled wanly and took a deep breath. She held it, as if using the moment to organize her thoughts. "I wanted you to know I had left James because I wanted you to know I'm now single. I don't know how you feel about affairs, but I've never had one and I might be old-fashioned but I don't really think they're right. But maybe that's just me being self-righteous because I never actually met anyone who I wanted to have an affair with, so it was easy enough to say I didn't believe in them."

Morgan opened her eyes wide at her understanding at where this rush of words was leading. But she kept quiet. Ally was still not finished.

"But I'm single now and for me that's good. Because right now I'm sitting here knowing that even if I wasn't and you asked me to your hotel room that I'd say yes and then I'd have to eat my words and admit I am the kind to have an affair. But since I *am* single, now all I have to worry about is that you *don't* ask me to your hotel room. And I really don't think I could deal with that because I've been thinking about what might happen tonight from the moment you called me. Even though I didn't know exactly what to think because I've never been with—"

Ally stopped as abruptly as she'd started, interrupted by the waiter who'd just arrived with their tapas selection.

They sat in silence while the waiter pulled up another little table hard to theirs and painstakingly organized the ten dishes around the jug of sangria.

Morgan took a long look at the feast, then an even longer look at Ally. "Would you like to stay here and have this, or would you prefer room service?"

Ally also looked at the food before settling her gaze on Morgan. Morgan didn't know which of them received the hungrier stare. "Why don't we ask them to package it up? Then we can have this . . . in our room."

Ally shivered a little as she and Morgan stood together in the elevator. They were on their way to the fifth floor. To her room, in her hotel, at her request. "It's closer," she had said as they finally exited the restaurant, each toting a bag containing five foil-wrapped packages. It actually wasn't closer at all. But if Morgan knew that she didn't argue, instead just smiling and telling Ally to "lead the way." Maybe she'd sensed her need to be in surrounds that were just a little bit familiar while she plunged into otherwise unknown territory.

Or maybe she was just lost.

"Are you cold?" Morgan asked her now, obviously having seen her shiver.

"A little." Ally cast a glance to the digital control panel as she spoke the lie. She was a lot of things right now. But cold was not one of them. Especially not now that Morgan had moved to stand a little closer. Close enough she could feel her body heat. Level four. One more to go. She shivered again as the digital display changed and the elevator ground to a halt on the fifth floor. This time a sudden rush of nerves was the primary cause. "Here we are," she squeaked, stepping out and heading quickly in the direction of her door. Twice the electronic entry system flashed red when she swiped her card. "I'm not very good at this tonight." She felt the heat of embarrassment spread up her neck as she handed the card to Morgan. "You try."

Morgan was much more successful and once inside she slotted the card into the system that activated the electrics. "Nice room," she said as she scanned the space. "Heaps better than my hotel." She lifted her bag of tapas a little and nodded to the long, low-lying wall unit that housed the mini bar and fridge. "Shall I put this over there?"

"Please." Ally handed Morgan her own bag and then just stood near the door, awkward, knowing she should do something. But what?

Offer the woman a drink, her brain suggested.

"Err . . . can I get you something to drink?"

"Sure."

Ally made a dash for the mini bar and squatted in front of it. She reached inside the fridge and pulled out a bottle of vodka and a bottle of cranberry juice. Both had previously been opened and some of the contents consumed. The vodka she'd bought at the airport in Milan. The cranberry was from the first supermarket she'd found after arriving in Barcelona. Now, she held up both for viewing. "Is this okay?"

Morgan had settled into a half-sitting position on the low-lying unit. She cocked her head and smiled. "Have I converted you to my favorite drink?"

Just having something to do with her hands served to calm Ally's nerves a little. She stood and reached for the two tumblers that sat on a tray next to some coffee cups. "Among other things."

Morgan removed herself from the wall unit and took a couple of steps so she stood directly behind Ally. Her hands came to rest on her hips and she bent her head so her breath was in her ear. "What else have I converted you to?"

Ally put the bottle of vodka down and closed her eyes. Morgan's breath was warm and it tickled, sending a fresh wave of shivers through her. And her body against her back felt so good, so soft, fitted so well, just seemed so . . . right. She turned slowly in Morgan's grasp and looked into those piercing gray eyes.

"You," she whispered, feeling a flood of emotion so strong it welled up in the form of tears. "You've converted me to you."

"Oh, Ally." Morgan lifted her hands to her cheeks and wiped gently at the tears with her thumbs. And her lips followed, kissing away any remnants, leaving a moist warmth in their wake. And then, almost without warning, Morgan's mouth was against her own.

Ally whimpered, Morgan's lips more tender, more melting than she remembered. Her mouth opened to the gentle pressure, inviting Morgan's tongue to slide inside and commence an erotic exploration.

Morgan's hands fell from Ally's cheeks to her shoulders, stroking up and down, up and down her arms, causing her skin to erupt into goose bumps and the fine hairs on her forearms to stand on end.

"Are you okay with this?" Morgan asked softly as her hands ceased their stroking and reached for the tie of Ally's halter top.

Ally felt weak at the knees. Her mouth was on fire and every cell of her being tingled. Never before had she been in such a state of arousal, and all it had taken was a kiss and a simple caress. She nodded, standing still, quiet, as the tie was released and the halter top fell away.

"Oh," Morgan breathed, her gaze almost as a touch to Ally's breasts. "You are even more beautiful than I imagined."

Shyly Ally smiled, accepting the compliment. And she bent her head to witness the first time her breasts were cupped by a woman's hands. Morgan's hands. It was an image she would never forget. So gently, reverently they were taken. Delicate fingers, long and slender, circled the tissue, traced an imaginary line around her nipples. Already hard with arousal, the almost-touch caused them to ache.

"Please." She pressed her hands against Morgan's, begging for more contact.

And Morgan complied, not only with her fingers, but with her mouth. Ally cried out in the pleasure of it. Of the lips that encased her flesh and the tongue that swirled and the teeth that nipped.

The sensation in her breasts grew and grew until it was almost too much. As if reading her body perfectly, Morgan withdrew her attentions and rose to Ally's height again. Her eyes were heavy-lidded and her pupils dilated. She took a step away, a step toward the bed. Then she held out her hand.

"Come?"

Wordlessly Ally answered, slipping her sandals off and padding to the bed.

With her heels removed and Morgan still in hers, their height difference was magnified. And with Morgan still fully clothed and Ally with her dress draped around her waist, she felt a sudden return of nerves, of being exposed and vulnerable.

But once again Morgan seemed to read her perfectly. She lifted one ankle and then the other, quickly undoing the straps of her own sandals and tossing them aside. Then she looked down to her dress and back to Ally, quirking an eyebrow.

It was an invitation to remove it. Ally did so, holding her breath as Morgan's skin was slowly exposed and imagining that this, surely, must be what men found so appealing in the act of undoing a woman's zipper. The planes of her back were firm and smooth, with a faint outline of the muscles that lay underneath. Ally swept aside a thick tress of auburn hair and kissed Morgan from nape to almost the base of her spine and back again. Then she turned her around and drew the straps of her dress from her shoulders. It fell around Morgan's feet, leaving her in only a little lacy bra and panties.

An unintelligible sound emerged from Ally's mouth as her eyes opened wide in appreciation of what they saw. Her musings on the train about Morgan having a figure befitting the cover of *Sports Illustrated* had been right on the mark. Put her on the beach in a bikini and she'd cause a riot. "You are a goddess," she breathed.

Morgan took the step to bring their bodies in contact. "And you are just perfect." Her hands settled gently at Ally's waist, but this time when she bent to her lips it was with a crushing passion.

They fell together onto the bed and, somehow, in between all the kisses and caresses and their tangled mess of limbs, their remaining clothes were removed. And somehow, in between more kisses and caresses, they molded into each other's naked bodies, breast against breast, thighs between thighs.

We're a perfect fit, Ally thought in wonder as she closed her eyes, enraptured by the sensation of Morgan's body against her own, the feel of her under her hands. Everywhere she touched was magic. The lines of her back, the curve of her waist, the fabulous swell of her buttocks. And . . . oh . . . the feel of Morgan's hands upon her. Upon her breasts, across her stomach and now, stroking up and down her legs.

Ally shifted, her thighs opening in response to the fingers that were moving ever and ever closer to the spot that was burning for attention. Never before had she felt so ready to be touched. Never before had she *needed* so badly to be touched. Her hips ground upward, seeking the fingers that kept advancing and retreating, advancing and retreating.

"Morgan . . . please!" she begged as she arched upward again, chasing relief to this exquisite torture.

And finally, finally it came.

"Ally . . ." Morgan's breath was hot, her voice heavy as her lips grazed against her ear. Her body moved in rhythm with her fingers, rising and falling, pressing and grinding. Ally was ardent in her touch, awash with sensation. The swell of feeling grew and grew until she was unable to hold it back. She cried out, clutching at Morgan's back, holding on for dear life as the waves of orgasm swept through her.

And then, mortifyingly, she just cried.

"Oh, Ally. Baby . . ." Morgan gathered her in her arms and rained light kisses on her eyes, her cheeks and her lips as she rocked her gently. "It's okay."

"I'm sorry." A little later Ally swiped at her eyes, still not quite through her rush of tears. "It's just I was not . . . expecting that."

Morgan's gaze flickered over Ally's face and she smiled. It was not quite confident, but it wasn't exactly a worried smile either. "What were you expecting?"

"I don't know," Ally admitted, turning out of Morgan's arms to lie on her side, her head on the pillow. "I don't have any reference points for this. It's totally . . . different . . . to what I'm used to."

Morgan smiled again, more surely this time. She trailed her index finger down Ally's arm to her wrist, then up her waist, to her ribs. "Different good, or different bad?"

Ally shivered as Morgan's finger found a breast. She glanced down to find her nipple hardening. And she glanced over to Morgan to find her biting on her lower lip, intent on the effect of her touch. "You tell me which one you think it is," she said, her voice breaking with renewed desire.

Morgan shifted her gaze back to Ally, her expression all innocence. "Would you mind if I try again, just so I can be certain?"

Ally reached to brush away a stray strand of hair from Morgan's face. "I don't think I would mind that at all."

Morgan shifted closer, close enough their nipples grazed. She slipped her knee between Ally's willing thighs at the same time she slipped her tongue into Ally's waiting mouth. "Oh . . . dear God." She groaned as her fingers again found Ally wet and ready. Then, suddenly, her mouth was gone.

Ally reached for Morgan's shoulders. "Don't stop kissing me."

"I'm not going to." Morgan slithered out of Ally's grasp, down her body. And as suddenly as her lips had left Ally's, they returned. But in a much more intimate place. And their attentions left Ally trembling.

Only this time, there were no tears. Instead, as the waves of her second orgasm had passed and Ally again lay in Morgan's arms, a thought pierced through her languid, soporific mind. *How did I not know that this was who I was meant to be?* She was thirty-three years old. Surely before now she should have had some clue, some inkling. Then, as she looked into eyes that were searching hers, no doubt wondering what she was thinking, Ally knew the reason. *Up until now I had never known Morgan.*

"What are you thinking?" Morgan asked the question Ally had predicted.

"That I love you," she said simply, unabashedly. And she held Morgan's cheeks in her palms, crushing her mouth against hers, not giving the opportunity for a spoken response. Words were unnecessary anyway, the passion of Morgan's kiss and the surge of her body against her own giving her all the response she needed.

Ally allowed her hands to wander where they wished. They ventured farther than before, discovering new curves, new softness. Finally, they found the inside of Morgan's thighs. In vain Ally attempted to replicate Morgan's stroking tease. But she couldn't. She had to discover the secrets within. Her fingers delved into intricate folds and she gave an involuntary groan, overcome by the evidence of Morgan's desire. Her fingers slid easily over and around the little bud she found, first in a process of exploration, then with the intent of giving pleasure.

In rapt fascination she witnessed the changes occurring as a result of her attentions. She felt Morgan building, the slick flesh swelling under her fingers, her body pushing harder against her, her hips grinding upward in an ever-increasing motion. Then Morgan stilled completely and Ally's heart leapt to her throat in the knowledge she was at the point of orgasm.

The stillness was shattered by a series of frenetic thrusts and an almost animal cry.

Ally rode the storm of Morgan's orgasm in wide-eyed awe. When it was all over and Morgan lay still except for the pronounced rise and fall of her chest, she climbed on top of her, straddling her thighs. She gazed down to the woman below, her heart fit to burst at her beauty, both inside and out.

Morgan raised a slow hand to cup Ally's cheek. "You do know that I love you too."

Ally didn't know why, but never before had she ever been so certain of the truth in another's words. She grinned impishly, newly confident in her success. "You're just saying that 'cause I'm good in bed."

Morgan's eyes twinkled with laughter as she grabbed Ally by the wrists and pulled her down on top of her. "Come here then and prove it."

Morgan carried the tray that had previously held the hotel room's coffee cups and tumblers over to the bed. She placed it in the middle of the mattress and sat down carefully so as not to upturn the open foil packages. "Dinner is served," she announced formally.

"Do you think that now we can hold our heads up high in Spanish society?" Ally asked as she selected a baby aubergine that—from the smell of it—had been cooked with a bucketload of fresh marjoram. She took a bite and held out the remainder.

Morgan chewed slowly on the morsel that was popped into her mouth. She'd been right; marjoram dominated the flavor. "Apart from the fact I don't think too many of them dine in the nude, I reckon we've outdone most tonight." She reached for her watch on the bedside table and presented the face to Ally. It read two thirty.

Ally grimaced theatrically as she read the time. "No wonder I felt like I was about to faint."

Morgan peered at the foil packages and selected a chicken croquette. "And here I was thinking it was me making you swoon."

"Oh, no." Ally's impish tone was back. "I was just hungry."

Morgan offered her croquette to the little vixen, watching as the crumbed ball disappeared between lips that were still puffy from being kissed so long and so often. And that had kissed Morgan back so long and often.

Everywhere.

And so well.

Morgan shivered at the memory of Ally's tongue rolling and swirling over her. And of the fingers that joined her mouth, slipping so easily inside, thrusting and pushing her to ever-increasing heights. Ally had played her body as if she already knew it intimately. Goodness only knew what would happen when she *did* have the benefit of experience. Morgan shivered again. She was in for one glorious ride.

If Ally would agree to the terms of a relationship with her, that is.

Morgan took the slice of cured ham that Ally had decided was next in line for consumption and set it back on the foil. "Ally." She took her hands within hers and raised them to her lips, kissing their tips. "I want to see you again . . . and again . . ."

"I'm glad," Ally replied, all traces of levity gone from her tone. "Because I want to see you again and again, too." She kissed Morgan's hands, which still encased hers. "I just wish it could be every day."

"Me, too." For the first time in a very long time, Morgan really wished she didn't have the job everyone else in the world wanted. "But you need to realize I'm gone more than I'm home—"

"I know that." Ally nodded, even though she slumped a little.

"And when I am home we can't exactly be open. Our relationship will have to remain . . . our secret."

"I understand."

"No, I don't think you do." Morgan tipped Ally's chin a little, forcing their eyes to meet. "We can do what we want when we're alone. But apart from that I have to . . . stay in my closet. No kissing in restaurants, no holding hands in public. No doing anything that may raise questions or speculation."

"But"—confusion crossed Ally's features—"on the train—you told me you were with a woman. How's that 'staying in your closet'?"

"She was a . . . moment of weakness." Morgan averted her eyes, not quite sure how Ally would react to the story of Marie. But she told it anyway, in its entirety.

"She really wanted money?" Ally asked at the end of the telling, her expression incredulous.

Morgan nodded.

"I don't want your money."

"I never thought you did."

Ally ran the tip of her index finger over Morgan's lips. "But I always wanted to see what it was like, living in a closet."

"It's a deep closet," Morgan warned. She was still not convinced Ally really understood what she was walking into. "If I was any farther inside it, I'd end up in Narnia."

"I read the book and I saw the movie. Narnia seems like a wondrous place." Ally took the tip of Morgan's finger into her mouth. "I'd go there with you anytime."

"And will you water my houseplants when I can't be there?" Morgan asked, tight-throated, her heart beating madly. She was imagining coming home, not to an empty echo, but to Ally.

Ally sucked Morgan's finger into her mouth. "I will create a garden of paradise for you."

Morgan took the tray of tapas and moved it to the carpeted floor, determined to make the bed theirs again. She kneeled on the mattress, motioning for the woman she loved to join her. She did. "Ally . . ."

"I have to go," Morgan said with a distinct lack of enthusiasm at six thirty a.m. She and Ally lay together under the covers, having finally succumbed to sleep just a few hours before dawn. The tray of almost untouched tapas was still on the floor.

Ally stretched like a cat and yawned widely. "I'll walk you to your hotel."

"You don't have to do that." Morgan stroked her hair. "Sleep while you can. You have a long journey ahead."

Ally stretched again then sat up. "I do have to. Or you might get lost."

"That is a distinct possibility," Morgan murmured, pulling Ally back down to pillow level. She buried her head into Ally's neck and breathed in deeply, committing her scent to memory. The floral fragrance of her perfume lingered. It mingled with the remnants of their night's passions, creating an intoxicating bouquet. Morgan moved her head just a little, enough to kiss her tenderly on the lips. "Good morning."

"Good morning." Ally smiled into her eyes. "Would you like a crappy instant coffee?"

"Yes, please." Morgan arranged her pillows and sat up. At eight a driver would arrive at her hotel to take her and the rest of the crew to some beach on the Costa Brava coast, where she would be filmed exploring the cliffs, caves and coves in a kayak. If the light that filtered through the curtains of Ally's hotel room was anything to go by, the day promised to be perfect for such an activity and, normally, she would be looking forward to it. But right now, as she watched Ally's bare behind wriggle away to make coffee, Morgan would have given almost anything to stay in bed and ignore the day . . . ignore everything except Ally and the feeling of euphoria she had in her presence. But that wasn't to be. Twenty minutes later, their crappy instant coffee had been consumed and they strode out into the bright Barcelona morning.

"Come up to my room?" Morgan asked as they walked into the lobby of her hotel.

"Try and stop me," Ally said seductively, reaching for her hand.

"Not here," Morgan murmured, tilting her head slightly in the direction of the reception desk. A group of men were standing around a cluster of suitcases, either checking in or checking out. In addition to the green and yellow rugby shirt that one wore—advertising he was a Wallabies supporter—their strong accents gave away their nationality. "Aussie alert to our right."

Ally turned to watch the group and then turned back, scowling. "What are they doing here? You haven't even finished filming your Barcelona segment yet."

Morgan chuckled. "Yes, I know. How dare they make a travel decision without my recommendation!" She headed for the elevator. "Let's go somewhere a little less crowded."

After a ride in a divinely empty elevator and a dash down a deserted corridor, Morgan opened the door to her room. The room's phone was ringing, but it stopped before Morgan could get to it. Not that she moved toward it with any great hurry. Her time with Ally was limited. She didn't want to waste a moment of it talking to anyone else.

"I told you my life wasn't all glamor and chic hotel rooms." Morgan watched Ally scan the quite small and utilitarian surrounds. She'd donned some casual-fitting jeans and a sleeveless shirt for their walk. Even in such a simple outfit, Morgan thought her beautiful beyond belief.

Ally pushed at the mattress as if testing it for firmness. She glanced knowingly up to Morgan. "So long as the bed works . . ."

"We won't get to find out." Reluctantly, Morgan pulled Ally away from the bed. She worked at the first button of her shirt, revealing the beginnings of cleavage. "I don't have time. But maybe you can test-drive the shower with me?"

218

Ally's response was to turn Morgan around in her hands and slowly undo the zipper on her dress. The room phone began jangling again as she brushed Morgan's hair to one side. "Are you going to get that?" Her voice was low and Morgan sucked in her breath when she felt a gentle bite on her earlobe. "Maybe it's the driver calling to say he'll be late."

"He'd call Kitty." Morgan's pulse quickened at the thought of some extra time, even though she knew the chances of getting any were next to nil. "It's probably her, since my mobile's still turned off. And knowing her, she'll keep calling till she gets an answer." She undid another of Ally's shirt buttons. "You keep going with this and I'll get rid of her as fast as I can."

It *was* Kitty, wanting to know why Morgan hadn't yet appeared for breakfast. Morgan told her she'd had a very late dinner and so wasn't hungry. She hung up on the promise she'd be downstairs at eight, as arranged.

"That was quick." Ally was just at the point of peeling away her shirt when Morgan hung up the phone.

"Hmm." Morgan's breath caught in her throat as she watched Ally undo the button and zipper on her jeans. She'd stepped out of them by the time Morgan had shrugged out of her dress. By the time they reached the bathroom they'd stepped out of their underwear. Morgan reached over to turn on the spray. She turned to Ally while she waited for the water to get to temperature. "Now, remember, we don't have much time." She wagged her finger at her. "Be good."

"Cross my heart and hope to die." Ally blinked innocently as she made the motions that went with the words. She tested the water with her hand, declared it as warm enough and stepped in. "Mmm." She sniffed at the open bottle of Morgan's almond body wash. "Now I know why you smell so good." She squeezed a good amount into her palm and rubbed her hands together. "Turn around and I'll wash your back."

"I thought you promised to be good," Morgan accused a

219

minute later. Her reprimand was not very convincing. She was too intent on the sensation of Ally's soapy body slithering and sliding up and down hers.

"Is this bad?" Ally whispered throatily into her ear.

"No." Morgan groaned as Ally's hands slid from her waist, to her breasts. Her lathered palms circled over Morgan's nipples in a slow rhythmic motion. Morgan shuddered and groaned again. "It's very good."

"So what's the problem then?" Ally asked, her mouth still at Morgan's ear. "You asked for good. I'm only giving you what you wanted."

"You're a vixen." Morgan closed her eyes as her breath caught in her throat. One of Ally's hands was traveling down her stomach. The promise in the slippery fingertips caused her desire to grow exponentially. "That's a technicality and you know it."

"Maybe." Ally slipped the tip of her tongue into Morgan's ear and pressed her body closer against Morgan's back, grinding lasciviously. Her hand slid lower. "All I know is I can't keep my hands off you."

"Oh, dear God!" Morgan threw her head back as Ally entered her. Morgan reached for the stability of the shower wall, laying her palms flat to the tiles.

"It's okay. I've got you." Ally held onto Morgan tightly when her hands kept slipping, unable to gain purchase on the polished surface.

Yes. You've got me. Morgan thrust more urgently against Ally's hand. So quickly the first waves of her orgasm approached. She closed her eyes tighter as sensation focused and then spilled to all points of her body. The explosion of energy came with a rush of emotion so strong that her cry of pleasure was accompanied by a choked declaration of love. And then, totally unexpectedly, tears rolled down her cheeks. "Ally . . ." She turned around in her arms. "I love you." She took Ally's face into her hands, punctuating each declaration with a kiss. "I love you. I love you. I love you."

Morgan laughed through her tears in pure joy when the words were repeated back to her, and under the warm spray of the shower they kissed and kissed again.

Kitty rang at ten past eight. "Where are you?" she demanded.

Morgan rolled her eyes at Ally, pointing to her phone and mouthing *Kitty*. "I'm just stepping out of the elevator."

It was true. By some miracle they had managed to finish their shared shower, get dressed and still have enough time for long good-byes in the privacy of Morgan's room. All without running too grossly over schedule. Of course, their lovemaking had been rushed, but still, Morgan was impressed with their efficiency.

Once outside the hotel Morgan pointed to the other side of the street. Mark and Nick were loading their gear into the back of a gleaming silver four-wheel drive. "There they are."

"I'll leave you here?" Ally tugged on the short sleeve of Morgan's T-shirt, bringing her to a halt.

"Don't you want to come and say hi?"

Ally shook her head, looking down to the ground.

"You've time for a quick hello," Morgan encouraged. "You said yourself you had a good hour before you had to leave for the airport. Mark will be disappointed if he finds out you were twenty feet away and didn't stop to talk to him."

"I know. It's not that." Ally shuffled her feet. When she looked up and met Morgan's gaze her expression was uncertain. "It's just . . ." She hesitated and scratched her head. "Won't they all think it a bit strange me being here at this time of the morning?"

A light switch turned on in Morgan's mind. Ally already knew she was out to all the crew. So she knew that they'd all know—or at least assume—the reason behind her early-morning presence. "Oh, honey. Don't worry. They like you and they certainly won't judge you."

"Even Kitty?"

"Kitty's different." Morgan tugged at the waist of Ally's shirt, encouraging her to cross the street, for the first time maligning her producer to someone other than Nick and Mark. "She disapproves of everyone and everything. None of us pays any attention to what she thinks, so neither should you."

In another five minutes Morgan was feeling the first sharp pangs of abandonment. She stood by the open door of the four-wheel drive, watching Ally walk down the street. Mark, who was puffing madly before getting into the nonsmoking vehicle, sidled up to her.

"How's it going?" he asked casually.

Morgan sighed. "I miss her already."

"It's not for long. Five days and we'll be back home."

"I know." Morgan sighed again. She turned to Mark when Ally rounded the corner and disappeared from view. "She's the one, Mark. She's it."

Mark took a deep, thoughtful drag on his cigarette before replying. "So does that mean from now on you won't be abandoning me every chance you get to go chasing after some tail?" When Morgan nodded in agreement he grinned. "I *knew* I liked that woman!" He threw his cigarette to the curb and stamped it out. "The drinks are on me tonight, Mogs."

By the end of the day Morgan was exhausted. "Not for me, thanks." She waved away Mark's offer of another drink. She set aside her empty glass and stood up from the too-soft club chair in the hotel bar. She stretched and yawned. "I'm sorry, but I can hardly keep my eyes open."

"But it's only just gone nine," Mark protested.

"I need an early night," Morgan insisted. "I had a late one yesterday."

"You're a pain in the ass, Morgan Silverstone."

"I know," Morgan agreed, happy to see that Mark accompanied his insult with a crooked grin. He wasn't *too* pissed off at her. "But I can't help it. I'm in love, remember."

Back in her room, Morgan made her preparations for the night. She also packed her suitcase. In the morning they were flying to Porto in Portugal. They'd fly out of Lisbon on Friday night, returning to Spain, this time for a quick visit to Seville, a city renowned for flamenco and bullfighting. Luckily they were there to film the former and not the latter. From there they were homeward bound, scheduled to arrive in Sydney midafternoon on Monday. Morgan smiled a little to herself, wondering what Ally would think when she saw her Monday appointments. She hadn't told her she'd set up an official meeting at her offices, deciding to leave her to find that out for herself.

Morgan slipped between the covers, resting one elbow on her pillow as she navigated for the umpteenth time to the single SMS Ally had sent her today. It had been sent from Milan, before she embarked on the second leg of her journey. "Boarding 4 Singapore. Am guessing ur bobbing around in ur kayak right now. Miss u. I love u. A." Morgan had indeed been bobbing in her kayak when the message arrived. Upside down, actually. She'd lost concentration, lost her paddling rhythm and lost her balance. Totally soaked, and with Mark and Nick laughing at her uproariously, she'd returned to shore to find the message waiting. It was too late to ring—Ally's plane would have left by then—so sent her a return SMS that she'd receive when she arrived in Singapore. "Am wet. Fell in the drink cos was thinking of you. Miss u. I love u. Speak soon. M."

Morgan read Ally's SMS once more before turning her phone off. Long ago she'd learned that no one, herself included, could keep up with what time zone she was in. To avoid friends or colleagues unwittingly calling her at all hours of her night she turned her phone off altogether, opting instead to set the teeny digital alarm clock that she carried with her. Tonight she set it to ring at two thirty a.m. By her calculations, at that time Ally should be one hour into her three-hour Singapore stopover. She wouldn't be expecting Morgan to call, assuming she'd be fast asleep. It would be a nice little surprise.

Morgan fell asleep smiling at the thought of spending the rest of her days giving Ally nice little surprises.

She had been deeply asleep and dreaming when a loud jangling woke her. Groggily she reached for her teeny alarm. "Wha . . . ?" The noise didn't stop when she pressed the "off" button. It took her a good few seconds to realize it wasn't her alarm at all. It was the room phone. "Hello?" she said sleepily, groping in the dark for the light switch. She blinked rapidly at the sudden glare and rubbed her eyes. They felt grainy with fatigue.

"Morgan. It's Kitty."

Morgan groaned. She picked up her teeny alarm and squinted at it. "It's midnight. What do you want?"

"I need to see you in my room, right now."

"It's midnight," Morgan repeated.

"Right *now*," Kitty insisted, her voice gaining her infamous "don't argue with me" tone.

Morgan argued anyway. "Can't it wait until morning? I'm dead tired."

"No, it can't. *Now*, Morgan." And she hung up.

Morgan threw herself into her pillow and stared at the ceiling, cursing Kitty and wondering what she was having a conniption over at this time of night. Ally, maybe? She'd thrown Morgan a tight-lipped glare this morning when she and Ally arrived together outside the hotel. But surprisingly, she hadn't said a word about it all day, maybe still clinging onto the belief that Ally was straight and partnered with a respectable *male* architect. But now . . . maybe she'd put the pieces together and was champing at the bit to remind Morgan how stupid she was to be playing with Australian fire. If that was the case, then she'd just have to tell her that Ally was different, that she was no one-night fling. That she was "the one." She'd tell Kitty that she and

224

Ally had already agreed on a discreet relationship. And that her days of casual dalliances were over. That fact alone should make Kitty happy. God knew, the thought made her happy enough.

Morgan threw the covers back and pulled on the jeans and T-shirt she'd laid out for the next morning.

"Okay, Kitty." She folded her arms when face-to-face with her producer. "I'm here. What's so important it couldn't wait?"

Kitty grabbed her by the arm and pulled her inside. "You're in deep shit, Morgan Silverstone."

CHAPTER FIFTEEN

Morgan had heard Kitty talk about deep shit on more than one occasion. She heard it when she and the rest of the crew were being lectured on making it to the airport on time; she heard it when she and Mark were about to hit the town and they were being warned to behave themselves; and she heard it when Kitty was present to witness Morgan in the process of chatting up—or being chatted up by—a potential bed companion. In all cases, however, Kitty said, "You *will be* in deep shit," and talked of some future catastrophe that may occur as a result of her behavior. This was the first time Kitty had said, "You *are* in deep shit."

The distinction stopped Morgan in her tracks. Obviously Ally wasn't her immediate concern. If she was, then she'd be getting the future-shit lecture. "What are you talking about?" she asked.

"I'm talking about that French floozy of yours."

"Marie?"

Kitty nodded somberly. "You remember that phone call you made to her on the train?"

"Yes."

"Well, she recorded it."

"What?" Stunned, Morgan sat down heavily on Kitty's bed. The conversation had been recorded? *Jesus.* She thought back to what had been said and realized that Marie now had a hold of the "undeniable proof" of her lesbianism that she had originally claimed. "And so she's back in contact wanting money again?"

"Unfortunately, no." Kitty took a step to the little table upon which her laptop sat. She pressed a key to reactivate the screen. "She didn't bother keeping us in the loop this time." She motioned Morgan over. "Look . . ."

Kitty remained quiet long enough for Morgan to sit in front of the computer screen and absorb the contents. She resumed talking as Morgan refocused on the headline of the scanned article: *She Used Me and Then She Threw Me Away.* Apparently Joseph, the executive producer of their show, had called Kitty nearly a half-hour previous, after repeatedly trying to get through to Morgan on her mobile phone. On arriving at work he'd been handed the just-released weekly edition of a nationwide tabloid by a representative from one of the network executives, whose message was an urgent "please explain."

He'd quickly scanned the article and whisked it off in an e-mail to Kitty. And they'd been in almost constant phone contact since. Morgan balked at what might have been said between the pair, but for the moment she was more intent on reading the article for the second time.

Star of leading travel show spends a night of passion with young backpacker and then sends her packing, announced the subheading.

"I was just sitting in the train minding my own business . . ." began a quote from Marie as she described the circumstances of their meeting. The way it was written made it sound as if

227

Morgan had targeted Marie for her amorous intentions and the "barely legal" traveler had little choice in the matter, being "persuaded" to join Morgan in her compartment.

"Jesus Christ!" Morgan exclaimed as time and again the words she used in her phone conversation with Marie were either twisted or taken out of context. To read the article one would think she was a sexual predator, using her influence and position to satisfy her "secret lesbian tendencies." She'd been quoted as threatening Marie with her "powerful contacts" if she dared to tell anyone of their interlude and of trying to "buy" Marie's silence by paying for her Sydney accommodations. The writer of the article was seemingly incredulous that Morgan, who "fetches one of the highest salaries in Australian television history," offered Marie nothing more than hostel accommodation. Of course no mention was made that she'd actually been put in a very comfortable four-star hotel right on the doorstep of Circular Quay. The article concluded by telling how Morgan refused to see Marie again, despite her attempts.

"I feel totally used," Marie was quoted as saying. "And I'm only going public with this because I don't want other young women to fall into the same trap that I did."

Accompanying the article was a photo of Marie, looking all innocent and downcast, hands in her pockets, her backpack beside her on the ground. Next to that was a file photo of Morgan, taken at this year's Logies awards. She wasn't looking into the camera but rather smiling at the other woman in the picture—one of the starlets in a popular long-running series. Morgan had her arm draped around the starlet's shoulder, and the starlet, who Morgan remembered as almost at the stage of being falling-down drunk, had a distinct "what's happening?" expression. In the context of this article, the image screamed "lecherous lesbian."

What didn't appear in the article was any reference to Morgan's side of the story. There was just a single sentence in the very last paragraph that read, "Morgan and her agent were unavailable for comment."

"Bastards," Morgan muttered under her breath. If the reporter who wrote the story had actually tried to contact either herself or her agent, then he or she hadn't tried very hard. Fair enough, she was deliberately difficult to get hold of, especially while on location, but it didn't take a super sleuth to seek out and find her agent. And if Michael *had* been contacted and questioned then he would have definitely told her about it.

She didn't want to look at the article anymore, but she couldn't help it. Like most all of her counterparts, she'd suffered at the hands of the media, having exaggerations and untruths printed at her expense. And, like most of her counterparts, she'd grinned and borne the publicity, acknowledging, for good or for ill, that the media machine was an unavoidable aspect of her job. But never before had she been targeted like this. With each word she read and reread came an increasing knowledge that she could be witnessing her career going down the toilet.

Kitty's voice intruded on her thoughts. "I don't know what the little tramp got paid for this, but I hope she thinks it's worth it."

Morgan turned to look at her producer. "Go on, Kitty," she said flatly. "Say it."

Kitty folded her arms and peered at Morgan over the rim of her spectacles. "Say what?"

"I told you so."

Kitty's continued gaze was steady, but Morgan was almost sure she saw her eyes soften for just a moment. Then they hardened again and Kitty said brusquely, "What's the point? What's done is done. Now we just have to do what we can to salvage the situation." Her mobile was sitting next to her laptop. She reached around Morgan to pick it up then started pacing across the floor. "Joseph's got his P.A. arranging your flights back to Sydney so she should be calling me soon. But in the meantime we should—"

"Hang on," Morgan interrupted, confused. "What do you mean my flights back to Sydney? When?"

"Hopefully first thing in the morning."

"But Portugal . . . ?"

"Morgan." Kitty paced back across the room, stopping to stand directly beside her. "Portugal will have to wait for another time. *If* there's another time." She sighed heavily. "They're thinking of pulling your segments from this week's show and getting one of the other presenters—Troy, I think—to reshoot the lead-ins you did last week."

"They're pulling me?" Morgan asked faintly.

Kitty shook her head. "They haven't decided exactly what to do yet. But they're making arrangements in case they do."

Kitty went on to describe what had been happening on the other side of the planet in the few short hours since the tabloid had hit the newsstands. The phone lines at the network had been running hot, some in support of Morgan, others enraged that anyone practicing such perversions be allowed on TV. The staff manning the phones had been instructed to give no more information than a "we're looking into it and until we have we're making no comment," but that hadn't stopped two radio stations from picking up on the story, or for reporters from all manner of publications to come crawling out of the woodwork, looking for more details, new angles, new dirt.

Kitty pointed to her laptop. "I can almost certainly guarantee you're the subject of lots of cyberspace discussion too."

"But I'm just . . ." Morgan's head was spinning at the level of attention this was getting. "All I do is present a travel show."

Kitty harrumphed. "Save the false modesty, Morgan. You're up there with Vegemite and Tim Tams. The Australian public has been watching you week after week for years. They care about you. A lot of them *idolize* you. So when something like this breaks, it breaks big. Remember that cricketer whose text mes-

230

sages were intercepted?"

Who could forget. The story of the married Australian fast bowler who'd been caught sending numerous X-rated SMSes to his mistress had been in the news for weeks. Australians were mad on their sports and took it—and their sports stars—very seriously. So seriously that the cricketer's off-field antics actually bounced other, much more newsworthy items right off the front page. But he'd survived the onslaught. After publicly apologizing to his wife . . . Morgan balked again. Surely the network wasn't expecting her to make a public apology to Marie?

Kitty snorted derisively when hearing this theory. "Hardly! Like I said, they don't really know what they want to do yet. But they do want to speak to you—in person—so that's why we're getting you back home as soon as possible. And hopefully, since the network's been actively spreading the word that you're over-seas and not due to return until Monday, you won't be trampled by reporters when you arrive at the airport." Kitty jumped slightly as the phone she still held in her hand began to ring. She looked at the display. "It's Becky."

Shit. Shit. Shit. Morgan set her elbows on the table and rubbed at her temples while she listened to Kitty speak to Joseph's personal assistant. She stared dismally at the computer screen. *What a difference a day makes.* To think that this time last night she'd been in a state of euphoria and now . . .

Ally! Morgan's thoughts leapt to her for the first time since being hit with the news. She had to talk to her, to warn her of what she'd arrive home to. Thank goodness there was nothing to connect them, so she would at least be saved the scrutiny of the nation. And thank goodness Morgan had already given Ally her side of the Marie story so it wouldn't come as a complete sur-prise. Morgan wasn't worried that Ally would actually believe this piece of journalistic trash, but who knew what else would be dragged out—or made up—about her. If enough mud about Morgan was thrown in Ally's direction, maybe some of it would stick . . .

Morgan leapt from her chair.

Kitty put her hand over her phone and demanded, "Where are you going?"

Morgan's standby excuse came in handy yet again. "My tummy's upset. I need the toilet." She dashed out of Kitty's room before she could offer the use of her own facilities.

Too late, she realized she was too early. Ally was still well over an hour away from arriving in Singapore. Morgan stamped her feet in frustration as she was switched to voice mail. She hung up and closed her eyes, gathering her thoughts, trying to think of a text message that would prompt Ally to call her with urgency, without unduly worrying her. "Pls call me as soon as u get this. It doesn't matter the time. Am awake here n thinking of u."

She pressed the key to send her message. Then she checked her own.

"Jesus." She muttered as she retrieved her missed calls. There were dozens. Four were from her agent, in each his voice getting more high-pitched and excited. Three were from her executive producer and another two from his P.A. There were also messages from a good number of her friends. And from her mum. From Lucas. From Audrey. It seemed just about everyone who knew her number suddenly wanted to speak to her.

Morgan's stomach turned into a tight knot. Kitty had been right. She really was in deep shit.

Ally sat in the transit lounge at Singapore airport, phone held to her ear, aghast at what she was hearing. "They're pulling you off the air?"

"They haven't actually decided on that yet, but apparently it's in the cards. I guess the network figures that maybe the less I'm seen, the quicker people will forget. You know, the short memory of the public and all that."

Ally's heart pulled at Morgan's too-bright tone. She knew it was purely for her sake, this trying to pretend the situation less than it actually was. But if the network was thinking of pulling her, even temporarily, obviously things were bad. "Morgan, I'm so sorry. What can I do?"

Morgan gave a long, drawn breath before she replied. "Just don't believe everything you read or hear."

"There's a reason I don't buy the tabloids," Ally said firmly. "If I wanted to read a piece of fiction, I'd pick up a book."

"Not all of it's fiction, Ally. That's the problem. They wrap their crap in enough truth to make it believable."

"Just as well I've got you then, to tell me which bits are the wrapping and what's just filling." Ally's heart skipped at the little pleased noise that came through the telephone. "But I actually meant, what can I *do* for you?"

The reply was immediate and determined. "Nothing, baby. I don't want you involved in this."

"But I *am* involved. I'm involved with you."

"No one knows that." Morgan hesitated for just a moment. "And I want to keep it that way."

"But—"

"Please just trust me on this," Morgan interrupted, her voice low. "I love you, Ally. All I need is for you to be there for me. I'll handle the rest."

"Can I at least be there for you when you arrive?" Ally clung tightly onto her phone, wishing she was already beside Morgan instead of having this conversation in the midst of strangers in one of the busiest airports in the world. But at least she didn't have to wait until Monday to see her. She was now arriving late Friday afternoon, flying back via London and Dubai.

"Baby, I've got a meeting with the network immediately after I arrive."

"I'll drive you there," Ally said immediately.

"My agent has already insisted he drive me," Morgan said

softly, apologetically. "He wants to talk to me before I speak to the bigwigs. But afterward . . . if it's not too late . . ."

"It doesn't matter how late it is. I want to see you."

"I can't wait to see you, either. I love you, Ally."

"I love you, too."

Ally disconnected from the call feeling quite bereft. This was definitely not what she'd been expecting when she'd found Morgan's SMS waiting for her on arrival at Singapore.

Just as she had on countless occasions during her long journey so far, she closed her eyes and concentrated on each glorious moment she had spent with Morgan in Barcelona. In the plane such thoughts had helped take her mind off the fact she was tens of thousands of feet above the ground, and combined with her preflight sleeping tablet and a shot of vodka, she'd spent at least a small portion of the trip in a warm and happy buzz. Now, however, even calling forth the most erotic image of Morgan could not lift her spirits.

Ally felt so bad for Morgan and what she must be going through, that she could almost cry. She walked the long corridors of the transit terminal, up and down, up and down, trying to figure out something she could do to help her out of this mess. Not a single thing came to mind. All she could do was be there with her love and her support. More to the point, she would be there—not just in the background—but unseen.

Which was exactly what she'd agreed to do, even before this disaster occurred.

For the first time Ally seriously considered the implications of the closet that she'd agreed to live in with Morgan. Sure, it had its upsides; not having to immediately think about the reactions of friends, family and colleagues to her sudden "change in lifestyle" was definitely one of them. But on the reverse of that, neither could she share with them her newfound joy. Ally wanted to shout her love from the rooftops. But instead she'd have to whisper it in secret.

Of course, Ally thought as she continued to pace the corridors, this whole catastrophe may just blow Morgan's closet to smithereens. Unless it was decided that she deny all the claims made against her—and given the existence of the recorded conversation Ally didn't see how that could be easily done—Morgan would be effectively outed. In that case, there would be no further need to keep their relationship a secret.

Ally smiled a little, imagining Morgan turning up at her offices on her days off and them striding out together for lunch at a restaurant where they would openly hold hands.

Then her smile faded at the edges. How could she be thinking of her own selfish desires at a time like this? From what Morgan had described, the article had next to painted her as some sort of sexual predator with a predilection for the young girls. Being able to hold hands in public was a miserly trade-off for suffering that kind of rumor.

That final thought took her to outside a large newsagent. Ally hurried inside and scoured the range of international publications for the tabloid in question. It wasn't there. She sighed. She'd have to wait until she got to Australia to pick up a copy.

"Jesus Christ," she muttered under her breath when she did finally get to read the article. She was reading it while waiting in the taxi queue at Sydney airport, having bought the tabloid at the first newsagent she found open after leaving immigration. The further she read, the more infuriated she became. The Morgan described in the article was not the Morgan she knew. Nowhere close.

When she was the next up for a taxi Ally tore the article from the page and handed the rest of the publication to the man behind her in the queue. He was so surprised at the offering that he accepted it.

Ally stepped into the taxi, gave her address and rode the entire distance with her chin resting on her fist, the suburbs of Sydney passing in a blur as she tried to focus her thoughts. But she was just too damn tired. She'd really had little to no sleep for the past forty-eight hours and hadn't slept a wink during the seven or so hours of her flight from Singapore to Sydney. The flight had been turbulent and so most of it had been spent in frozen terror. The rest of it had been spent turning Morgan's situation over and over in her mind.

It was nearly midnight when she stepped gratefully out of the taxi and headed wearily toward the entrance of her apartment block, dragging her suitcase behind her. With each step, each sleepless hour caught up with her a little more and she was tired to the point of exhaustion, so much so that the light shining from her lounge room window on the third floor did not register.

That didn't happen until she unlocked her front door. Fear clutched at her stomach. Had she disturbed a prowler? She stood, frozen with fright, as a shadow moved across the hallway floor.

"James!" She exhaled in pure relief when his familiar figure appeared in the doorway leading to the lounge. Relief just as quickly turned to annoyance. "What are you doing here?"

He took one step closer. "I came to get my things."

"At midnight?" Ally frowned. She'd called him the night before she left for Spain, advising him of her unexpected trip and suggesting it might a good idea if he came to collect his belongings while she was gone. "You've had nearly a week to do that, yet you choose to do it now?"

James nodded toward her bedroom door. "And I brought all yours. They're in there."

"Thank you." Ally rubbed at one of her temples. "But I'm really tired and I've got a big day at work tomorrow. So I'd like to go straight to bed. *Alone*," she added, in case James entertained any ideas she was extending an invitation.

"Did you hear the news about your little friend?"

"Pardon?"

James took another step closer to her. "Your friend. Morgan."

He reached inside his jacket and pulled out a folded sheet of newspaper. "This was in today's news."

Ally controlled herself from snatching what she already knew to be the tabloid article. Instead she calmly took the paper from his hand and opened it slowly, scanning it as if seeing it for the first time.

She handed it back. "This is rubbish, James. And since when did you start reading the tabloids?"

"I don't," James said evenly. "Phil rang me this morning. Barbara had seen the article and thought I might be interested . . . since you bought Morgan at auction just the other week."

Ally could feel the blush of guilt creep up her neck. "I fail to see the connection—"

"Neither did I." James opened out the paper again and pointed to the paragraph that gave details of the train—right down to the date—where Morgan met Marie. "Until I saw this. This is the same train you were on, is it not?"

Ally bit on her lip. Then she straightened her shoulders and said airily, "So she was on the same train as me. So what?"

James rubbed at the stubble of his day-old beard. "And you didn't think of mentioning that to me at some stage? Like maybe *before* you paid five thousand dollars for a bit of her time?"

Ally was at a loss for an explanation, so she pounced on the money issue. "Will you quit it with the five-thousand-dollar thing! I told you . . . it's my money. I can do what I like with it!"

James looked at her long and hard. "Is she the woman you kissed?"

Ally's mouth went dry. Judging from his expression, he knew. Or at least he *thought* he knew. She turned back to the front door, not only to grab at the handle, but to avoid having to hold his accusing gaze. "I'm through with this conversation. Please leave."

Just as with all the other times Ally had thrown him out of her apartment, he left without further argument. But he did turn around in the moment before Ally closed the door. "Good-bye, Alison."

It was said with finality. Ally held the door open for a moment longer than she needed, watching him walk toward the stairwell, knowing it was probably the last she'd see or hear of him. She closed the door quietly, getting the distinct feeling she was also shutting the door on her old life.

Ally was not exactly sure how she felt about that. And right now she was just too damn tired to figure it out. She left her suitcase where it was and put herself to bed.

CHAPTER SIXTEEN

Morgan wished she'd been able to shower before her meeting. It certainly would have helped boost her confidence a bit. That had been well and truly rattled by the presence of reporters at the airport. They were waiting for her, so word must have leaked out about her altered travel plans.

"Ready?" Michael, her agent, asked when she emerged from the bathroom located near the conference room where she was to meet her fate.

"Ready as I'll ever be to face a firing squad." She smiled wanly. She'd had a quick freshen-up and pulled on a clean but slightly crumpled shirt that she'd packed into her cabin bag. But her confidence was still at a low, low ebb.

Michael placed his hand at the small of her back and steered her toward the large double doors. "Stick to your guns and you'll be fine."

"You'll back me up?" Morgan asked him for the fifth time since they'd met at the airport and discussed how they were going to proceed.

"Of course," Michael said, applying a little more pressure with his hand. "All the way."

They entered the conference room to find the gathering a near replica from when her last contract had been signed. Around the table sat Joseph, her executive producer; Maxwell and Sophie, two network directors; Claude, from legal; and Carlo, from public relations. The circumstances of this meeting had set their expressions in a completely different manner to that of the contract signing.

Morgan, donned in her day-old jeans and crumpled shirt and feeling the grit and grime of long-haul travel on her skin, acknowledged their guarded greetings and took a seat, preparing herself for the onslaught.

The very first question—posed by Maxwell as he pushed an enlarged computer-printed version of the article across the table toward her—was totally unexpected. "Is there any truth in this?" he asked.

It was unexpected because Joseph had already asked her exactly the same thing when he spoke to her by phone in Barcelona. She'd have thought he would have relayed the reply to his superiors by now. Maybe he had and Maxwell just wanted to hear it from her own mouth. Or maybe Joseph hadn't yet told him, giving her a last opportunity to change her mind. She hadn't. Against Kitty's and Joseph's—but thankfully not Michael's—advice, she had decided it was high time she stood up and be counted.

As she'd told Michael and Kitty and Joseph, she was sick of lying, sick of hiding, sick of denying who she was. She'd declare herself today and ride out the consequences, whatever they might be. What she hadn't told them about was Ally. Seeing no advantage to dragging Ally with her through the media-slung mud, she'd decided to keep their relationship a secret, at least until the dust settled and the public's interest turned in a different direction. Only three people knew of Ally's existence: Kitty, Mark and Nick. Only Mark knew of Ally's importance to her.

"There is some truth to it," she said slowly, trying very hard to maintain eye contact with Maxwell. "I *am* a lesbian and I *did* sleep with Marie. But all the details around those two facts have been twisted and embellished to such an extent they bear no resemblance to what actually happened."

Morgan held her breath as she waited for Maxwell's response. He leaned forward in his seat, clasped his hands together on the desk and looked at her intently. "Who else have you told this to?"

"My producer, Kitty Bergen. To Joseph"—Morgan nodded to her executive producer and then to Michael—"and to my agent, Michael Potter."

"That's it?"

Morgan held her gaze steady. "That's it."

Maxwell glanced to director Sophie and legal Claude, who both nodded slightly, as if confirming some predetermined agreement. Then he fixed his attention on Morgan again. "We'll issue a statement tomorrow saying you have denied everything. And, just to show how seriously you're taking these accusations, you'll initiate legal proceedings against the company who produces this rag."

Morgan's mouth fell open. "But I don't see how . . . what about the recording of the conversation? That's physical evidence. I can't deny that, even if I wanted to."

Claude shrugged. "We can get proof it's been faked."

"No," Morgan said firmly, wondering blackly just how this "proof" would be obtained. "I won't do it."

"You've hidden it all these years," Sophie interjected. "What's the problem now?"

"The problem now"—Morgan looked in turn to each person

around the table—"is that while I may have hidden my sexuality, I never outright denied it. Now the proof is out there and I can't take it back. In fact I *refuse* to take it back. I'll make whatever statements are necessary to expose the article for the rubbish it is. But I won't tell the world I'm not a lesbian."

"You don't have any choice," Maxwell said gravely.

It was at this point Michael cleared his throat. "Err, excuse me. But I think Morgan does have a choice here." He pulled a copy of her contract from his briefcase. "I've been over this with a fine-toothed comb, and nowhere does it state you have control over what she does in her private life."

Claude began flipping pages of his copy of Morgan's contract. Nearly an hour later, after he had stopped flipping pages because there were no more left to flip, it was acknowledged that Michael was "technically" right. Like it or not, they couldn't dictate what Morgan did outside business hours.

It was then that Sophie, who Morgan was fast pinning as homophobic, came up with the brilliant idea that since she'd been on location when this incident occurred it wasn't techni- cally "private life" time. It was company time. This prompted everyone to start talking at once, debating where the workday ended while on location. *If* it ended at all. To Morgan's dismay there was general agreement that—since the network paid for everything except their personal expenses while they were away—they were constantly on company time and should be acting in an appropriate manner. Sophie even spouted Kitty's favorite line: "We must keep the reputation of the network intact."

"Oh, puh-leese!" Michael interjected with a roll of his eyes. "If that's the case then half your people should have their con- tracts canceled just from their behaviour at the last Logies after- party." He pointedly tapped the picture of the extremely drunk starlet that had accompanied the tabloid article. "If I'm not mis- taken this underage little angel still wanders up and down these

242

hallowed corridors. Does she not?"

No one said a word.

Michael directed his next question to Maxwell. "Just exactly what action do you plan to take if Morgan refuses to participate? You can't revoke her contract for refusing to lie. And neither can you revoke it because she's gay. Everyone here *knows* that's illegal." Before Maxwell could reply, Michael continued, "And it may also be a very, very bad idea from a P.R. perspective."

"Carlo . . . ?" Maxwell turned to the representative from the public relations department. "What's the latest take?"

Carlo, who Morgan had known and liked for the three and a bit years he'd been with the network, scratched nervously at the back of his scalp. If Morgan didn't know better she'd interpret the action as portent to bad news. But she did know better.

She practiced deep-breathing before every performance. Carlo scratched himself.

He flashed a brilliant smile around the table and a covert wink in her direction.

For the first time since the meeting started she allowed herself to relax a little. Obviously, it wasn't all bad news.

"The vast majority of calls taken since yesterday have been outstandingly in Morgan's favor," he said as rose and took a step behind him to the panel of controls on the wall. He dimmed the lights a little and then returned to his seat, where he pressed a single key on his laptop. The large screen at the narrow end of the conference room was suddenly lit with figures and graphs. "As you can see, the number of calls to the network has increased by over six hundred percent of normal. Of this increase ninety-eight percent were in direct relation to Morgan. And of these"— he paused and smiled in Morgan's direction—"over *eighty-nine percent* have been in her support."

Carlo's expression sobered and again he looked in turn to each person around the table.

"As you are all no doubt aware, word quickly got out that

Morgan's presence on *Bonnes Vacances* is currently in question. These are some of the reactions we received." He pressed a key and the screen changed. Text this time. Some caller comments.

Morgan leaned forward, reading the screen faster than Carlo read it out loud. "Keep Morgan on the air. My Friday nights would be ruined without her." From Steven, in Ringwood, Victoria.

"So what if Morgan is gay. She still gives the best travel advice. And she's easy to look at too." From Tim, in Esperence, Western Australia.

"Eight years I've been watching *Bonnes Vacances*. Take Morgan away and I'll never watch it again. You go, girl!" From Jenny in Sydney, New South Wales.

"Morgan, bless her, is one of the kindest women I have ever had the good grace to meet. She is the main reason *Bonnes Vacances* is such a wonderful show and I would be proud to call her my daughter." From Marge, in the Adelaide Hills, South Australia.

Morgan blinked. Surely that couldn't be *the* Marge? From the train.

Carlo scratched his chin before he read out loud the comment from Marge. "This woman insisted that she traveled on the same train as Morgan—a fact we have since verified through the train company. She was very . . . verbose . . . in her praise, telling us that Morgan's conduct was exemplary"—he scratched again, this time near his temple—"and that she couldn't do enough to help out a friend and fellow traveler of hers who was in a bit of strife."

Jesus. Morgan felt her insides tie into a tight knot. *Please, please, please don't mention that I offered Ally to bunk in with me.*

Carlo gave her the merest of glances and a teeny eyebrow raise, then he pressed a key and the screen changed to a new set of positive caller comments. Morgan exhaled in relief. Carlo was on her side. And, like the public relations specialist he was, he focused on the positives. He didn't deny the existence of the negatives; he just didn't give them any undue attention. In actual fact, he probably would not have given them any attention at all, had Sophie not directly asked about negative feedback from the viewers.

Morgan mentally prepared herself for a dose of bigotry and hatred while Carlo rustled through a sheaf of papers. From his comments while he continued to sort through his papers, it seemed that the percentage of people against her was relatively small.

Small maybe, but extremely vocal in their opposition. Morgan cringed when Carlo began to read an excerpt from one such call.

"Miss Silverstone should be removed immediately and permanently from our screens," he quoted a woman who hailed from the same area as Marge. "It's the promotion of this type of perversity that is the root of all the problems in our society."

"Stop it right here." Maxwell held up his hand to Carlo. Then he waved it in the direction of the screen. "I think we've seen enough from the public. Obviously their views are skewed"—he peered at Morgan—"in your favor. But there are other issues at hand here."

"What could be a bigger issue than the opinion of your viewers?" asked Michael.

Maxwell stared for a moment at Michael, a superior look on his face. He obviously thought it a stupid question. "There's the small matter of our advertisers . . ."

Oh, hell. Morgan inwardly cringed. *Here we go. Money.*

Worse yet, Sophie was the director in charge of advertising and sponsorship. Morgan watched her rustle through the sheaf of papers that sat in front of her. And her hopes struck bottom with Sophie's expression before she commenced on her report. It was smug and self-satisfied.

Things were no longer looking so good.

Ally was unable to sit still. She moved from the couch to her drafting table, wondering at the possibility of concentrating on some work, just to take her mind off this awful waiting.

It seemed forever since she'd received a call from Morgan advising her plane had landed.

"Good luck," Ally had said softly, matching Morgan's hushed tone.

"Thanks, baby," Morgan replied. "I'll speak to you as soon as my meeting finishes."

That call had been over four hours ago. What on earth could they have to talk about for all this time?

Although, Ally thought as she moved away from her drafting table again, if they were picking through everything that had been written or said since the tabloid hit the newsstands, then they could be at it well into the night.

Ally sat at her dining table, where she'd strewn copies of every daily paper she'd found during her out-of-office excursion to buy a lunch of takeaway Japanese. Of these, at least half had made mention of the tabloid article. To what end, Ally wasn't sure, since they had nothing new to report, except to say the network had issued a firm "no comment" and that the star herself was not available to confirm or deny the story, being on location "somewhere in Europe."

At least she won't get pounced on by the media when she arrives, Ally had thought as she read the reports while picking at her box of sashimi.

Once home and flicking from channel to channel trying to catch every one of the evening television news reports, she realized her assumption had been premature. A news presenter announced, "Troubled star of *Bonnes Vacances* Morgan Silverstone is back on Australian soil this evening . . ." The image of the presenter disappeared to be replaced by footage

246

shot at the airport. Morgan, wearing dark glasses and with her head down, was pushing silently through a mass of reporters, all sticking their microphones in her face, shouting questions at her.

Ally's heart went out to her. She was already stressed enough as it was, without having to suffer a mob of rabid reporters. And how on earth did the media find out, not just that she was arriving early, but on which airline and at what time?

All the network channels—with the exception of Morgan's own—made mention of her return to Australia. And all speculated over her "immediate future," one even mentioning "the star, rumored to be next year's presenter at the Logies" was also "rumored to be at threat of being dropped from her show."

"Where do they get this stuff from?" Ally wondered out loud as she shifted her attention from television screen to computer screen, firing up her laptop and Googling "Morgan Silverstone."

"My God," she exclaimed as she started delving into the results. Kitty had not been exaggerating Morgan's popularity. Whole sites were dedicated to her, created by fans who'd taken their Morgan-worship to the extreme. They had picture galleries and video clips, Morgan message boards and downloadable screensavers. Ally was currently most interested in the message boards. As expected, all were humming with new activity. The majority of the comments were highly positive, the participants declaring their continued devotion and announcing dire consequences for the network ratings if they dared pull Morgan from their TVs. Others had taken great umbrage at the possibility that their idol was a lesbian, with one particularly prolific messenger posting comment after comment about the evils of homosexuality. He or she made constant reference to an episode of *Bonnes Vacances* aired a few weeks prior, one that had featured family-friendly holidays. Morgan's segment had focused on a five-star camping ground where she was filmed going down a kid-sized waterslide, the final person in a chain of laughing, excited children. "Those types of people should be kept as far away from our future generation as possible," the post announced. Ally noted with satisfaction that the messenger was shot down in flames by others making subsequent posts, but still she was both surprised and saddened to discover that such rampant homophobia still existed.

That discovery prompted Ally to temporarily shift her attention from Morgan to herself. Were any of her friends, family or acquaintances homophobic, she wondered? And would their opinion of her change from one moment to the next because she announced herself as a lesbian? Offhand she couldn't think of anyone who might be that narrow-minded, but maybe she was just being naïve.

"Too bad for them if they do," Ally said resolutely as she rose from her computer. "If they can't see I'm exactly the same person I was before they knew, then that's their problem."

Still, as she settled back in front of the television to see if the network had prematurely carried out their threat and pulled Morgan from this evening's show, she began to feel worry niggling at the back of her mind. After all, she wasn't *exactly* the same person anymore.

For one, she was rapidly turning into a liar.

She'd lied to Josh about the demise of her mobile phone; she'd lied to James on goodness knew how many occasions since she'd left the train from Kalgoorlie. And today she'd lied to the entire office, both about what she'd done on her last night in Barcelona (early dinner and an early night), as well as throughout the Morgan-related conversation when Kirsty announced at their staff meeting that a woman she hadn't recognized at the time, but who turned out to be Morgan Silverstone ("you know—the one who's all over the news at the moment") had made an appointment to see Ally the following Monday. Ally's surprise at the appointment was genuine, Morgan not having mentioned anything about it to her. But surprise soon turned to anguish when Josh subsequently brought up Ally's purchase at auction and the newspaper photo showing her and Morgan together. Kirsty had already mentioned that Morgan made the appointment based on a friend's recommendation, so Ally thought madly for an explanation to this apparent contradiction.

"Actually," she said, smiling a little nervously. "I recommended myself when we met after the auction. When she discovered what I did for a living she mentioned she was looking to build and so I thought a little self-promotion wouldn't hurt." Ally shrugged and this time her smile was self-effacing. "Probably she decided not to advertise the fact I have a big head."

Her lie worked a treat, everyone laughing and then commencing a debate on just how big Ally's head had become since one of her houses had been featured in *Architectural Digest*. Ally relaxed, grateful she'd gotten away with it, but already thinking to her next lie—the one that would be needed to explain why Morgan wasn't going to proceed with a new house after all.

Then again—Ally rolled her pencil between her fingers as the meeting progressed around her—designing a house for Morgan would provide a very good excuse for her to keep visiting the office. She could be a difficult client who demanded lots of design changes and lots of meetings. Ally entertained this fantasy for a couple of minutes before conceding that designing and building a house was a pretty extreme—and expensive—method of dating.

Stop being so ridiculous! She chided herself angrily. She excused herself from the meeting and stomped to her office to gather what she needed for her site visit. Under normal circumstances, she would never entertain such outrageous thoughts. She wouldn't normally lie to everyone who crossed her path either. Ally stomped back out of her office, plans in hand, and left for her site visit without saying another word to anyone.

To top off her day, her mum called not too long after she got home from work. "How are you, dear?" she asked.

I'm in love, Mum . . . with a woman. I've never been so happy and I can't wait to introduce you to her because I just know you'll love her too. But I've also never felt so frustrated because she's in trouble at the moment and I can't do anything to help her.

"I'm fine, Mum. How are you?"

Right toward the end of the conversation, Ally mentioned she'd split with James. "I realized he wasn't the right one for me," she told her. Apart from saying that she'd loved every minute she'd spent in Barcelona, that was the only complete truth she told in that conversation.

Lies, half-truths and evasions. Ally had hung up from her mum feeling strangely desolate.

The feeling returned now, as Ally recalled their conversation. Then, just as suddenly, her spirits leapt along with her heart. Her mobile was ringing. And it was Morgan.

"How did it go?" she asked without saying hello, desperate to know the outcome of her meeting.

"It was long . . . and difficult." Morgan sounded drained. Ally was not at all surprised. Straight off a long-haul flight and straight into a marathon meeting. Nasty. "I've never been so glad to be home in my life."

"You're already home?" Ally frowned. Morgan had said she would call as soon as the meeting had finished.

"Mmm. Michael drove me home. I didn't want to speak to you in front of him, so I waited until I got back."

"He came to the meeting with you?"

"Yes. He sat in on it. And I'm glad he did since he's much better at arguing the terms of my contract than I am. In fact, he's just better at arguing than I am full-stop."

Ally balked. They were talking contracts? That didn't sound too promising. She wanted to be there, beside Morgan, if there was any bad news to impart. "Honey, don't tell me over the phone. I'm all ready to go, so I can leave for your place straight-away."

250

Morgan drew a long breath. "Baby," she said gently, "I don't think that's a good idea."

"Why not?" Ally frowned.

"Did you see the news tonight, about the reporters at the airport?"

"Yes."

"Well, some of them moved camp to outside my apartment building. Building security keeps moving them on, but they keep coming back. And even from a distance they can see anyone who comes or goes."

"I don't care!" Ally cried. "If they ask me anything I'll just tell them I'm your friend. You are allowed to have *friends*, aren't you?"

"It's not that simple at the moment, baby. Any woman seen in my company is going to be the subject of *intense* public speculation. I don't want that for you."

"Or you don't want it for *you*," Ally blurted, suddenly blinded by tears and too upset to be the caring, supportive lover she'd promised to be. Anyway, how could she be loving and supportive? She wasn't even allowed to be *there*. "This is bullshit!"

She clutched her mobile tightly then threw it across the room.

CHAPTER SEVENTEEN

Morgan jerked her head in fright at the sudden crashing sound that came through her phone. It was over as quickly as it happened. She held her mobile in front of her, staring at it in stunned shock. She put it back to her ear. Nothing. Ally had hung up.

Tears sprang to Morgan's eyes. She should have predicted the presence of reporters at her home from the moment they welcomed her at the airport. But she hadn't, too intent on other, more immediate problems. Like the potential nightmare that was waiting for her at the network. So she'd kicked herself when Michael drew up to the entrance of her building and she'd stepped out of his car to the sound of pounding feet, of figures emerging from the shadows, of more shouted questions and blinding camera flashes. Had she predicted this, she would have insisted to Michael that she take a taxi home and then instructed the driver to go instead in the direction of Ally's address in Croyden. But she hadn't. And it was almost guaranteed she'd be followed if she was seen exiting her apartment building's underground garage. So she couldn't go to Ally and Ally couldn't come to her. Either way she would be immediately targeted. Morgan didn't want that. She wanted to protect Ally, keep her safe, keep her well out of the ruthless hands of the media. Much as she found the thought of not seeing Ally tonight both distressing and disappointing, she decided on it anyway, and she'd called her the moment she was safely inside her apartment.

Now, realizing what an error in judgment she had made, she tried calling Ally back.

"Don't do this to me again, please," she prayed softly, dismayed to be switched through to Ally's voice mail. She didn't leave a message, instead hanging up and immediately redialing. Voice mail again. She hung up again.

Morgan stood motionless in her lounge-room, looking out to the glittering arch of the Sydney Harbor Bridge and wondering what the hell to do next.

Quickly she decided.

Her phone rang just as she was about to redial and leave Ally a message. The caller ID was one Morgan had entered in the minutes before she and Ally left her hotel room in Barcelona. *Ally-Home*. It seemed she was calling from her landline.

"I'm sorry." Ally's voice was choked with tears.

"It's okay." Morgan wished she could reach through the phone and pull Ally directly to her. Then she could kiss away her tears, the tears she knew she had caused by her efforts to protect. "I'm sorry, too. I should have known—"

"I broke my mobile." Ally sobbed. "That's the second in as many weeks." There was a muffled sound as if she'd covered the mouthpiece while she blew her nose. In the next moment the sound clarity had returned. She sniffed and then sighed heavily. "God knows how I'm going to explain this one to Josh."

So *that* had been the crash. Ally must have hurled it at something. "Somehow I think that's going to be the least of your worries soon." Morgan closed her eyes, vacillating one final time over her latest decision. She made up her mind once and for all. "Would you like me to come to you tonight, or do you want to come to me?"

Ally snuffled and then made a little noise that conveyed she was surprised but very happy with the change in plan. "I'll come to you."

"Are you sure?" Morgan asked, still hesitant. Just like the closet Ally had promised to live in—and was already wanting to evict herself from—Morgan was pretty sure she really had little understanding of just what she was letting herself in for. Maybe Ally could check into a hotel and she could arrive an hour or so after?

But no, Ally insisted she wanted to be there for Morgan and not skulking around like a thief—or worse, a mistress. And the paparazzi would probably follow Morgan to the hotel and then the papers would be full of her "secret late-night rendezvous."

Morgan had to admit she was right. She gave her the codes to enter the building and access the elevator. She'd have preferred she enter via the underground garage instead of the main entry, but remote control access was the only means of opening the garage door. Obviously Ally didn't yet have a remote control and since she no longer had a mobile she couldn't call to advise when she was waiting outside. So the main entry it had to be.

"See you soon, my love."

Morgan disconnected from the call as she ascended the stairs to the mezzanine level of her apartment and to her bedroom. For that long-awaited and much-needed shower.

"Coming!" Morgan called loudly about forty minutes later. She threw her hairbrush aside and dashed down the stairs. Her hair was still a little shower-damp, but apart from that she was ready to receive visitors. Ready to receive Ally. She opened the door and there she was. Morgan took a second to drink in the sight of her then threw herself into her arms. "Oh, Ally! My God, I've missed you."

"Ditto." Ally clung onto her tightly. "I'm so glad you changed your mind . . . and I'm so sorry for what I said to you earlier. I was wrong. I was thinking only of me and what I needed when I—" She looked up to Morgan with tears pooled in her eyes. "When I should have been thinking of you . . . how you felt."

"It's okay." Morgan ran her hand down Ally's cheek and bent to kiss her softly on the lips. "You're here now and I'm very, very happy about that." She held her at arm's length, worriedly searching her face. "Did you get ambushed at the entrance?"

Ally pulled a tissue from the cuff of her shirt sleeve and dabbed at her eyes. "Not ambushed. I got approached by two reporters wanting to know if I lived in the building . . . if I didn't, who was I going to visit . . . was it you? That sort of crap." Ally smiled, although not quite confidently. "I did what you did at the airport—head down and don't say a word. Although I doubt I looked half as good doing it as you did."

Morgan rolled her eyes. "Come off it!" She kissed Ally on the nose. "Congratulations. You've just survived your first brush with the press."

"Such good fun it was too." Ally grimaced. "Anyway, that's more than enough about me." She pressed her index finger to Morgan's breastbone. "I want to hear about you. How did it go?"

Morgan tugged at the sleeve of her shirt. "Come in and I'll tell you all about it."

Ally dabbed at her eyes again and smiled. "I thought you were never going to ask."

Morgan stood aside for her to enter and then watched Ally look all around her, at the bits of the apartment that could be seen from the entrance—essentially just the passage leading to the kitchen and living areas, and the staircase.

"Wow!"

"I'm guessing that's a great compliment coming from an architect." Morgan laughed. "I'm also guessing that architect's mind of yours won't be able to concentrate on a word I say until you've taken the tour?"

Ally shrugged noncommittally. But her eyes lit up at the suggestion.

"Come on then." Morgan tugged at her shirt sleeve again and herded her in the direction of the stairs. "We'll start with the best bit."

"The bedroom?" Ally blinked innocently.

"Exactly." Morgan laughed again, already feeling the stresses of the last forty-eight hours melting away. This woman did wonders for her spirit. She wagged her finger at her. "But be good."

Ally blinked again. "Aren't I always?"

An hour and a half later—a good portion of which had been spent admiring the architecture of the bedroom from various positions on Morgan's bed—Morgan handed Ally her second vodka and cranberry juice. They'd moved downstairs and were settled on Morgan's oh-so-very-comfortable couch. They had made a nice little arrangement of the oversized cushions near the divan end so they could sit close together with their legs stretched out in front of them. They were both donned in T-shirts and tracksuit pants that Morgan pulled from her wardrobe. They were too large for Ally's petite frame and she looked so cute, so vulnerable, that Morgan felt her heart tug as she sat down again.

"Thanks." Ally took a sip of her refreshed drink then placed it to the side, on the coffee table. "Now please, *please* don't keep me in suspense any longer. You were saying that the bitch from hell—"

"Sophie," Morgan offered, thinking "vulnerable" was maybe not the best description of Ally.

"Yes, her. You were saying she was looking smug about the advertising."

"Exactly." Morgan also took a sip of her drink and set it aside. "Although I really have no idea why, because since this happened only one advertiser has requested their ads be pulled from our timeslot. Sophie was adamant it was due to the controversy surrounding the show and warned of more to come. Then Carlo jumped in and reminded everyone, because we're prime time, advertising costs are at their peak. Many companies run ads for a while in the expensive slots to gain the initial reach, then they drop to either lower frequency or less expensive slots."

"But that would all be booked in advance, wouldn't it? If this advertiser suddenly pulled, it's probably because they *are* worried about the controversy."

"You're absolutely right." Morgan nodded. "And Sophie did point that out. But then Carlo asked how much longer the ads were to run in that timeslot."

"And?"

Morgan grinned. "Just two more weeks. After that the campaign was scheduled to go to a slot at half the price—and that particular booking still stands, so it's not like the advertiser has got their back up too badly with the network. Honestly, Ally, if you could have seen Sophie's face! And then, to top that off, in the very next minute Maxwell received a call announcing that the phones were currently jammed with viewers up in arms because I was conspicuous in my absence from my usual presenter role of the at-air episode of the show. Carlo, who had already said he thought the decision to keep my scheduled on-location segment but replace me with Troy for all the lead-ins was a big mistake, went on an 'I told you so' rampage. Apparently, he'd already advised them that to be seen to be reacting to what was still essentially tabloid rumor was a big mistake. But to be seen to be reacting in a half-assed manner—which is essentially what they did by keeping my segment but not my lead-ins—was nothing short of a public relations disaster."

"It does sound like a pretty stupid thing to do." Ally nodded, her expression wry. "Did they think that if everyone saw just a little of the lesbian they'd be less likely to be offended?"

Morgan laughed. "Something like that."

"I wish I'd thought to ring the network and add my voice to the protest," Ally mused. "All I did was swear at my television and throw a cushion at it."

Morgan kissed her on the cheek. "You're making a habit out of throwing things tonight."

"Yeah, well." Ally reached for her drink. She dipped her finger into it and pushed one of the ice cubes around and around the glass. "I got frustrated." Her dipped finger was removed and held to Morgan's mouth, an invitation for her to suck. "Anyway, keep going." After a few seconds she pulled her finger from Morgan's mouth. "I meant with the story, silly."

Morgan laughed again. How she adored this woman. "Well, as I said, the phone lines were jammed. But of course not all the calls received today were so great . . ." She explained the polarized views that had been expressed and how difficult they had been to see and hear.

Ally agreed, telling of her similar reaction that evening when reading some of the comments posted on the Internet. "It's so sad to think there are still people out there with such archaic views." She met Morgan's gaze directly. "But surely that small percentage isn't going to be enough to convince the network you're a liability, especially in the face of such obvious support for you?"

"I don't know yet," Morgan admitted. "As Carlo said, there's a whole heap of reasons why they shouldn't. For one, they've got a couple of shows that already have either gay or lesbian characters in them, so dumping me—even though I'm a 'real' lesbian as opposed to someone just acting like one—would look rather hypocritical. And like I told you earlier, they can't just 'get rid of me' because of this. And Michael, in his inimitable way, made it very clear that if they suddenly find a loophole in my contract it will be glaringly obvious that that's the real reason behind my dismissal. They'd find themselves slapped with a discrimination suit so fast, their collective network heads would be spinning. So if they want me out, they'll have to pay me out."

"And how would you feel about that?" Ally asked quietly.

Morgan hesitated. "It's nice to think I'm protected in that regard. But it's a bit akin to someone getting a dishonorable discharge from the military when they've done nothing wrong. Moving on from that would be difficult."

Ally gave her a comforting squeeze on the arm and a gentle cranberry-flavored kiss on the lips. "I don't think it's going to be something you'll have to consider, honey. From what you've said, the wind is blowing in your favor."

Morgan smiled into Ally's eyes. "It must be. I met you."

"Ooh, what a smooth talker!" Ally kissed her again, more firmly this time. "So, what's the final outcome?"

"Well, believe it or not, they've decided to 'suck it and see.'"

Ally's eyes widened. "*Suck it and see?*"

"Mm-hmm." Morgan nodded, her smile quickly turning into a grin. She was sure she'd had the same wide-eyed expression as Ally did now when Maxwell announced it may be best if, for the moment—while they continued to gauge viewer reaction and monitor advertising revenues—she return to the screen in her full capacity. "'We've never dealt with a situation like this before so I guess we should just suck it and see.'" Morgan did her best to imitate Maxwell's heavy, gruff tone. But as usual her acting skills let her down. "A somewhat 'interesting' turn of phrase, don't you think?"

"Very." Ally giggled. "So you're still on TV. Congratulations."

"For the moment." Morgan, while very, very pleased with the initial outcome, refused to get too confident. She couldn't help but think to her somewhat "active" past and feel it coming rushing up to greet her. "Like I said before, if there's one thing certain in TV, it's that nothing's ever certain."

Ally scooted around on her bottom until she sat at the foot of the divan, opposite Morgan. Morgan closed her eyes to the warmth of Ally's hands as they cupped her face. "Look at me," Ally whispered. When Morgan complied she found her eyes filled with concern. "What's wrong, honey? I thought you'd be happier at the outcome than this."

"I *am* happy." Morgan bit on her lower lip. Half of her wanted to tell Ally everything. The other half was fearful of what would happen if she did. Ally had fast become such an important presence in her life, she didn't want to do or say anything to jeopardize that presence. She studied Ally's face while she weighed up the pros and cons of telling versus not telling. Under normal circumstances there would be no need to dredge up her past and lay it bare. But these weren't normal circumstances. It may be true that up until Marie she had been discreet, so the chances of that aspect of her private life being opened up for public scrutiny were slim. But not nonexistent. Better she tell Ally before she received a blown-up, half-true or maybe even completely inaccurate version via the media. Morgan took hold of Ally's hands, holding them gently in her own. "Ally, there are some things about me I want you to know . . ."

Morgan told Ally everything. About Audrey and the threats each had issued during their breakup. About the shared veil of secrecy surrounding her other Australian lovers and about the freedom her travel with *Bonnes Vacances* had afforded. She didn't—in fact she couldn't—give an exhaustive list of her lovers, but she provided enough detail for Ally to get the general picture.

"So." Morgan smiled a little unsurely as she drew to a finish. Ally had remained quiet throughout the telling, forcing Morgan to gauge her reactions via subtle changes in her expression. "Now you know."

Ally, whose latest expression almost exactly replicated the one she had worn when Mark first left the two of them alone in

Barcelona, shifted a little uncomfortably in her seat. "Why are you telling me all this?" she asked.

Morgan couldn't help but notice Ally's movement had left a little more space between them. On purpose? she wondered. She decided to use Ally's own words. "In case things get written or said, I wanted you to know beforehand what was the wrapping and what was just filling."

Ally gave the smallest of nods but her eyes searched Morgan's, as if looking for another explanation. "That's it?"

"What other reason would I have?" Morgan squeezed Ally's hand reassuringly. "Trust me—this is not the kind of thing I discuss with just anyone. In fact, you're the first."

Ally gave another teeny nod. Her lashes were lowered and she seemed to study her hand as it lay in Morgan's. Her head lifted suddenly and she blurted, "I told you I don't know anymore exactly where I stand on affairs. But I do believe in monogamy."

"Wha . . . ?" Morgan felt her insides tie into a knot. She'd admitted that two of her Australian lovers—one a high-profile newscaster and the other a professional golfer—had been married. "I told you I wasn't proud of those decisions, but—"

"I don't care about them." Ally shook her head vehemently. As if reading what Morgan was thinking, she said, "They're in the past and what's done is done. You can't change it. I'm talking about *now*."

Morgan frowned. She knew without a doubt that Ally wasn't married and she'd believed it when she had said James was no longer in the picture. Then, suddenly, she knew what Ally was driving at. She was still employed with *Bonnes Vacances*. She'd still be traveling all over the world. So Ally was wondering if she'd still be taking advantage of the fringe benefits.

"Oh, baby." Morgan grabbed for her other hand so she held them both. "You don't have to worry for one second about that. I haven't thought about—or even looked at—another woman since I met you." Given that they had only met two weeks ago, and given that she had just told of her track record while on location, Morgan was well aware that wasn't a particularly strong argument in her defense. "I love you, Ally, and I don't want to be with anyone but you. But the only thing I can offer you in proof of that is time."

There was an extended silence when again Ally seemed to be studying her hands as they lay in Morgan's. Again her lashes were raised but this time she spoke softly, slowly. And her expression was uncertain. "I'm not just another 'moment of weakness' . . . like Marie?"

"Oh no, baby, no!" Morgan drew Ally into her arms, holding her close and kissing her hair. "I've had a weak spot for you since the minute we met. But there was nothing momentary about it. I know we've only known each other a short time, but it's been long enough for me to know I want to spend the rest of my days getting to know you better."

Ally responded by giving Morgan a squeeze that rivaled the rib-crushing one of Marge. Then she giggled.

"What's so funny?" Morgan asked, confused by the sudden change in Ally's mood. She pushed her far enough away that they were eye-to-eye.

Ally giggled again. "God knows how you ever graduated from journalism school. Your vocabulary sure needs a bit of work. Four *knows* in one sentence. That's really sad."

"Cheeky girl!" Morgan laughed, grabbing for Ally as she slipped from her arms and off the couch.

"I *know*." Ally poked her tongue out and ran out of the lounge, toward the stairs.

Morgan launched herself off the couch and after her. She caught her just as they reached the bed.

"I love you," Ally said simply as she was lowered onto the mattress.

Morgan climbed on top of her, straddling her hips and sliding her hands under Ally's oversized T-shirt. Her skin was deliciously warm and silky to the touch. Morgan smiled crookedly under the weight of her increasing desire. "I know, baby. I know."

"I don't know about you"—Morgan grinned at what had quickly become their first private joke—"but I'm starving."

"I know you are." Ally was curled up on her side with her head resting on Morgan's abdomen. She tapped at Morgan's stomach. "There's a very loud protest going on in there. Shall we go see what we can rustle up in the kitchen?"

"I'm not sure we'll find anything much worth eating." Her fridge was next-to-empty, her housekeeper having cleared out all the food likely to spoil at her last visit. Usually she'd arrive home from her travels to a freshly stocked fridge, but since she'd arrived early and unannounced, that hadn't happened and her housekeeper's next visit wasn't scheduled to occur until Monday. "Unless of course you'd like a bowl of ketchup with a Spanish olive garnish?"

Not surprisingly, Ally screwed up her nose at the offer. "Do you think anyone is still delivering pizza?"

Morgan picked up the alarm clock that sat on the bedside table. It was nearly four a.m. "Not likely. There's an all-night food place a couple of suburbs down, though. I can go pick us up some burgers."

Ally sat up and tousled her already tousled hair. "You must be exhausted by now. I'll go."

"No, I'll go. You don't know where it is and it's complicated to explain."

"If it's that complicated you'll get lost."

"I have been there before," Morgan pointed out, smiling. "My sense of direction isn't *that* bad."

"Why don't we both go?" Ally suggested, looking Morgan

263

straight in the eye.

Morgan drew in her breath, hesitating. There may still be reporters lurking. They were nothing if not persistent.

"Fine." Ally read her own interpretation into Morgan's silence. She shunted off the bed and pulled her borrowed, over-sized T-shirt over her head. "I'm going downstairs for some ketchup."

"Can you bring me an olive?" Morgan asked, trying to lighten the suddenly heavy mood.

It didn't work.

"Get your own damn olive." Ally pulled on her borrowed oversized track pants and stalked out of the bedroom and down the stairs.

For a full minute Morgan sat on the bed, chewing on her knuckles. Then she pulled on her own T-shirt and track pants and followed Ally.

"Narnia doesn't look so wondrous now, does it?" she said quietly as she eased onto a stool on the opposite side of the island bench to Ally.

Ally poked around in the jar that she'd placed on the bench in front of her and picked out an olive. She studied it before popping it into her mouth. "I wouldn't know. I've never been there. I'm stuck in the netherworld called the closet." She sighed and pushed the olive jar away from her. "And it sucks."

Morgan released a sigh of her own. "I know."

Ally glanced sharply at her but seemed to sense this was not a comment made in jest. She reached for Morgan's hands. "I want to be with you, Morgan. I've never wanted something so badly before. I want to hold you and cherish you and love you. And I know I can do all of that, here, in this apartment. But I want more than that. I want you to meet my friends and I want to meet yours. I want to have people over for dinner and not pretend you and I are just friends. I want to be able to talk to my friends and family about you as my partner. I want everything I just took for granted before but never appreciated. I want a *life*—a normal life—with you." Ally fell silent, as if considering her words. "And I know that because of what you do and who you are—even if we were a traditional couple—that 'normal' life wouldn't be as normal as other peoples' . . . but it would be nice if we could at least pop out for burgers together."

Morgan leaned against the low back of the kitchen stool, not quite sure what to say. Actually, because she'd never had a girlfriend since she'd "made it" in television, she'd never really considered the full implications of what it would be like to be the "silent partner." What would she do if the shoe was on the other foot? How would she cope if Ally was in the spotlight—either rejoicing or suffering—and she could do nothing but whisper her praise or her condolences. Not very well, she imagined.

"You know," Morgan said slowly, "I've been thinking about your mobile phone."

Ally pulled the jar of olives back toward her and peered into it. "What about it?"

"Well, since I was able to get through to your voice mail, the SIM card still works. So if you bought another phone of the same model then you could just put your SIM in and your boss wouldn't be any the wiser about your destructive tendencies."

Ally shrugged, obviously uninterested in the topic. She dug into the jar and picked out an olive. "Yeah. I guess I could do that."

"You and I could go looking for one together later this morning."

That suggestion stopped Ally in her tracks. The olive she held never made it to her mouth. "Together? To the shops?"

Morgan nodded. "But you know what they say about shopping on an empty stomach. What say you and I go grab a burger together?"

"Together?" Ally repeated, dropping her olive back into the jar. "But what about the reporters and the tabloids and getting into the news and your reputation, and all of that?"

Morgan shrugged. "Maybe being seen with you will give me an air of respectability."

Ally scoffed. "I can hardly see how—"

"Do you want to go or not?" Morgan interrupted.

"Yes, I want to go," Ally said quickly.

Morgan rounded the bench and pulled her to her feet, patting her bottom and leading her in the direction of the stairs. "Then you'd better get changed. It won't do my reputation any good if you're photographed looking like a lost little waif."

"A *young* lost little waif," Ally said slyly, referring to the inference made by the tabloid article. Then she bolted up the stairs.

For the second time that night, Morgan bolted after her. She didn't know what would greet them once they got outside, and she certainly didn't know if Ally was either aware or prepared for it. But she knew for sure, whatever it was, she and Ally would face up to it together.

And that knowledge alone made Morgan happier than she'd been in a very, very long while.

EPILOGUE

Ten months later

Ally started when she felt hands across her eyes. She put down her pencil and ruler and leaned back a little, feeling the familiar curves. "Hello, you."

"Hello, baby." Morgan kissed her on the top of her head. "Sorry to disturb the genius at work, but you looked so cute there—all concentration—that I just couldn't help it."

Ally smiled as she swiveled her stool so she sat with her back to the drafting table. She checked her watch. "You're early."

"Hmm." Morgan peered at the drafting table, casting her eye over Ally's latest design. "I took a leaf from your book and concentrated really hard. So I got most of the lead-ins done in one take. So, if you're ready . . . ?"

"I'm ready." Ally nodded. It was past six on a Friday and there was nothing she'd like better than to leave the office for the week. "But Paterson's not here yet, and you know he'll be totally bummed out if he misses you." Ally laughed when Morgan visibly slumped her shoulders. "Come on, sweetheart, he's catching the bus just to see you."

"He's catching the bus because he lost his license." Morgan pouted. "It's got nothing to do with me."

Paterson, Josh's son, had had his driver's license revoked for twelve months after being charged with driving a stolen vehicle under the influence of illegal substances. He was now only two months away from being able to apply for his license again, but in the ten months since his court appearance he had rediscovered the joys of public transportation. He had also discovered that Morgan Silverstone was a regular visitor to his father's offices. And, ever since the first time he met her, he had been smitten.

"He's coming just to see you." Ally grinned. She could completely understand Paterson's crush, even though he, along with the rest of the nation, knew that Morgan was not interested in the opposite sex. "We should wait. Just a few minutes."

"Fine," Morgan said, resignation in her voice. She took a seat in one of the plush chairs that now flanked Ally's desk. They hadn't been there ten months ago. But a lot of things had changed in the past ten months, one of them being the number of visitors to her office.

That had increased exponentially from the time she went to get late-night burgers with Morgan. They'd been followed and they'd been photographed getting out of Morgan's Mercedes. They'd also been questioned as they headed into the burger bar, but they hadn't said a word. This hadn't stopped their picture making it into the papers—along with an accompanying photograph of Ally as she had entered Morgan's building earlier that same night. Media speculation about their relationship ran high and Ally had to fight through a forest of reporters and photographers to get into the offices on Monday morning. Then the calls to the office started, and it was almost impossible to distinguish between who was the press, who was a genuine customer and who was just curious to speak to "Morgan's lesbian lover."

After three days of constant bombardment, Josh called an emergency meeting and declared the office closed to all but established clientele. Ally shrank in her seat at the announcement and nervously followed him when he asked to see her in his office. But rather than being angry at her for the disruption to business, Josh shook her hand and said, "I always knew you had it in you to finally be honest with yourself." Then he smiled. "And I always knew you'd be the best thing to happen to this company." Ally had left his office totally bemused. *How had he known when even I didn't?* she wondered. And why wasn't he pissed that the commotion surrounding her private life had spilled into the offices?

After a few months she knew why. After all the public attention, including interviews with herself and Morgan, she had unwittingly become the poster girl for sustainable housing design. Suddenly everyone wanted to know about the best aspect for positioning a house on a block of land, about flow-through ventilation, about thermal mass, about gray water and solar power. And they all wanted to hear about it from Ally.

The offices were inundated. Business had never been better. Hence Josh invested in some very posh and very comfortable chairs for Ally's clientele.

He had, however, left it up to Ally to sort the wheat from the chaff. She sat through many a meeting with supposed new clients only to discover they were, at best, just interested onlookers or, at worst, reporters looking for some new "Morgan and Ally" gossip. But there was a solid core of genuine customers. Ally had never been busier.

Which was just as well. It helped keep her mind off the fact she didn't get to see Morgan half as much as she would have liked.

Contrary to Morgan's original fears, she had been in no danger of losing her job. If anything, her already strong position became even stronger. The ratings for the show soared—not only for the period immediately following her very public coming-out, but consistently week after week. The media speculated over why and came to a "lesbian chic" conclusion. Being lesbian was definitely "in." One publication even questioned if Morgan was indeed lesbian at all or if she had just fabricated the whole story to boost her popularity.

"Jesus." Morgan had thrown aside that particular publication during one of her and Ally's regular media sweeps. "And I thought *you* were the only one I had ever needed to convince about the fact I was gay."

They'd ended up laughing over both the story and Ally's initial disbelief about Morgan. But not all the media coverage was taken so lightly. Ally was upset to the point of tears upon reading that she was a "gold digger" out to benefit from Morgan's current popularity and ongoing wealth.

"I don't want your money," Ally, still teary, cried that night in a phone call to Morgan, who was in Ireland at the time. "What gives them the right to say something like that?"

"Oh, baby," Morgan soothed over and over. "I know you don't. Just ignore it."

"I'm trying." Ally fingered the extremely expensive gold chain and diamond pendant Morgan had presented her with for their three-month anniversary, and her hand moved to the matching bracelet she'd gotten for their six-month celebration. She looked around Morgan's multi-million-dollar apartment and out of the expanse of glass to its priceless views. She'd moved in two months prior, giving up her apartment in Croyden the day her lease expired. And she thought to the environmentally friendly hybrid car that Morgan had given her just two weeks after that, to mark the fact that another of her houses was to be featured in *Architectural Digest*. "But you've given me so much . . ." Ally swiped at her eyes, trying to stem the flow of tears. If she were an outsider looking in, she might describe her as a gold digger too.

"I wish you were here. I miss you right now."

"I miss you right now too, baby," Morgan whispered. It was one of their more often repeated phrases, spoken via phone each day she was on location.

As was usual, that sentiment had led to a discussion of what they would do together when next they met. On that occasion it was a Sunday afternoon barbeque at Ally's folks' place. As Ally had predicted, her mum, and her dad too for that matter, had taken immediately to Morgan, and invitations for them all to spend time together were offered frequently. The first time Morgan came to dinner they'd gone to the extreme of laying the table. But they'd reverted to form for all subsequent visits, and casual, plate-on-the-lap dining was now the order of the day. Morgan loved it. And Ally loved it that Morgan had been so readily accepted as part of the family. She also loved the fact her parents had so readily accepted her "lifestyle change," announcing that their only desire was to see their daughter happy. Which she obviously was.

This evening, however, Ally wasn't exactly brimming over with happiness at their plans. Because what they had planned to do a few hours down the track was even more unsettling to Ally than the constant media attention that surrounded their relationship. They'd finally scheduled the activity she had successfully bid on at auction all those months ago, and tonight she and Morgan were to do the Sydney Harbor Bridge Climb.

"Come on, Ally," Morgan urged her when, after another ten or so minutes, they were still purportedly waiting for Paterson to show. "If you want to have dinner before we 'do it' then we need to get going soon."

"I don't suppose you'd believe me if I said I was feeling sick?" Ally said, only half joking.

"Nope." Morgan pulled her to her feet.

"What if I said I am medically unable to go more than a meter above sea level?"

Morgan smiled wickedly. "Then I'd wonder why you were able to perform so brilliantly each time you're in our 'way above sea level' bedroom."

Ally couldn't help but smile back. "What if I said I just didn't want to do it?"

"Then I'd remind you of all the other things you didn't want to do this year but have." She drew Ally into her arms. "For a person who hates being the center of attention, you've certainly handled it very, very well."

"Only because you've been there to hold my hand," Ally murmured, reveling—as she always did—in the feel of Morgan's body against her own. She still could not get enough of her. "What say we have a nice dinner then an early night? You'll need it, what with your day of rehearsals tomorrow. We can't have the host of the Logies looking like a worn-out wreck . . ."

"Nice try." Morgan laughed. She held Ally at arm's length. "Do you remember what you said the first time we ever had a shower together?"

Ally thought hard. It was in Barcelona, she remembered. But she'd been in such a state she could hardly think at all, never mind concentrate on specifics. "No," she admitted.

"You said 'I've got you,'" Morgan said softly. "And tonight, when we climb that bridge, I'll be right behind you. So if you feel you're going to slip or fall, you need not worry, because I've got you too."

Publications from
BELLA BOOKS, INC.
The best in contemporary lesbian fiction

P.O. Box 10543, Tallahassee, FL 32302
Phone: 800-729-4992
www.bellabooks.com

ASPEN'S EMBERS by Diane Tremain Braund. Will Aspen choose the woman she loves . . . or the forest she hopes to preserve . . .   978-1-59493-102-4 $14.95

THE COTTAGE by Gerri Hill. *The Cottage* is the heartbreaking story of two women who meet by chance . . . or did they? A love so destined it couldn't be denied . . . stolen moments to be cherished forever.   978-1-59493-096-6 $13.95

FANTASY: Untrue Stories of Lesbian Passion edited by Barbara Johnson and Therese Szymanski. Lie back and let Bella's bad girls take you on an erotic journey through the greatest bedtime stories never told.   978-1-59493-101-7 $15.95

SISTERS' FLIGHT by Jeanne G'Fellers. *Sisters' Flight* is the highly anticipated sequel to *No Sister of Mine* and *Sister Lost, Sister Found.*
          978-1-59493-116-1 $13.95

BRAGGIN' RIGHTS by Kenna White. Taylor Fleming is a thirty-six-year-old Texas rancher who covets her independence. She finds her cowgirl independence tested by neighboring rancher Jen Holland.   978-1-59493-095-9 $13.95

BRILLIANT by Ann Roberts. Respected sociology professor Diane Cole finds her views on love challenged by her own heart, as she fights the attraction she feels for a woman half her age.   978-1-59493-115-4 $13.95

THE EDUCATION OF ELLIE by Jackie Calhoun. When Ellie sees her childhood friend for the first time in thirty years she is tempted to resume their long lost friendship. But with the years come a lot of baggage and the two women struggle with who they are now while fighting the painful memories of their first parting. Will they be able to move past their history to start again?   978-1-59493-092-8 $13.95

DATE NIGHT CLUB by Saxon Bennett. *Date Night Club* is a dark romantic comedy about the pitfalls of dating in your thirties . . .   978-1-59493-094-2 $13.95

PLEASE FORGIVE ME by Megan Carter. Laurel Becker is on the verge of losing the two most important things in her life—her current lover, Elaine Alexander, and the Lavender Page bookstore. Will Elaine and Laurel manage to work through their misunderstandings and rebuild their life together?   978-1-59493-091-1 $13.95

WHISKEY AND OAK LEAVES by Jaime Clevenger. Meg meets June, a single woman running a horse ranch in the California Sierra foothills. The two become quick friends and it isn't long before Meg is looking for more than just a friendship. But June has no interest in developing a deeper relationship with Meg. She is, after all, not the least bit interested in women . . . or is she? Neither of these two women is prepared for what lies ahead . . .   978-1-59493-093-5 $13.95

SUMTER POINT by KG MacGregor. As Audie surrenders her heart to Beth, she begins to distance herself from the reckless habits of her youth. Just as they're ready to meet in the middle, their future is thrown into doubt by a duty Beth can't ignore. It all comes to a head on the river at Sumter Point.   978-1-59493-089-8 $13.95

THE TARGET by Gerri Hill. Sara Michaels is the daughter of a prominent senator who has been receiving death threats against his family. In an effort to protect Sara, the FBI recruits homicide detective Jaime Hutchinson to secretly provide the protection they are so certain Sara will need. Will Sara finally figure out who is behind the death threats? And will Jaime realize the truth—and be able to save Sara before it's too late?
                                                  978-1-59493-082-9 $13.95

REALITY BYTES by Jane Frances. In this sequel to *Reunion*, follow the lives of four friends in a romantic tale that spans the globe and proves that you can cross the whole of cyberspace only to find love a few suburbs away . . .   978-1-59493-079-9 $13.95

MURDER CAME SECOND by Jessica Thomas. Broadway's bad-boy genius, Paul Carlucci, has chosen *Hamlet* for his latest production and, to the delight of some and despair of others, he has selected Provincetown's amphitheatre for his opening gala. But Alex Peres realizes the wrong people are falling down, and the moaning is all too realistic. Someone must not be shooting blanks . . .   978-1-59493-081-2 $13.95

SKIN DEEP by Kenna White. Jordan Griffin has been given a new assignment: Track down and interview one-time nationally renowned broadcast journalist Reece McAllister. Much to her surprise, Jordan comes away with far more than just a story . . .
                                                  978-1-59493-78-2 $13.95

FINDERS KEEPERS by Karin Kallmaker. *Finders Keepers*, the quest for the perfect mate in the 21st century, joins Karin Kallmaker's *Just Like That* and her other incomparable novels about lesbian love, lust and laughter.   1-59493-072-4 $13.95

OUT OF THE FIRE by Beth Moore. Author Ann Covington feels at the top of the world when told her book is being made into a movie. Then in walks Casey Duncan the actress who is playing the lead in her movie. Will Casey turn Ann's world upside down?
                                                  1-59493-088-0 $13.95

STAKE THROUGH THE HEART: NEW EXPLOITS OF TWILIGHT LESBIANS by Karin Kallmaker, Julia Watts, Barbara Johnson and Therese Szymanski. The playful quartet that penned the acclaimed *Once Upon A Dyke* are dimming the lights for journeys into worlds of breathless seduction.   1-59493-071-6 $15.95

THE HOUSE ON SANDSTONE by KG MacGregor. Carly Griffin returns home to Leland and finds that her old high school friend Justine is awakening more than just old memories.   1-59493-076-7 $13.95